APACHE MOON

JAMES POWELL

Luther Cordalee, on the run from both Mexican bandits and the U.S. Army, is finally out of chances. Mexico's become a little dangerous for him, since he killed a man in a fight in a *cantina*. But he can't go back to the States, where the Army would try him for desertion. So he's on the run through what used to be Apache territory, before the last of them had been rounded up and sent to Florida. At least he doesn't have to worry about them . . .

But Cordalee has even more problems than he thinks he has. He's picked up by the last remaining band of Apaches in the Southwest and taken to their secret home on Stronghold Mountain. Cordalee doesn't like Apaches much — and the Indians, for their part, have learned from bitter experience just how treacherous a "White Eyes" can be. But common enemies often create unlikely alliances, and when Cordalee and the

(continued on back flap)

By *James Powell*

APACHE MOON
THE HUNT
THE MALPAIS RIDER
VENDETTA
DEATHWIND
STAGE TO SEVEN SPRINGS
A MAN MADE FOR TROUBLE

APACHE MOON

JAMES POWELL

DOUBLEDAY & COMPANY, INC.
GARDEN CITY, NEW YORK
1983

Excerpt from *The First Hundred Years of Niño Cochise* (Abelard-Schuman) as told by Ciyé "Niño" Cochise to A. Kinney Griffith, copyright © 1971 by Ciyé (Niño) Cochise and A. Kinney Griffith. Used by permission of Harper & Row, Publishers, Inc.

Library of Congress Cataloging in Publication Data

Powell, James.
Apache moon.

(Double D Western)
I. Title.
PS3566.O82A84 1983   813'.54
ISBN: 0-385-18748-3
Library of Congress Catalog Card Number 82-48709

The name of the full moon in the Apache language is *Klego-na-ay*, but the crescent moon is called *tzontzose*, and *hoddentin* (the sacred pollen of the tule) is always offered to it.

The women of the Chiricahua throw no *hoddentin* to the moon, but pray to it, saying: *Gun-ju-le, Klego-na-ay* ("Be good, O Moon").

—John G. Bourke, Captain, Third Cavalry, U.S. Army

. . . It [the full moon] is called the Apache Moon. The old-time Mexicans called it Apache Moon because it is big, bright, and red. They said there was blood on the moon and that the Apaches put it there.

—Ciyé "Niño" Cochise, "grandson" of Cochise, Chiricahua Apache chief

APACHE MOON

CHAPTER 1

Luther Cordalee stopped suddenly along a slight rise that overlooked the river from the Fronteras-to-Bavispe trail, which he had been following ever since early the night before. He had seen something move within a dense canebrake across the river. Quickly sinking to one knee beneath the outstretched arms of a huge mesquite, he continued to watch the spot where he had seen the movement. Tangled mats of sacaton mixed with willow, cane, and ash grew everywhere. But nothing moved, not even a limb or a blade of grass waving in the breeze. In fact, there was no breeze —only the glaring rays of the white-hot Sonoran sun beating down from high noon above. Finally he decided he had seen nothing of consequence . . . maybe only a bird flitting from branch to branch. Probably it had been nothing worse than that.

But he did not hasten to leave the shade of the mesquite. He wanted to; his exhaustion was matched only by his desperate desire to keep going, to stay alive. But he needed the rest. He had gone without food or drink since early that morning, and he knew he could not keep it up without at least a brief respite from the tortures of the trail.

His skin, naturally dark to begin with, was nearly black from sweat-caked dust and the effects of five long years spent beneath the desert sun; his coal-black hair hung almost to his shirt collar; the whites of his shockingly gray eyes were bloodshot and his pupils contracted; his two-day-old beard was streaked with dirt; and the clothes he wore—a blue flannel shirt over a sweaty undershirt, faded blue trousers, and the campaign hat of a cavalry trooper—were tattered and smelly. His boots, an almost soleless pair of regulation "No. 8s," should long since have been thrown away. In the crook of one arm he carried a Springfield carbine, .45 caliber, and at his hip was holstered an Army Colt revolver of the same caliber. Strapped to his back was a rolled-up rubber poncho, inside of which remained the balance of his earthly belongings—virtually all of it being standard Army issue. At least it had been—a month ago when he'd left Arizona. . . .

But that was then. Luther Cordalee no longer considered himself a member of Troop E, 4th U.S. Cavalry, stationed at Fort Huachuca, Ari-

zona Territory. He was many miles away in Mexico, somewhere, he calcu-
lated, on the Río de Bavispe a good fifteen miles southeast of where he'd
crossed its northernmost tributary, the San Bernardino, at sunup that
morning. And he was on foot and in trouble, growing worse all the time.

It was an uninviting prospect, but he was forced to take stock of his situation. Four miles back, his horse had dropped from under him, dead of a
bursted heart. Also back there, still not in sight but no doubt gaining fast
now that Cordalee's horse was gone, were men who pursued him—a dozen
or so self-styled Mexican national guardsmen from Fronteras, friends and
family of the man he had fought with and killed there early last evening.
Once he had been certain he had lost them, but then he had seen them
coming again and knew he had been wrong. He didn't know how far
back they would be now, but his last distant sighting of them had come
several miles this side of the Batepito Springs crossing of the San Bernardino. That had also been before his horse had gone down on him. Now
his only hope was that their horses, too, would soon be playing out. He
dared not bank on that, for he doubted they had pushed their mounts as
he had his—likely the only reason he had gained his early lead in the first
place—but at least he could hope.

In any event, he knew well enough what was behind him. But what lay
ahead? The trail he was on led straight down toward the river. A ford,
perhaps one of many as the trail wriggled its way up the narrow canyon to
the tiny river towns that lay along the way, would probably be found
there. Cordalee knew from maps he had studied of the area that he must
be near the initial curvings of the Bavispe River Bend, the stream flowing
originally down from the south, then swerving sharply westward until it
at last met with the San Bernardino and finally turned south on its long,
weary way to a confluence with the mighty Yaqui, largest of all rivers in
western Mexico.

To the southeast, as far as he could see, towered hazy blue sierras, a ma-
jestic barranca-cut and haughty upheaval that could only be the heart of
the mighty Sierra Madre itself. Directly to the south and somewhat west,
inside the river's great bend, more mountains loomed. These were not as
large as the more prestigious range to the southeast, but they were nonetheless typically Sonoran in character—rugged, imposing, unfriendly, and
wild.

It occurred to Cordalee as he looked at it that this had most recently
been Apache country, and the thought gave him a little shiver. Were this
not May 1887, eight months after General Nelson A. Miles, Commander
of the Department of Arizona, had taken the surrender of the last of the
infamous Chiricahua hostiles and sent them to Florida to stay . . . well,

Cordalee still could not help shrinking from the sight of what he knew to be the Apache's last and most desperate stronghold. He began to wonder if there might not be another direction in which he should go to make his escape.

But he knew there was not. Back to the west and some north were his pursuers; due north lay the United States and Arizona, where he was already wanted for desertion; to the east loomed more mountains, then the open plains of Chihuahua on the other side, where hiding places would become few and far between.

He looked back the way he had come and was hardly surprised to see a thin dust cloud rising above the Fronteras trail: his pursuers closing in. It would not be long now until they were upon him, he knew.

Getting to his feet, he once again stared across the Bavispe at the sierra vastness, wondering which was more fearsome—the mystery of the mountains or the volatile hatred of those Fronteras "guardsmen" who hounded him. The question unresolved, he hefted his rifle and checked his pack, then began making his way down toward the river crossing.

Although he was aware how much easier it probably made it for his pursuers to follow him, he was glad he had stuck to the well-defined trail when it came to fording the crystal-clear and cold waters of the Bavispe. Even then, he suspected he was lucky that the summer rains had not yet come to swell it beyond its banks, an occasion upon which even a good swimmer might have his troubles getting across. As it was, the *vado*, or ford, was waist deep and the current not to be laughed at.

Nevertheless, Cordalee paused only long enough to slake his thirst before quickly making it on across to the other side. He drew up, sloshing and dripping, within a canebrake, wondering if now would be a good time to forsake the trail. Through a break in the cane, he could see the mountain foothills, cloaked primarily with mesquite, cactus, and agave. Within a comparatively short distance, however, a massive formation rose steeply, cut everywhere by mean-looking, vertical-walled canyons, and he couldn't help questioning if any part of it was scalable.

Suddenly a brightly colored bird fluttered within the cane not twenty feet away, and Cordalee recalled the movement he thought he had seen earlier. Then, for the first time, he noticed a damp spot on the ground a few feet to his right, very much like the one at his own feet, only not so fresh. Actually there were three such spots. Alarmed, he went quickly over to them and felt the ground. The spots could hardly be more than half an hour old. Someone or something had crossed the river not long before Cordalee had, and then had stood there drying off just as he had done.

The realization gave him a start, and he began looking around for tracks along the trail. The ground was hard packed at this point, showing only old tracks of horses and mules, none of which had been made within the past several days.

But then, a few yards farther to the right, in softer dirt and heading in the direction of the mountains, he found a human footprint. Then he found what he thought was a full set—no, two sets, three! One track was smaller than the other two but all were freshly made and all were headed in the same direction. And they had been made by moccasined feet!

A cold feeling came over Cordalee. He looked quickly all around. He saw no one. Still, he couldn't help being made considerably nervous by the situation. He decided to move on up the main trail until he found a good place of his own to leave it, hoping to avoid whoever had preceded him at the river crossing. Maybe if he left them alone, they would do the same for him. . . .

Then he noticed something about one of the tracks: A foot had been dragged, toe first. . . . He looked farther. Yes, there it was again. Someone seriously crippled had made that track. And something else: One track was too small to be anything but that of a child, while neither of the other two seemed large enough to be that of a man. Could it be they were two women and a kid, one of the women suffering an injured foot or leg. . . ?

He thought about it. He really should know who was lurking about in that canebrake. He decided to follow the footprints, at least for a way. He went carefully, watching for snakes almost as much as he did for whoever had made the tracks, stopping frequently in order to listen for the telltale sounds of either stirring. The canebrake he was in became almost impassable, and had he very far to go in it he would have given up entirely. But then he found himself at the outer edge of the thickest growth, looking out at a mesquite-covered foot slope that angled sharply up onto a rocky knoll. Although after the canebrake this looked like open space, the brush ahead was still thick enough to hide twenty people with ease.

The tracks were plainly heading straight for the heaviest growth of mesquite, located about halfway up the rocky knoll. Whoever it had been had obviously made an effort to leave the canebrake as quickly as they could and had probably done so while Cordalee was still debating whether or not to cross the river. He had not been able to see them go from the other side due to the height of the cane growing between him and the base of the mesquite thicket, but he wondered if they had seen him. . . .

"Damn," he muttered to himself. Who were they? Were they alone, or were there others somewhere in the brush, waiting for them? Were they

Indians, or was there such a thing as moccasin-clad Mexicans? And could they possibly be armed and dangerous . . . ?

He studied the mesquite thicket for a while longer, detecting nothing. Checking once again to make sure of the direction the tracks took, he decided on a short dash for the nearest mesquite bush. Bent low, he burst forward and made the bush without incident. He crouched there, waiting, listening. Nothing moved.

Quietly he moved around the bush and sprinted toward the next. Then the next and the next. Now, he, too, was well within the thicket. He stood upright amid several tree-type mesquites, then moved a few steps farther and stopped to listen. Again he saw and heard nothing.

He began to wonder if the tracks were not several hours rather than minutes old when he'd found them. But no, the wet spots along the bank belied that. And both tracks and wet spots had to have been made by the same persons; after all, he hadn't seen a human soul other than his pursuers since leaving Fronteras. The land was virtually deserted—a lingering result of past depredations committed by the Apaches, no doubt.

He was still debating his next dash forward when suddenly he heard a sharp cry ring out from across the river. Several excited voices followed the cry and Cordalee's heart suddenly seemed to stick in his throat. He whirled, but was unable to see anything other than cane and mesquite.

Quickly, he made for higher ground, making sure to stay within the thickest growth of mesquite and somehow managing to scramble to a vantage point that was well above the top of the canebrake without starting a rock slide. Crouching low, he gazed back across the river. Again his heart jumped. Gathered along the rise, almost at the same spot on the trail where Cordalee had rested earlier, were at least a dozen mounted men. All wore huge sombreros and looked to be armed to the teeth. They were milling excitedly around at least one or two others who had dismounted and were pointing at something on the ground.

Instinctively, Cordalee gripped his rifle, then began easing farther back into the brush, thinking to slip on around the knoll toward the steeper foot slopes and canyons beyond. He was backing along, feeling his way with one hand and holding his rifle with the other, when a sharp gasp, then a muffled little cry, caused him to spin around. At first he saw nothing, but then, beneath a twisted, arching tangle of mesquite limbs, two round eyes stared both fear and anguish back at him.

"Good God," he breathed, half in surprise, half in relief. It was a kid. Just a dark-eyed, dirty-faced, long-haired little Mexican kid.

Then he saw the woman; she was huddled next to the child . . . an old woman, her hair long and graying, her bronzed face wrinkled and her black eyes expressionless but cutting. Neither she nor the child moved, even though they were only a few feet away.

"Who are you?" Cordalee asked instinctively in English. Then, "¿Quién es usted? ¿Qué está haciendo usted allí?" If he had learned nothing else in his five years of soldiering in Arizona, he had at least learned a passable command of the Spanish language. He had a bent for such things, it seemed.

"Who are you?" he repeated impatiently. "What are you doing there?"

He got no answer and was about to repeat the question when suddenly something hit him from behind—a flailing, kicking something that was less big and heavy than pure fury. He went forward and down under the on-slaught, dropped his rifle, and only barely managed to turn in time to see his attacker, apparently unarmed, going for the weapon behind him.

It was the second woman, much younger, a slender, black-haired she-devil if there ever was one. Lunging desperately, Cordalee managed to make a grab around her hips and bring her down before she could grasp his rifle fully. The Springfield clattered on the rocks as both Cordalee and the girl rolled into a mesquite, its thorns gouging deeply into Cordalee's back and shoulders above his rolled-up poncho.

Just as he thought he had a grip on the girl's arms, she squirmed free and came catlike to her feet, her nostrils flaring and her black eyes blazing. She aimed a lightninglike kick at his groin, which struck all too accurately home and sent Cordalee moaning doubled-up to the ground.

But he sensed her going for the rifle again and somehow managed to get a hand on her arm before she could bring it to bear. He wrenched her around, jerking the rifle loose with the other hand and out of her grasp. Then he flung her into a bush and brought the rifle barrel around so that its business end stared her in the face.

"Freeze, damn you!" he uttered in English, still half breathless and un-able to stand due to the pain below his belt. Then, in Spanish, "Don't move! Don't move, I said! Damn you, can't you understand your own lan-guage?"

Then it hit him: The girl didn't quite look Mexican . . . her features maybe, but not her dress, her hair, or the unmistakable wildness in her eyes. The same, he realized now, was true of the old woman and the kid, a boy, both of whom remained like statues where they had been all along. Indians . . . they were Indians! But what kind? Opatas, Yaquis . . . ?

He looked hard at the girl. Although something about her expression indicated that she had understood his Spanish, she only spat on the ground in front of him and did not say a thing.

The old woman uttered a guttural few words then that Cordalee had no hope of understanding, and the younger one turned quickly to look toward the river. Cordalee instinctively followed suit.

The Mexicans were still over there, only now several of them were pointing toward Cordalee's hill . . . or was it the mountainside beyond? Cordalee couldn't tell, only that they were more excited than ever. Surely they couldn't have seen him or the Indian women and the kid. Had enough noise been made for them to have heard? Well, maybe. Sounds carried far on a clear day. . . .

One fellow, dismounted, seemed to be looking back across the river through a set of binoculars. The rest milled about indecisively, as if in disagreement about what to do next. The one with the binoculars pointed urgently toward the mountain. Or was it the knoll after all? Damn them, what were they doing?

Suddenly the one on the ground remounted and they all began moving off, looking back, their huge hats wagging one way then the other as they went. Cordalee looked on in disbelief. They were going back! Just like that, they were going back the way they had come!

He looked over at the Indian girl, who still crouched where he'd left her. Only now her eyes were back on him.

"¿Por qué?" he asked sharply. "Why did they go back? Those men were after me. They wanted to kill me. . . ."

Something about the girl's expression caused him to break off. He watched as she cast a quick look over at the older woman and the boy. She uttered something guttural, then looked past Cordalee's shoulder toward the mountain.

Cordalee turned to try to follow her gaze, though he kept her in sight out of the corner of one eye. All he saw on the mountainside where she seemed to be looking was a canyon cutting well back between two towering bluffs.

"What is it?" he asked. "You understand me; I know you do. What are you looking at?"

Then he saw something moving halfway down one side of the steep canyon. Horsemen! Just close enough to be seen, they were coming single file down what looked to be an almost impossible trail.

Cordalee whirled on the girl. "Who are they?" he demanded hoarsely.

She didn't look at him. She never once took her eyes off the thin line of tiny figures coming down the mountainside. But finally she spoke in clear, concise Spanish, with only one strange, very Indian-sounding word thrown in:

"They are Indeh," she said. "They are Apaches."

Luther Cordalee's disbelieving ears could not keep his blood from suddenly running very, very cold.

CHAPTER 2

For almost a minute Cordalee watched the line of horsemen as they toiled slowly downward over a tortuously zigzagging route. Still, he found it hard to believe they were Apaches. Every official statement he had seen or heard over the past eight months denied the possibility. But who were they, then? The girl had seemed so positive.

He turned to find that she had not moved except to shift her position slightly away from the bush he had thrown her into. Her eyes met his without wavering.

"I don't think those are Apaches," he announced suddenly in Spanish. "I think you are either guessing or lying. I don't think you know who those riders are at all."

For a moment he thought she wasn't going to reply, but then she tossed her head and said confidently, "They are Apaches." Beyond this, it seemed clear that she didn't care a whit for whether he believed her or not.

"Are you an Apache? Are this old woman and the kid Apaches, too? Is that how you know?"

This time she said nothing.

He looked at the old woman, but she gave no sign of having understood any of it. The boy's expression remained one mostly of fear.

Cordalee turned his gaze back to the mountainside. At first he couldn't relocate the horsemen, then he saw them, still small figures coming one at a time around a bend. He estimated that in straight-line distance they could be little more than a mile away, yet at the pace they were coming they could also be as much as an hour from reaching the river—plenty of time for him to get out of there before they arrived.

Or was it? What if the two women and the kid were waiting to join them? Wouldn't they tell of the white man who had run off into the brush? And how far would he get—on foot against a group of wild Apache horsemen?

He turned once again to the girl. She had struggled to her feet now and was looking down at the old woman and the kid, both still hunkering inside the mesquites.

Cordalee said, "Get them out of there. There's no use them hiding anymore; I'm not going to hurt them."

The girl bent to help the boy out of the bush. The youngster, probably no more than nine or ten years of age, scrambled to her side, his big eyes still fastened on Cordalee in both suspicion and fear. The old woman, however, did not move and the girl did nothing to help her.

"What's the matter with her?" Cordalee asked impatiently. "Can't she get out?"

"She is hurt. It is her leg, a gunshot wound. And she is very tired. She thinks she should be left to die." Her Spanish, in an elongated speech, was better than his.

He shook his head. Well, that sure sounded like an Apache, all right. Who else, after all, went off and left their old and injured to die? Damn them. It was only one of the things he didn't like about them. Matter of fact, after five long years serving the Department of Arizona, the only thing he had learned to dislike more than Apaches was the Army itself. God, how miserable they both could be!

And yet, he couldn't help feeling sorry for this poor old woman cowering feverishly before him. The miserable creature obviously needed help. He looked back at the girl. "Here, help me get her out. Let me look at her wound."

The girl looked suspicious at first, then without a word, began to help him. Together they managed to drag the old woman out into the open, getting only a resentful stare and a painful grunt in return for their trouble. After much urging, they got her to let them raise her dress above the knee. The wound, in the muscle of the right leg just above the knee, was badly infected and swollen. Pus oozed freely and there was a huge bruise around the ugly round hole where the bullet had entered and apparently lodged against the bone.

"Who did this to her?" Cordalee asked.

The girl hesitated for a moment, then shrugged. "It was the Mexicans. Two days ago we were seen from a distance by a group of *soldados* from Chihuahua. They shot at us. We ran into the brush and they were unable to find us and they finally gave up. But the old woman was hit and left hurting. She did not want to come with me. She wanted to stay behind. She would not tell me how to dress the wound with the proper poultice of herbs, but I would not take the child and leave unless she came too. It made her mad, but she came. She had not spoken to me for those two days, until a while ago when she spotted those Mexicans turning back across the river."

Cordalee frowned. "Well, I suspect she's going to have to have that bullet out pretty quick, or it won't make any difference." It amazed him that the old hag had been able to walk at all, even with help. She's tough, he thought, tough like only an Apache can be.

Again his eyes drifted back to the mountain. The thin file of riders was still coming, although they seemed to have made only slight progress since he had last seen them. The question as to what he should do for his own protection returned, and no better answer than before came to him. To try to escape on foot seemed pointless; to hang around waiting seemed even worse.

But was it really? His own natural impatience to get away said to him only a fool would stay where he was even one minute longer. But what did it matter unless he could do something to keep the two women and the kid from giving him away? Somehow he would have to keep them quiet. The question was, how could he?

He addressed the girl. "You didn't answer me when I asked if you were an Apache. I think you must be, for you seem to know those people coming down the mountain. I think when they get close enough you will call to them. I think you will give me away to them."

She stared at him with fathomless eyes. "What would you have me do instead?"

He wagged his head. "I don't know. I just don't want to get killed. I'm trying to figure out a way to protect myself. I want to know what you are going to do."

She was silent a moment before saying, "We have come a long way to find those people. They are our people. We have no one else to go to. Why wouldn't I call to them?"

"If I went away and hid in the brush, would you tell them where I was?"

She was silent, noncommittal.

Cordalee pressed to make his case, struggling somewhat with his Spanish as he did. "All I'm asking is to be left alone, to be allowed to go my own way unharmed. Is that asking too much?"

Still, she said nothing.

"I have not harmed you," he said. "If I leave you here without hurting you, can't you do the same for me?"

She shook her head uncertainly. "I don't know. You have seen them up there on the mountain. You have seen that there is a trail. No white man is supposed to know. You might come back with more Americans. You are even dressed like an American *soldado*. The Americans have come into Mexico after our people before, and they have taken many away. There are only a few free ones left. If they, too, are taken, there will be no more."

"But I would promise not to do that. I would never bring soldiers, or anyone else, to these mountains. I would promise that."

"The Americans have always promised. My people become especially worried when that happens. The promises have seldom been kept."

He didn't know what to say to that. He hadn't thought of it that way. In his mind, the Apaches had always been the ones to break faith; they were the ones who had promised so many times to be good, only to break loose from the reservations again and again to murder and steal. Such had been the case with Gerónimo. Had he not matched every broken promise with a broken promise of his own several times over?

But Cordalee sensed he would get nowhere fast if he argued the point. He must find another tack.

"Listen," he said. "I couldn't bring the Americans here if I wanted to. I am a deserter from their Army. If they catch me, I might be imprisoned or shot. I only want to be left alone, just as you do."

Once again she chose to answer him with silence, her expression glazing over so that Cordalee couldn't even tell if she was thinking about what he had said. Then the old woman grunted something and the girl bent down beside her. A few clipped phrases passed between them, and the girl turned to the boy, standing close at her shoulder now.

To him she uttered a few more words; then she reached down and ripped a piece of cloth from the hem of her dress and handed it to him. He hesitated a moment and she spoke some command, harshly this time. The boy turned as if aiming to go back down through the canebrake to the river.

"Wait a minute!" Cordalee barked. "Where is he going?"

"To the river. The old woman is feverish and the pain in her leg is growing unbearable. The boy is only going to dampen the cloth so that I can tend to her at least a little bit."

The boy stood, unsure if to go ahead, waiting for some word of instruction in a language he could understand.

Finally Cordalee said, "Okay. I lost my canteen this morning somewhere on the trail. He'll have to go to the river for water. But tell him to hurry it up."

The girl turned to the boy and said something that sounded like *"Ugashe!"* and the boy scampered off through the mesquites toward the canebrake.

Looking back to the mountain once more, Cordalee struggled to locate
the file of riders. Scaling downward from where he had last seen them, his
eyes finally picked up movement again. Suddenly he realized how much
closer they had come—almost having reached the narrow band of foothills
that separated the mountains from the river. Coming much faster than he
had at first anticipated, they looked to be no more than fifteen or twenty
minutes away.

Cordalee said to the girl, "Do they know you're here? Will they come
this way?"

Her features, though lacking the typically prominent cheekbones and
straight mouth of the average Apache, were nevertheless Apache glum as
she watched the line of riders make their way down onto the foot slopes
and disappear into heavy brush.

"Well?" Cordalee persisted. "Do they know you're here?"

"No," she said. "They do not know. Not unless they saw us crossing
the river, and I doubt if that was the case. I think they were too far away
then."

"Then where are they going? Will they pass close by?"

"I don't know where they are going, except that they will probably
cross the river at the *vado*. The trail passes just the other side of this little
hill. They cannot see us from there, but we can see them for part of the
way as they go around."

He eyed her curiously. "You've been here before, then. Maybe you've
even been up on that mountain." His eyes narrowed. "Maybe you've even
lived there and plan to do so again."

She looked at him darkly. "Yes. I have lived there."

"When?"

"Not long ago. A year maybe, but then for only a very short time."

"But you could find your way up there alone, couldn't you? Am I not
right about that?"

She gave him a puzzled look. "Yes, I could find my way there alone.
Why?"

"Because I want you to let them go on by. I want you to give me time
to get away. Then, later, you and the old woman and the kid can either go
on up the mountain the way you must have planned to do in the first
place, or you can wait for those riders to come back from wherever they're
going."

Her eyes flashed. "The old woman will never make it up the trail on
foot now. It is too steep and rough for one in her condition. Those riders
are our best chance of making it, but if we let them go on by now that
chance will be gone. You are asking too much of us."

Cordalee had caught just a glimpse of the horsemen again, coming at a trot now through the brush of the foot slopes. He had not yet been able to count them, but his guess was between ten and fifteen. And they were getting close; time was fast running out on him while he stood there arguing uselessly with the girl.

"Okay," he told her. "I'm just going to have to force you." He raised the rifle threateningly. "You keep quiet while those Apaches pass by, or I'll kill the both of you. And the kid, too . . . if he ever gets back. Where is he, anyway?"

All but the bitterness in her eyes was masked as the girl said, "He will be back."

"Well, he'd better hurry. Those riders will be here damned quick. And you—you understand what I'm telling you? Not a sound from either of you, or I'll . . . I'll bust you in the mouth with this rifle butt. And here, get farther behind these bushes. I don't want to take any chances on being seen."

The girl spoke to the old woman, then they grudgingly moved in behind a nearby mesquite clump. Cordalee came over to crouch near them, making sure he had room to keep his rifle trained on them and also that he was in a position to see past the edge of the knoll. He had picked out the general area where he expected the Apaches to show themselves, and he didn't want his view obstructed any more than was absolutely necessary.

Several minutes passed and still nothing happened. Then, suddenly, the first of several horsemen appeared coming out of the brush about three hundred yards away. They were coming straight on at a good gait. Cordalee finally counted twelve riders in all, at least half of whom led pack mules behind their horses. One look, even at that distance, was all Cordalee needed to dispel any lingering doubts as to who they were. Everything from the way they sat their wiry, sure-footed ponies to their raven-black hair worn long and held away from their coppery-skinned faces by broad, flat headbands of variously colored cloths spelled Apache. Cordalee's heart became a pounding turmoil inside his chest, and he wondered again why the kid had not returned from the river. He knew now that he should never have been so stupid as to let him go, and he cursed himself for it.

But it was too late to fret about that; all he could do was to sit and watch the small caravan make its approach and keep an eye on the two women at the same time.

It seemed to take forever for the Indians to close the remaining distance between them and the knoll. Twice they dipped down to cross arroyos, disappearing only briefly before coming back into view again. In and out of the brush they came, until finally they were almost upon the rocky knoll. Then, just as it looked like they would continue right into Cordalee's hiding place, they swerved to follow the trail around the hill, passing between it and the steeper foot slopes beyond before going out of sight on the other side. They had gone exactly the way the girl had predicted they would. Cordalee listened as the clatter of hoofs died away, then he heaved a controlled sigh of relief.

He looked around at the two women, both of whom met his gaze with stolid ones of their own. Somehow he was surprised that they had remained quiet; he had almost expected them to yell out at the last moment when the Apaches had been their closest. He knew, and he suspected the two women did too, that he could have done nothing at that point to stop them. He doubted he could have brought himself to kill either of them. He would have been completely helpless . . . still was, for that matter, assuming the riders were yet within earshot of a good healthy scream.

Then he thought once more of the boy, and he turned on the girl. "Why didn't that kid come back? I told you to tell him to hurry."

The girl said nothing; in fact, she looked away from him for the first time with a strong reluctance to meet his gaze.

A sound in the brush behind Cordalee caused him to rise and whirl around. Fear rose in his throat as another sound off to his right, and another to his left, came to him almost simultaneously. Instantly he recognized the sound of a cartridge being levered into a firing chamber. He all but forgot his own rifle as something moved in the mesquites not twenty feet in front of him. He simply stood, staring helplessly as all of a sudden the brush around him seemed to come alive with bronze-faced, breech-clouted forms, armed and deadly looking to a man.

Central among them was a slender, straight-shouldered Apache, the missing boy standing resolutely at his side.

CHAPTER 3

Cordalee could no more move a muscle than he could take his eyes off the somber-eyed young Apache standing in front of him. No more than twenty-two or -three years old, the Indian nevertheless exuded importance from every pore. He was a good two inches shorter and perhaps fifteen pounds lighter than Cordalee, yet he was not small for an Apache. He was almost perfectly proportioned: lithe, muscular, large-chested, and straight. His face did not look savage; rather, he was almost handsome, and his expression was more one of curiosity than anything else. His long black hair was held in good control by a dark blue headband, and his clear black eyes were both bright and bold. His clothing was typically Apache: a loose-fitting gray shirt worn beneath a dark leather vest, a pair of cotton trousers that looked more like underwear, a knee-length breechclout, and as perfect a pair of roll-topped Apache moccasins as Cordalee had ever seen. All around them, similarly attired figures came out of the brush, their dark eyes coolly taking in the strange white man and the two Indian women still hunkering within the mesquite clump.

None of the Indians wore paint on their faces, but all were armed with rifles and revolvers, and each wore at least one cartridge belt filled with ammunition. Cordalee was quickly relieved of his own weapons.

Finally the slender warrior who Cordalee had instantly taken for the group's leader, said something to the girl, now rising from the bush to stand upright not three steps from Cordalee. She responded in Apache and the young leader grunted. For a few moments they carried on a lively conversation, during which the young woman gestured first to the old woman and the kid, then to the northeast, to herself, back across the river, and finally to Cordalee. The warrior followed her every gesture with much interest, his eyes at last coming to rest firmly on the white man.

When he spoke this time, it was in Spanish. "This girl tells me you understand *español*. She says you can speak for yourself as to what you are doing here and what is your name."

Cordalee, half surprised to be still alive at this point, tried to answer through a mouth and throat so dry he could hardly croak. "Cor . . . dalee . . ." he managed. "My name is Luther Cordalee."

"Cor-dah-lee," the Indian repeated, cutting the name into syllables in typical Apache fashion and somewhat after the manner Cordalee himself had first pronounced it. "Cor-dah-lee. Huh!" He looked around at some of the other men, most of whom were little, if any, older than he was. "Cor-dah-lee," he repeated. The sound of it seemed to please him. "Okay, Cor-dah-lee, tell me what you are doing here."

Cordalee hesitated, trying to think it out in Spanish as well as to figure out the tack this Indian meant to take with him. Thus far, he wasn't having an easy time of either undertaking.

Finally he decided it best to be candid, while at the same time elaborating no more than seemed absolutely necessary. "I am a deserter from the American Army," he began. "About a month ago I came into Mexico hoping to find a place to hide as well as maybe to do a little prospecting. I wound up spending most of my time near Fronteras. I got along all right there until last night when I had a fight with a Mexican in one of the cantinas. The fellow drew a gun on me and I was forced to shoot him. I left town with a dozen or so of his amigos close behind me. I lost them during the night, then discovered they had found my trail again somewhere this side of the San Bernardino this morning. I still had a good lead on them, but then I rode my horse too hard and he played out on me before I reached this river. My pursuers were just arriving about the time I found these women. They turned back for Fronteras when they saw you Apaches coming down the mountain." He looked the Indian in the eye. "Maybe you saw them go."

"We saw them," the Apache acknowledged, "but they did not go as far as you think. They only went beyond the first ridge, where you cannot see them. I think you are not saved yet."

Cordalee didn't know how to react to this. He had all but forgotten about the Mexicans as he waited for the Indians. And he still had not figured out the young Apache standing before him, except that somehow he did not seem as savagely ferocious as one might have expected him to be. Quickly Cordalee decided on a position of boldness.

"I have told you my name," he said. "What is yours? And what are *you* doing here? I thought all Apaches had surrendered and left Mexico months ago."

The Indian's eyes narrowed. "I am called Miguelito. This is my home. I belong here. As you can see, I have surrendered to no one. Nor will I ever. That is why these women were coming to me. I am the chief of the only clan of Apaches who are yet free."

Cordalee looked over at the two women. "And where were they coming to you from?"

Miguelito also looked over at the two women. He seemed to be deciding whether to give an answer. After a moment, he brought his gaze back to rest on Cordalee, apparently having concluded that it could hardly hurt anything to tell this lone white man what he wanted to know. After all, he could always kill him later. . . .

"They were with Mangus, the last war chief of the Mimbreno Apaches, son of Mangas Coloradas, their greatest chief ever. She tells me that Mangus did not join with Gerónimo and Chief Naiche of the Chiricahuas when they surrendered to the White Eyes' *nantan*—the one you call General Miles—in Arizona. These two women and the boy are all that is left of Mangus' small band, and they only because they hid in the hills in Chihuahua while Mangus and the others raided a ranch near Los Corralitos and then got themselves caught."

Cordalee looked at the girl. He had heard of Mangus, supposedly the last important Apache to be taken into captivity—last October it had been, although not nearly so prestigious or newsworthy an event as the surrender of Gerónimo a month earlier. But that had been almost seven months ago. . . .

He looked at Miguelito. "How do you know all that? How do you know yours is the only free Apache band left?"

The Indian shrugged. "Some of it this girl has just told me, of course. The rest we have learned from this or that bronco Apache who comes now and then to visit us from Arizona. We have been told that all of our people are on reservations somewhere—all except those few broncos and us. We do not doubt that this is true."

Cordalee glanced once again at the two women. "It has been months since Mangus was captured. Where have these two and the boy been since then?"

"They say they were captured by some *Chihuahuenos* who took them to a rancho east of Janos and made them slaves. It wasn't until ten days ago that they managed to escape and begin their journey here."

"And 'here,'" Cordalee concluded quickly, "is actually someplace atop those mountains there. These women knew about a secret Apache stronghold up there, and they were heading for it. Your stronghold, Miguelito. Your band of free Apaches."

Miguelito met his gaze for a moment, then gave an impatient grunt as if he had already said more than he wanted to. He turned to one of his men and said something. The man replied, as if in concurrence, then turned and motioned to another man standing nearby. Both disappeared in the brush.

"Where are they going?"

The young chief said, "To get their horses. The old woman, here, has been wounded. Someone must take her up the mountain to our shaman."

"And the rest of you? Where are you going?"

"To Magdalena to trade for goods and horses."

Cordalee wasn't sure he'd heard right. Apache Indians, the most accomplished thieves and raiders in all the Southwest—in the world, maybe—*trading* for goods and horses! He would believe that when he saw it!

Then his eyes settled on the old woman as two men moved to help her up. She moved slowly and with great pain. Cordalee began thinking of the Mexicans waiting for him across the river; he wondered if he might be able to delay the Apaches' departure long enough that his pursuers might finally give up for good and leave.

He said, "That woman needs a doctor, Miguelito. She has a bullet buried in her leg. Can your medicine man take it out? I don't think the wound will heal without it. She may even lose the leg, or die, if the bullet is not removed."

Miguelito scowled impatiently. "Our shaman knows about such things. He can heal her."

Cordalee shrugged. "*Bueno.* Good for the shaman. Just thought I'd mention it, since I've already seen the wound and you have not."

The Indian eyed Cordalee thoughtfully, then asked, "Are you a White Eye *médico?* Can you take the bullet out?"

"I worked with the post surgeon a few times," Cordalee replied warily, knowing better than to appear too anxious. "But that doesn't make me a doctor. No, I don't think I could do it. Especially without the proper instruments. No."

"But you saw your White Eye doctor take out bullets?"

"Yes. Yes, I did. But watching and doing are two different things. Besides, what is this old woman to you? I've always heard that you Apaches simply leave your old and weak behind to die. . . ."

Something in the Indian's eyes made him stop. The Apache said tersely, "It is important that this old woman lives. I have recognized her as an aunt of mine, a half-sister to my mother. It will go very badly if she dies."

"Well, good luck to you and the shaman," Cordalee said.

Miguelito studied him coolly for a moment, then turned abruptly to give instructions to another of his lieutenants. This man took off into the brush, as had the two before him.

"Now what?" Cordalee asked.

"You and I are going up the mountain with the others."

"Now wait a minute . . . !" Cordalee had thought to detain the Indians, not to *join* them. "I don't know that I want to go up on that mountain."

"Would you rather we turned you over to the Mexicans?" the Apache asked icily.

Cordalee looked around uncertainly. Every gaze he met was deadly serious. He had no doubt that they would give him over to his enemies in a flash, or kill him themselves, if he resisted them. Neither thought appealed to him. For a while he'd been lulled by their apparent lack of ill will, but now the words of an old Army scout he'd known came to him: "Once an Apache always an Apache, boy. Don't ever forget that. They'll smile at you one minute and sull on you the next. And when they sull, well, just you look out. You damn well better look out."

Cordalee made his decision quickly. "Do I get a horse," he asked of the young chief, "or do I have to make it up that trail on foot?"

Cordalee was escorted down the hill by one of the young men to where three horses and a mule stood waiting. He was handed the reins of a rawboned buckskin and told to wait until the others were ready to leave.

Presently, two men—Miguelito and one other—came out of the mesquites carrying the injured old woman between them; following them came the younger woman and the boy. The balance of the group apparently had gone off some other way.

Cordalee watched as the Apaches helped the old woman painfully aboard a small blaze-faced roan mare, then brought around the mule for the young woman and the boy to share. Miguelito swiftly mounted the remaining animal, a dark bay that did not have a marking of white anywhere on it.

"Get on your horse, Cor-dah-lee," he ordered.

Cordalee heaved himself into the big-horned Mexican saddle worn by the buckskin and reined the horse around to face the Indians. Looking on around the edge of the knoll, he now could see the other group mounting their horses and taking up the lead ropes of the remaining pack mules, apparently to continue on with the "trading trip" to Magdalena. Miguelito, the two women, the boy, Cordalee, and two young men on foot watched the larger group disappear in the brush as they made their way toward the canebrake and the river *vado*.

"These men will walk," Miguelito said matter-of-factly, nodding toward the two sturdy young Indians on the ground. "We can spare only one mule for riding. You will follow me, Cor-dah-lee." Then he kicked his bay forward and moved into the brush in the direction of the mountain trail. By the time they actually reached the base of the steepest incline and Cordalee began to get a close look at the zigzag trail that led up the mountain, he had to wonder again if any of it was really scalable.

"How long will it take to reach the top?" he asked.

Miguelito glanced back. "This is a hard climb and we must rest often. It will be night when we get to the ranchería."

Then he looked back across the river, which was already a couple hundred feet below them. A smile crossed his face. "There go your Mexican friends. See? They have spotted my men."

Cordalee located the first group easily—a small cluster of horsemen moving out at a good pace from the shelter of a wide, flat wash cutting across the Fronteras trail. A low ridge back from them, along the near edge of the broad plain that stretched toward the San Bernardino, came another group of riders—Miguelito's Apache warriors with their small packtrain. The first party was obviously taking pains to put all the distance possible between them and the second. The Apaches, on the other hand, seemed content to maintain a steady pace and let the Mexicans go. Cordalee could imagine them actually laughing at the fright they were putting into their longtime enemies as they went.

But Miguelito was no longer smiling when Cordalee turned back around. Something about the scene must have begun to bother him. But he said nothing more; he simply reined his horse around and continued on up the trail. The rest of the small party formed behind him, going single file because that was all the room there was on the trail. There was no further talk for the moment.

Cordalee soon realized that no matter how rugged the trail looked from below, there was no comparison between that and how it really was. The horses and mule labored constantly upward, over and around rocks, through dense brush and around small cedar trees, and always along the narrowest of trails. Many times they overlooked sheer precipices that dropped off as much as several hundred feet into the ever-deepening maw of a canyon below them. The height, mixed with the constant sensation of being on the verge of falling, gave one a heady feeling, and only the complete lack of a sound alternative kept Cordalee on his horse and climbing.

Higher and higher they went. Below, the trail wound back and forth, in and out of shadows along the edge of the canyon. Above, the mountaintop seemed to sway permanently beyond their grasp, sometimes hidden entirely by treetops—the first tall pines now—and jutting rock outcrops and ledges that at times blotted out substantial portions of the sky as well.

Cordalee, glancing back, saw the girl and the boy coming right behind him, then came the old woman with one of the two young men striding alongside her mare and helping her to stay on. The other men brought up the rear, his tireless legs set in a perpetual shuffle, his impassive face revealing nothing as to how tired he really was. Talk came infrequently and usually only during the brief stops taken so the horses could be allowed to get their wind. The afternoon passed in the paradoxical manner of swiftness blended with action that seemed bound to continue into eternity. Both extreme hunger and thirst gnawed at Cordalee's insides, and he felt weak and even more light-headed than ever.

As Miguelito had predicted, dark was upon them by the time they finally ceased climbing and found themselves crossing a relatively level maze of shallow canyons and glens surrounded by tall pines and oak brush. A guard challenged them at one point, then acknowledged who they were and let them pass on by, and finally they broke out into what appeared to be a flat tabletop about half a mile wide and no telling how long. Stars blinked in a clear sky overhead, and the skyline before them was broken only by the towering tops of the pines that rimmed the flat expanse on all sides.

Shortly they broke out upon a clearing, and the ranchería lay before them. Small cookfires illuminated an area of scattered brush arbors, or wickiups; voices chattered excitedly; dark figures came to surround the small party and follow them into the camp. They dismounted in front of one of the wickiups, located at one end of the village, and a dark-eyed older woman emerged. Behind her came a gray-haired apparition who was both thin and shriveled, with the deep-set eyes of the wildest coyote and a gap-toothed grin that was easily more a smirk than a smile.

Miguelito was the first to speak. His words were in Spanish. "Cor-dah-lee, this woman is my mother. Her name is Nah-de-glesh. She will feed you and give you a chance to rest. This one standing beside her is called Old Man Din; he is our shaman. He will tend for now to my aunt, E-kon-sen-de-he. Later, when you are rested, we will talk of taking that bullet out."

CHAPTER 4

Food was served to Cordalee in a large shallow bowl just outside the wickiup of Nah-de-glesh. Joining him were the young woman and the boy from the Bavispe. The meal consisted of boiled venison, black coffee, and a kind of flat pancake resembling a Mexican tortilla. Cordalee ate ravenously, and Nah-de-glesh silently refilled his bowl and tin coffee cup the moment he finished the first helping.

Across the way, children were playing, and just moments ago Miguelito had disappeared inside what Cordalee assumed was the chief's own wickiup, followed by a slight, very young Apache woman whom Cordalee took to be the chief's wife. E-kon-sen-de-he, in graver pain than ever now, had immediately been carried to another wickiup somewhere beyond the chief's, the medicine man trotting alongside, chanting and dusting her with a kind of powder or meal that Cordalee assumed carried some significant religious importance.

After finishing with his second bowlful of venison, Cordalee looked over at the girl who sat across from him.

"How do you ask for more coffee in Apache?" He did not know if Nah-de-glesh understood Spanish and, feeling unsure of himself in the presence of the chief's mother, hesitated to address her directly anyway.

"*Tu-dishishn*," the girl said, then added in Spanish, "It means black water. And don't worry, Nah-de-glesh understands Spanish, more or less, though many of the Apaches here do not."

"*Gracias*," Cordalee told Nah-de-glesh as she came over to refill his cup. She grunted something unintelligible and retook her seat near the entrance to the wickiup.

Cordalee looked back at the girl. "Miguelito said you were captured and made a slave by the Mexicans. Over in Chihuahua, near Janos. Isn't that a long way from here?"

"Yes, it is a long way."

"Ten days on foot, I think he said. You must have had to cross the mountains north of the main Sierra Madre. Quite a rough trip for two women and a kid, I'd think."

She stared at him impassively. "Yes, very rough. We came by way of the Sierra Enmedios, through what is now known as Crook's Pass, then south to the Bavispe. It was at Crook's Pass that E-kon-sen-de-he was shot by the *Chihuahuenos*."

"And then you ran into me on the Bavispe. What did you think when I came stumbling into the brush where you were hiding? Besides landing square in the middle of my back the way you did, of course." He smiled thinly.

She shrugged. "Any other time I would have had a knife. I would have killed you"—she paused before adding—"of course."

Again Cordalee marveled at the girl's Spanish. "You aren't really an Apache, are you? Something just isn't right about you—your features are too fine, your Spanish too perfect. Am I not right?"

The line of her mouth grew thin and her eyes flashed. "I don't want to tell you about that," she said in a low voice.

He was just finishing his coffee when a voice came from inside the wickiup. It was a feminine voice, speaking in Apache, yet somehow less guttural, clearer, than most others he had heard. Startled, Cordalee turned his gaze on the darkened entrance to the domelike structure, but could see nothing inside. He wondered who on earth would be sitting, apparently alone, in the dark like that. Possibly someone sick, he thought.

As Nah-de-glesh rose and disappeared inside, Cordalee looked quizzically over at the girl. Getting no reaction from her, he was just about to voice his question when a lithe form came stalking across the compound and interrupted them.

"I see you have eaten," Miguelito said, coming up to squat before the fire. "I hope you do not mind the small variety we have to serve. We are out, or nearly out, of many things—sugar, salt, flour, mescal—and have been using what supplies we have of these things very sparingly for some time now. That is why my men went on to Magdalena. When they return, things will be better. It is our first chance to get supplies since the leaves were red and Gerónimo surrendered. As a tribe, it will be our first such trading trip ever."

Cordalee allowed silently as to how he could well believe that! But at the same time this Indian's frankness—not exactly an Apache-like trait around white men—was beginning to intrigue him deeply. It had also begun to bother him. The Indian didn't seem to be worried in the least how much Cordalee knew. It was as if the white man would never be allowed the chance to tell of it anyway.

"The meal was fine, Miguelito," he said. "It's what happens next that has me wondering."

35935

The young woman and the boy elected at this point to get up and leave, and the two men were suddenly left alone.

Miguelito watched them go, then turned back to Cordalee. "You are, so far as we know, the only *norteamericano* who knows about this place—and us. Your future has to do with what we decide you might do because of that."

"You think I might bring the American Army down on you?"

"You are an American," the young chief said simply. "You wear American Army clothes and you carry American Army weapons."

"But I told you, also, I am a deserter. I left Fort Huachuca over a month ago. I am a wanted man in my own country and cannot go back to it."

"I don't know anything about that," the chief insisted. "Only that you are an American—"

"And not to be trusted," Cordalee filled in.

The Indian shrugged lightly. "I am still trying to decide about that."

"You could have killed me when you first found me, you know. Then you wouldn't have had to decide anything."

Miguelito nodded, his eyes narrowing. "Yes. That's true."

"But you didn't. At first, you were curious; then you thought I might save your aunt's life, so you brought me here instead. You are a strange Apache, Miguelito. I never encountered your like before."

The young Indian's body stiffened and his expression darkened. "I still might kill you. That would be more like an Apache, wouldn't it? Maybe I will let you save old E-kon-sen-de-he's life, then I will cut your throat and hack you up in little pieces and leave what is left of your body for the Mexicans to find. Would that not be more the Apache thing to do?"

"The Apaches I've heard about and seen, yes," Cordalee answered, although not at all comfortably.

Miguelito rose abruptly. "I do not think you know much about Apaches. I thought I might like you, but now I am not so sure."

Cordalee also got to his feet, but he could think of nothing to say.

"No matter for now," Miguelito said. "You are still a guest here. I will find you an empty wickiup and some blankets, for it will be cold on the mountain tonight. Tomorrow we will talk more."

Cordalee stared at him. "But what about the old woman? You wanted me to try to take the bullet out of her leg. What if I decide to run away during the night? I mean—"

"You won't run away. There will be someone watching to make sure of that. And the old shaman will not yet hear of anyone fooling around with his patient. He has mixed the proper herbs and made a poultice, and is singing and doing all of the other things shamans do. He will be all night with her, and we will just have to be patient and see what he decides."

"You mean I'm going to have to stay here indefinitely?"

"Until something different is decided, yes . . ." The young chief broke off as Nah-de-glesh came out of the wickiup and said something in Apache. He murmured a reply, then turned back to Cordalee.

"Are you ready to go to your wickiup?"

Cordalee was staring once again at the opening of the brush arbor. "Yes . . . but first tell me who is in there. Why won't she come out?"

"Why do you want to know that?"

"I don't know; just curious, I guess."

"Well," Miguelito said bluntly, "you will just have to stay that way, because I am not going to tell you."

Cordalee, hardly surprised, shrugged and turned his gaze across the compound. Cook fires burned low and voices coming from the various wickiups nearby were muffled. Even the children had ceased scampering about and calling to one another now.

The Apache said, "Come with me, Cor-dah-lee. Your wickiup is over this way."

Acutely aware of the many dark and suspicious stares that would follow him every step of the way, Cordalee sighed deeply and followed the young chief toward the far side of the rancheria.

Had Cordalee been anything but dead tired when Miguelito showed him to the empty wickiup and gave him blankets, he would have found it a long, cold night indeed. He noticed that a fire had been started for him inside and was burning low, and that a bed of skins awaited him against one wall; but beyond that, he was quickly oblivious to all but his own desperate need for sleep and rest. He was in deep slumber within minutes of being left alone and did not even know when his fire died a few hours later.

When he awoke, it was to a cold, clear morning and a flood of sun's rays shining in through the open doorway of the wickiup. For a moment he wasn't sure where he was. Then he saw his rolled-up poncho lying off to one side, and memories of yesterday's extraordinary experience came flooding back. Outside, a mule brayed and children's voices rang. A bird whistled shrilly, the sounds of people bustling about a camp grew distinct, and the smell of wood smoke filled the air. From somewhere came the cheerful gurgle of water running, and someone outside was calling his name.

"Cor-dah-lee, are you awake?" the voice queried in Spanish. "I have you some coffee and some food."

Cordalee ran a hand through his tousled hair and lurched to his feet, wrapping as he did one of the blankets around his shoulders in an effort to keep warm and to avoid the necessity of unrolling his poncho to look for his coat. It was hard to believe it had been so hot the day before.

Miguelito stood just outside, a fire already going and a coffeepot sitting perched atop two flat rocks in the center of the pit. He held two bowls, one of which he proffered to the sleepy-eyed Cordalee. "More venison and ashcakes, I am afraid. But even that is better than going hungry. Here, sit down. I have come to eat with you."

Cordalee took the bowl and squatted down across the fire from the Indian. He noticed two brimful coffee cups sitting on a rock next to the cook fire, their contents steaming in the crisp air. "I thought you had decided not to like me," he said, reaching for a cup.

"I have decided to try harder," the Apache said, looking even more youthful than he had the day before, but no less solemn. Somehow, though, Cordalee sensed he was being laughed at. It made him feel uncomfortable, but he couldn't help smiling.

"How is your aunt this morning?" he asked as he tested his coffee. "Has the medicine man's magic helped her any?"

Miguelito shook his head seriously. "Her leg is swollen and has turned almost black. I don't think the shaman is very happy with his medicine. When I went to his wickiup at dawn, he met me at the door, growling and snarling like a pregnant wolf."

Cordalee, following the Indian's example of eating with his fingers, asked, "What are you going to do?"

"I am unsure. I think I will talk with my mother and . . . and another one who is also wise. It is ticklish business, dealing with shamans."

Cordalee eyed him thoughtfully. He was wondering, among other things, if this other one who was "also wise" might not be whoever had sat mysteriously inside Nah-de-glesh's darkened wickiup last night. "Do you still think I might take the bullet out?" he asked.

"Yes. Because you have helped the White Eye doctor do such a thing before, I believe you can do it for E-kon-sen-de-he. But I cannot make such a decision alone. It will depend on the shaman and maybe a full council of our elders."

"But what if I fail? What if I cannot help E-kon-sen-de-he and she dies?"

Miguelito was silent for a moment, then said, "We would not let you try if we did not think she would die otherwise. It would simply be the will of Ussen if that happens."

Cordalee frowned. "Who is Ussen?"

"Ussen is the Apache God. He is the Life Giver, the Creator of All Things. It would be He who would have you succeed or fail."

Cordalee couldn't help a slight shiver at this. Miguelito had been right; he really didn't know much about the Apaches.

He looked around at the ranchería, finding nothing terribly different in the immediate scene from what it had seemed to him last night. There were maybe thirty or thirty-five brush-walled, hide-covered wickiups, all facing the morning sun and arranged in a large, loose circle of perhaps a hundred yards in diameter. Children were playing here and there, dirty, ragged, and half-naked but somehow not the models of impoverishment one might have expected. There was a purity about them, a raw beauty ordinarily reserved for the most natural of creatures; and they were bright-eyed and happy—nothing like the sad, silent little things Cordalee had seen on the reservation back in Arizona. . . .

He wagged his head, letting his gaze move to take in the larger scene. Beyond the wickiups, to the south and arranged on the opposite bank of a small, gurgling stream, two large brush and pole corrals held maybe fifteen or twenty horses and mules, most of which were obviously of inbred mustang stock although several were just as plainly well bred. Beyond this, in fact surrounding the entire village, were thickets of oak brush and pine, interspersed with small openings. Grass grew abundantly out away from the camp where it had not been stomped and grazed away, and the soil was a deep red clay that Cordalee imagined could become quite sticky when wet, maybe staying that way for days at a time after a good rain or snow. Through one opening, Cordalee even spotted a couple of skinny Mexican cows and a calf, and he was fairly sure he had seen several others moving in the brush beyond these.

But, as his eyes came back to the closer surroundings, he knew something was missing. He had sensed it last night, but had been too tired and confused to think it out. Suddenly it came to him.

"There are no dogs, Miguelito," he said. "I never heard of an Indian village without dogs."

The Apache almost smiled. "You have not seen us moving around trying to stay one step ahead of the American Army and scouts for days, even weeks, on end. You don't realize how we have had to learn to live. It has become our habit not to keep dogs, even though we are no longer hounded. Dogs bark and give us away, and even now we are within twenty miles of the Mexican villages on the Bavispe. They don't know we are here, and we do not want dogs running through the hills and howling at night to give us away."

Intrigued, Cordalee said, "I'd like to learn more about that, Miguelito.

You must know how curious a thing you and your people are to me—especially when all you Apaches were supposed to have given up with Gerónimo last fall."

The young chief shook his head. "It goes back much further than that. But this is not the time for me to tell you of it. Here, you are through eating; I will take you to meet some people and we will check with the shaman as to the state of old E-kon-sen-de-he's health."

Cordalee rose, tossed his blanket aside, and followed the Apache across the compound.

Two wickiups away from that of Nah-de-glesh, he spotted the young woman and the boy from the Bavispe putting out a fire; Miguelito was striding a couple of steps in front of him and seemed not to pay the twosome any notice.

"That girl and the boy," Cordalee called ahead. "Who are they? I mean, what are their names? And the girl . . . she isn't an Apache, is she?"

Miguelito drew up and turned back. "Why? What makes you think that? Why must you know?"

"Because I just don't think she is. And I am curious. Can't I simply be curious?"

Miguelito grunted. "I have never seen anyone so curious," he said. "Anyway, the girl is called Paulita, and the boy is Nito, her younger brother. I do not remember them from when they were with us before, but my mother tells me the girl is full-blood Mexican, although the boy is only half, for his father was an Apache warrior who once rode with Mangus. Both father and mother were killed in a battle with *soldados* from Chihuahua about a year ago."

So, Cordalee thought, he had been right. The girl was Mexican. Not that it mattered much now; no full-blood Indian could have become any more an Apache than she.

Miguelito turned and started forward again, asking, "Are you interested in the girl, Cor-dah-lee? Are you in need of a wife? Do you see how her hair is made into a bow in back? That means she is *nah-lin*, which in Apache means an unmarried girl of marriageable age."

Cordalee caught stride beside him. He said with a grin, "That one is a little too wild for my blood, Miguelito. Thanks, anyway."

It was the Apache's turn to smile as he stopped before a wickiup, then called something inside, apparently announcing their presence. In a few moments, a wizened, gray-haired old man appeared, his breechclout dangling almost to his ankles and the tops of his moccasins unrolled and

pulled up over his knees. A second old man wobbled out behind the first, and finally a third appeared, bow-legged and shriveled.

Miguelito introduced them in the order of their appearance. "This is Say-la, Cor-dah-lee. This is his wickiup. These other two are his visitors, as is their custom every morning at this time. This one is Tan-ta-la, and this other one is Nah-go-ta-hay. They are among our tribal elders and they sit at our every council no matter how minor the business may be." Then he proceeded to bestow an equally long speech in Apache on the solemn-faced threesome, each of whom squinted curiously up at Cordalee as the young chief spoke. When he finished, Say-la grunted something and stimulated a similarly unintelligible response from the other two.

"Is there something I should say?" Cordalee asked.

"No, *nada*," Miguelito advised, his eyes still on the old ones. "I have said it for you." Then he nodded to each old man in turn and motioned for Cordalee to come with him. They walked toward the next wickiup, where Miguelito again announced their presence. This time, however, a muscular youth of about the chief's age stepped out.

"This is Juan Tomás, Cor-dah-lee. He is a relative of old Juh"—he pronounced it "Hō"—"the Nedni chief who once ruled the Sierra Madre like a mustang stallion does his mares. Juh is dead now, but Juan Tomás carries his blood very well and has only recently become a full warrior. He was with the trail guards who challenged us on the north trail last night."

Juan Tomás apparently understood Spanish, for Miguelito did no elaborating in Apache this time. The young warrior grunted and stuck out his hand. Cordalee met his grip firmly and said, "*Tengo mucho gusto en conocerlo*, Juan Tomás."

Juan Tomás grunted as if satisfied and released Cordalee's hand as Miguelito said, "Okay, Cor-dah-lee, now we shall go to visit Old Man Din. It is back that way. Come."

They were almost there when Cordalee happened to glance toward the wickiup of Nah-de-glesh. A girl, dusky and dark-haired, had just stepped outside and was simply standing there, looking nowhere in particular. No more than fifteen yards separated them, but it still wasn't clear at first to Cordalee what so immediately impressed him about the girl. She wore a two-piece calico dress, its skirt long and full with the blouse worn outside the belt; she was no taller—though she was more slender—than the average Apache woman, and her hair was worn, as was Paulita's, put up in a vertical bow at the back of her head; the several strands of beads that encircled her neck were unimpressive, and her moccasins looked worn and of no special design. Yet there was something about the way she stood there,

the almost regal way she held her head and shoulders, and the high-cheek-boned features of her face that seemed finer, prettier than any Apache woman Cordalee had ever seen.

He was about to ask Miguelito about her, but he didn't get the chance, for the skinny, bow-legged figure of Old Man Din came waddling toward them from the direction of his wickiup.

The old shaman spoke brokenly in Apache, almost every word requiring a deep intake of breath before he went on to the next. He gestured and stamped, pointed toward one of the wickiups, then at Cordalee.

After a few moments of this, Miguelito looked around at Cordalee. "The shaman says he has done all a shaman can do for old E-kon-sen-de-he. He says she will die if more is not done. He has appealed to Ussen and has seen a White Eye _médico_ cutting into the wound with an Apache skinning knife and an awl. The White Eye doctor in his vision had an indistinguishable face, but he believes you are the one he saw. He wants to tell this to a council of our elders so they can decide if his vision truly tells us what we should do. He says the old woman is in such pain that she has already passed out several times."

Something inside Cordalee suddenly turned very cold. _A skinning knife and an awl!_ God!

"Listen," he said. "I don't think I can—"

But Miguelito held up a hand. "Don't say it. Ussen has spoken to the shaman—at least that's what the shaman thinks, which is good enough. The council will decide."

"But—"

Again the young chief cut him off. "You cannot change what is started. I am not very old or wise, but I do know that much. Here, go to your wickiup and wait. I will call you when the council has decided. _Enju!_" The word was Apache. It seemed to mean that enough had been said for now.

Cordalee numbly did as he was told, only vaguely noticing as he went that the maidenly vision he had seen standing outside Nah-de-glesh's wickiup had once again disappeared inside.

CHAPTER 5

Somehow Cordalee never doubted what the outcome of the council would be, and an hour later when its representatives came to stand before the door of his wickiup, he managed to meet them calmly, fully prepared for what they had to say.

The delegation consisted of Miguelito, Old Man Din, Say-la, Tan-ta-la, Nah-go-ta-hay, and, surprising to Cordalee, the chief's mother, Nah-de-glesh.

Cordalee said, "You have decided something, I see."

The obvious spokesman was Miguelito. "Yes. And we feel the sooner it is done the better. Are you ready?"

"There are some things I will need. And you must understand that I make no promises as to the outcome. I think the bullet is not very deep and should not be too difficult to extract, once it's located. But there are risks—infection, a severed vein or artery, hemorrhaging . . ."

"We understand this," the young chief said. "You will not be held responsible if you fail. We ask only that you try and promise much gratitude if you succeed."

"Fair enough," Cordalee said, glad to have this established. "Now, here is what I will need. I have my own knife, which I carry inside my poncho and which your braves did not think to search for when my weapons were taken yesterday. It is a narrow-bladed stiletto that I often use to make holes in leather and is about the right size. But I will need a pot of boiling water, some clean rags, something for disinfectant, such as mescal or *pulque* if you have it. And because I have had time to think about it—*and* because of your shaman's vision from Ussen—I think I can use one of those awls you mentioned. Something at least that has a handle and is very narrow and that can be used along with my knife to work the bullet away from the bone."

Miguelito seemed especially pleased with this latter request, and he quickly turned and said something to his mother, who grunted affirmatively and headed off in the direction of her own wickiup.

"Is there anything else?" Miguelito asked then.

"Only some strong helpers who can hold the old one down. This is likely to be very painful."

The Apache nodded. "That can be arranged. My mother has gone to get the things you have asked for and the shaman will prepare the patient. We should be ready very soon."

"Fair enough."

From that moment on Cordalee had precious little time in which to entertain second thoughts. In less than half an hour he was escorted to a wickiup next to that of the medicine man, where old E-kon-sen-de-he had been deposited on a bed of skins to await the operation. A kettle of boiling water hung over a fire built in a small scooped-out place in the center of the floor, and a blanket, on which were spread the things Cordalee had asked for, was spread near the fire. He thought wryly to himself that if the post surgeon had been able to acquire even half this kind of cooperation in his own hospital, no telling how many more soldiers' lives could have been saved over the years. Even a jug of mescal had been arranged, and someone had already thought of plying the patient with it in order to reduce her awareness of the pain. Old Man Din sat chanting near her head, the jug in his one hand and a small leather bag full of *hoddentin*—which Miguelito explained was the sacred pollen of the tule or cattail—held tightly in the other.

Once the makeshift instruments were adequately cleansed and readied for use, the actual probing and extraction took less than fifteen minutes. Very carefully Cordalee felt with the awl for the metal inside the wound while the old woman moaned and tried to squirm away from the grasp of the several helpers Miguelito had rounded up. Then, the bullet found—snugged firmly against the large bone of her leg above the knee—he used both the stiletto and the awl to gently work it loose and finally out. When finished with this, he cleansed the tortured and bleeding flesh, poured liberal amounts of mescal over it, and pressed clean rags against it to help stop the bleeding. The old woman at first screamed at the burn of the mescal, but presently she relaxed and seemed to heave a sigh of relief. Finally Cordalee fashioned bandages out of the remaining rags and wrapped them carefully around the leg.

"It's about all I can do," he told Miguelito, wiping the sweat from his brow. "If we're not already too late, I think she has a good chance. Time will tell."

They went outside, Cordalee pleased with how smoothly it had gone, yet at the same time nagged by the thought that it might have been almost too easy. Nevertheless, by the time Nah-de-glesh emerged a few minutes

later and announced with typical Apache brevity that the old medicine
man had already predicted the patient's survival and eventual return to
good health, the self-styled physician was feeling quite good about his
achievement.

Miguelito, too, reflected the elation of success. "Well, Cor-dah-lee, I
promised you much gratitude. Tonight you shall see what I meant. We
will have a feast and a celebration. We will butcher a cow and bring out
the last of our mescal. Tonight you shall see!"

From that time on, the ranchería buzzed with preparations for the evening's festivities. Cordalee was resting inside his wickiup when he all of a
sudden heard a bellowing bawl coming from just outside the village. He
looked out just in time to see a couple of mounted braves dragging a two-
year-old steer—most likely a member of what Miguelito had said was a
Mexican herd stolen and left on the mountain by Gerónimo's renegades
shortly before their final surrender—at the end of a braided rawhide rope
over near the horse corrals. Just as suddenly a third brave dashed into
sight astride a swift bay pony, a lance held poised for throwing. He made
one, then a second, high-speed sweep past the desperately balking steer.
Then, with his third pass, the young brave made his throw, shafting the
steer perfectly through the heart and bringing it down. Quickly the
beast's throat was slit and the animal bled where it had fallen. A few minutes later the carcass was dragged to the center of the ranchería where the
skinning and butchering commenced with a flurry.

In only a short time, the beef was halved and two pits of coals were
readied, each large enough to roast an entire side of beef within itself. By
sundown, the aroma of cooking meat was strong throughout the ranchería,
and with the exception of the four or five trail guards who apparently did
duty at selected approaches to the village at all times, the inhabitants had
gathered to the last man, woman, and child. Somehow an enormous potful
of pinto beans had made it through the winter, and were now cooking
over an open fire near the beef pits. Bread was baking on hot flat rocks,
and a surprising number of jugs of mescal were cropping up all over the
place.

Well before any food was served, however, three braves, in the persons
of Juan Tomás and the two who had walked up the trail from the Bavispe
the day before, presented themselves at Cordalee's wickiup. In reasonably
good Spanish, the young relative of the Nedni chief, Juh, called to Cordalee and then proceeded to escort him to a place near the center of the
gathering Apaches, of which Cordalee estimated there were no fewer than
sixty present. It wasn't the largest such gathering he had ever witnessed,

but seldom had his heart been made to pound more wildly than it did then at the sight before him.

For a few minutes everyone stood expectantly around a large firelit circle, on one side of which Cordalee was told to stay, somewhat separated from the nearest person on his either side. Before he'd had a chance to figure out what was happening, a cheer went up and Miguelito, Old Man Din, and Nah-de-glesh appeared in their midst. The young chief was dressed in what looked to be his festive best—fancy buckskin shirt covered with decorative stitching, beaded, pug-nosed moccasins, and a two-strand necklace of beads with coyote or cougar teeth evenly spaced between beads and a large obsidian arrowhead hanging point downward from the bottom strand of the necklace. The shaman and Nah-de-glesh were also decked out in finery, although the balance of the tribe seemed to have shown up in their everyday dress.

Miguelito ceremoniously raised his hands to the cheers of the gathering, then said something in Apache as the serving of food began. Someone motioned for Cordalee to take a seat between the chief and the shaman, while Nah-de-glesh moved over to sit at Miguelito's other side. All were served steaming bowlfuls of meat, beans, and bread, and jugs of mescal were passed around, plenty for everyone.

"You like this feast?" Miguelito looked over and asked at one point.

Cordalee did not hesitate to say, "¡Es muy grande! ¡Maravillosa! As good as I've had in a long, long time, chief."

The Apache grunted his satisfaction and took a long pull from his mescal jug. Then, shortly, his meal finished, he got to his feet and signaled something to the shaman. Old Man Din waved approvingly, and the circle of people opened up to make room for their chief, who, followed by Juan Tomás and the two braves who had accompanied Cordalee to the feast, pranced out into the center of the circle and began dancing to the beat of several drums. A chorus of voices, chanting and singing, rose to the tempo struck by the musicians, and shortly half a dozen others joined in the dancing.

After going exactly four times around the circle, the young chief and his original three followers retook their places in the outer circle. This seemed to relieve the proceedings of some measure of formality. Both men and women got up to dance, and the drums gave off dull thump-thumps to the beat of over one hundred per minute, blending perfectly and creating a fascinating harmony with the singing that actually sent chills up and down Cordalee's spine. It was an almost eerie scene, there under a moonless sky and in the dancing light of the campfires, and though Cordalee had briefly witnessed Indian dances before, he had never been allowed to attend anything quite like this.

Still, remembering the many suspicious stares he had received when he had come into the village last night, he turned to Miguelito and asked, "Does my presence here mean I am to be trusted now?"

Miguelito offered up his jug of mescal and Cordalee let him fill the tin coffee cup he had been drinking from. Then the Indian took a long pull from the jug, grimacing and going "*Agh!*" in mixed pain and pleasure from the raw, warm burn of the fiery liquid. Finally he said, "It means we are grateful for what you have done for one of our band, and thus for all of us. But it does not change the fact that we know very little about you." His expression became unreadable as he suggested, "Maybe you will tell me once again why you came to Mexico, why we found you as we did on the banks of Bavispe yesterday."

Cordalee shrugged. "I've nothing to hide. As I told you, I deserted from the American Army about a month ago. I served five years with the Fourth Cavalry in Arizona, most of it stationed at Fort Huachuca. My home, originally, is in the East—a place called Indiana. Possibly you have never heard of it. Anyway, I never really liked the Army, but it grew unbearable for me only after Gerónimo was captured and all we had left to do were things like drill endlessly, do fatigue duty, or ride out on useless patrols across the countryside *practicing* how we might fight Apaches if any ever left the reservation again. I could have asked for a transfer to another department, but there wasn't anything going on anywhere else either, so I just stayed on in Arizona. I even reenlisted, once, last year, and it was the dumbest thing I ever did. I don't even know why I did it. In fact, I kept asking myself that and not getting an answer, until one night while my troop was camped down near Calabasas close to the border, I took a horse and stole away to Mexico. Eventually I drifted on over to Fronteras, took up prospecting there, wound up in that fight I told you about, and then ended up running for my life. That's when you found me on the Bavispe."

"Did you ever fight Apaches?" Miguelito wanted to know, his eyes narrowing.

Cordalee smiled thinly, hesitant to be totally candid about this subject. "Not much. Mostly we chased their shadows and wild rumors about where they had been. Once we were on the verge of running down Gerónimo himself, only to surround a camp of peaceful Papagos after tracking them for three days and half killing our horses trying to catch up. And one time, back in '83, I was with a patrol that was close on the heels of Chato's band. The Indians seemed just to melt away in the rocks and we never caught sight of them. But at least we had a reason for going out, a reason for being around. It wasn't like that anymore after Gerónimo surrendered and all we had were General Miles's silly war games, a lot of tiresome duty, and bullying sergeants with nothing to do but make life miserable for enlisted men. That's the part I finally couldn't stand."

"Well," the young chief said, "I am sorry there are no more Apaches for you to chase and fight. Maybe a few of us free ones should make a little raid now and then. That would give you something to do again, eh?"

Cordalee shook his head. "Not me, it wouldn't." Then he looked at the Indian. "But what about you? I sense you are at least partly joking about making raids again, but the fact that you are here . . . well, you still haven't told me anything of your story, the story of this last free tribe of Apaches. Surely it can't hurt for me to know at least some of it."

Miguelito thought a moment, then took another pull at his jug. "No," he said, "I guess it can't hurt. Just what do you want to know?"

"Well, first," Cordalee said, thinking, "how come you aren't on a reservation? How come you never surrendered with the other Apaches?"

The young chief smiled. "Because we did not want to, it is that simple. It was when General Crook, the White Eyes' *nantan* or head officer, came with his soldiers into the Sierra Madre in search of the escaped Chiricahua and Warm Springs people four years ago"—May 1883, Cordalee knew, remembering vividly the fanfare that had surrounded the event. "There were over seven hundred of us then, most but not all being fugitives from the reservation. Our many rancherías were a long way south of here, on the headwaters of the Bavispe. We did not think anyone could find and attack us there. But there was this Tonto Apache called Tso-ay who had lived with us then later surrendered to the White Eyes, and who finally led the Americans to us—he and almost two hundred San Carlos and White Mountain Apache scouts who were paid to fight against us. They found us, surprising two of our larger rancherías while many of our fighting men were away raiding in Chihuahua. They attacked and scattered our people, frightening them and discouraging some of our leaders. We had thought ourselves safe in Mexico; we were little afraid of the Mexicans and we did not think the Americans would cross the line after us as they did. But suddenly all that was no longer true. A truce was called, then there was talk between Nantan Lupan, the Tan Wolf Chief— which is what we called Crook—and our chiefs about surrender; councils were held. The decision to give up was made by almost all . . ."

"'Almost'?" Cordalee said. "Meaning your tribe here being the exception, Miguelito?"

"Yes, but we weren't a tribe then. We were members of several scattered and separate bands. Our leaders did not want to see every last Apache herded into captivity. They wished to see at least a few of us left free to maintain the lifeblood of our race. They were afraid that someday the White Eyes would manage to destroy us completely if they got us all on reservations. I know all of these things because what I did not observe myself the shaman, my mother, and others of the elders have told me about. A plan was discussed for leaving a few of us behind. A few that Nantan Lupan and his soldiers would never miss. Not even the Indian agent at San Carlos would miss these few. And we were so scattered it would take days, even weeks, for us all to be brought in by the various leaders, thus giving us more time to carry out our plan in an organized fashion.

"The main thing was, only relatively unknown Apaches could be left behind. All the important leaders—Loco, Chihuahua, Nana, Juh, Benito, Gerónimo, Naiche, Mangus—had to come in with their people, or the White Eyes' *nantan* would become suspicious. Our leaders were determined to convince Nantan Lupan it would take quite a long time for all the people to be rounded up and brought back to Arizona. Actually, he could do nothing about that. Had we not given up voluntarily, he could never have taken us. But our people were tired, and we could see how hopeless our future was; we could not remain even in the Sierra Madre if the Americans were going to be allowed by the Mexicans to come after us there also. They had hounded us out of our homelands in New Mexico and Arizona, and now they had come to hound us here, too. It was decided that we had a future as a free people only through subterfuge and secrecy, and no longer through fighting and running."

"So a surrender was effected," Cordalee said, a deep-seated thrill beginning to course through his veins. Even wily old George Crook had been taken in—understandably, to hear the Indian's tale—but taken in just the same.

"Yes. Many of our people went back to Arizona with Nantan Lupan—all of those who could be rounded up, including most of the principal leaders. My own father was among that group. But many stayed behind, Gerónimo and Juh among them, on the basis that they needed more time to bring their people in. Those who would never come in, most of whom you see here tonight, were already being selected among many volunteers. Families were to be kept intact wherever possible, old wise ones as well as young ones of both sexes were picked, and we were brought here to what we call Stronghold Mountain. Gerónimo and most of his band gave themselves up later in Arizona. Juh was to come in too, but he had an accident and was killed. Only we were left here, few more than sixty of us alto-gether, and we dedicated ourselves to starting a new life."

Cordalee was fascinated. "But the scouts, the Apache scouts—didn't they realize all of you had not come in?"

Miguelito shrugged. "A few of them did, most did not—especially those stupid Tontos and San Carlos. The ones that knew, however, did not know how many we were and even they were still Apaches; they sympa-thized with us—at least, that is what we have always assumed. No White Eyes' *nantan* has ever come to get us, anyway. Not even after Gerónimo and some others escaped the reservation again just two years later. We have never raided and fought from this place—not even against the Mex-icans. We have lived a primitive life much of the time, but we remain peaceful, determined to cast off the old ways of the Wild Ones—the *Net-dahe*, we call them—those whose vow has always been to fight the whites and the Mexicans until one side or the other is forever destroyed. We still do not like our old enemies, but we know now that we can only lose if we fight with them. We only wish to be left alone to live in peace."

"And all this time we Americans thought we'd defeated the last Apache!" Cordalee marveled, remembering the rumors—always the rumors —to the contrary that had circulated throughout Arizona ever since Ge-rónimo's surrender. But he had never put any faith whatsoever in those ru-mors. Now, here was proof that they had been true, living proof! "Ge-rónimo did come back here, though—later, when he broke off the reservation again?"

"Yes. At one time there were half a dozen other rancherías within a few days' ride of here. Those of Gerónimo, Chihuahua, Mangus, Naiche—all involved in that final breakout. They even brought us booty from their raids, kept us supplied with food, clothing, and much mescal. But finally we became afraid they would also bring us trouble that we didn't need or want. We held a council and decided all the *Netdahe* should leave Stronghold Mountain. Not long after that, Nantan Lupan came again. There was another surrender, this time at Cañón de los Embudos, well to the north of here. Gerónimo and Naiche ran away with a few followers while the others went in. Mangus was not involved at the time. Later, as you know, even these surrendered to Nantan Miles. We have seen none of them since."

"That's because all the Chiricahuas were taken to a place called Flor-ida, far, far away from here. Have you ever heard of Florida?"

"No," Miguelito said, but interested just the same. "Where is Flo-rida?"

"It is in the east, a little boot that sticks out between the Atlantic Ocean and the Gulf of Mexico."

Miguelito shook his head; he did not understand. "How far?"

"Two thousand miles, maybe more."

"Huh! That is very far. Maybe it is good. The *Netdahe* will never come here again, I think."

"Probably not," Cordalee agreed. "But listen, you talk of the Tontos and the San Carlos, and of the Chiricahua and Warm Springs. Are all of you here one of those?"

"Except for one or two Aravaipas," Miguelito said, "we are of the *Chihinne* or Warm Springs, the *Chokonens* or Chiricahua, the *Bedonkohes* or Gillaenos, the Mimbrenos, and the *Nednis*, who have always lived in the Sierra Madre. I myself am *Chokonen* or Chiricahua. We are a hodgepodge, but we are all Apaches."

Cordalee had just seen Paulita and Nito appear among the dancers inside the circle. "Or Mexicans," he added.

"They are Apaches, too—now," Miguelito insisted.

"Peaceful Apaches," Cordalee continued to marvel. "Which is why your men went on a trading trip rather than a raid. But that brings up a point, too. I saw your mules yesterday. Not a one carried a load; their *aparejos* were empty, or at least nearly so. What on earth were you going to trade?"

Miguelito frowned at this. "I don't think I'm ready yet to tell you that."

Cordalee might have pressed him further, except suddenly something changed with the drumbeats and the dancers, and Miguelito looked away, toward one side of the big ring. The shaman had gone over that way just moments before and disappeared inside the crowd, accompanied by Nahde-glesh. Now the crowd was parting to let them back through, leading someone between them. It was the girl Cordalee had seen in front of Nahde-glesh's wickiup that morning. Excitement stirred within him.

"Who is that, Miguelito? Who is that girl?"

The young chief sighed as the drums and the dancing stopped completely. "I guess you will never give up without knowing," he said resignedly. A roar went up from the gathering, and he waited for it to subside. Then he said, "She is my sister. Her name is Mistan. She is highly revered by our people, especially so for a woman."

"Why? What is it about her?"

"She has a power that only a very few have, the ability to perceive certain things about the future. She is considered an important woman because of it. She is four years younger than I, but she is honored just short of our shaman himself for both wisdom and goodness. She is among the most beloved of all our people here."

The girl was standing just within the far side of the circle, the medicine man and Nah-de-glesh still at her side. She made a small gesture and the drums, the singing, and the dancing began anew. Cordalee, impressed to the point of awe, croaked ridiculously, "Is she *nah-lin*, Miguelito?"

The Apache eyed him. "Yes, she is *nah-lin*. She had her womanhood ceremony two summers ago, but has never married."

"But why? She—she is beautiful. Don't Apache men like beauty in a woman?"

"Apache men like beauty; many have left good horses and presents at my mother's wickiup, but Mistan never feeds or grooms their horses, the presents are always left outside. She is *nah-lin*, but no man has come that she will have."

"Unbelievable," Cordalee breathed, then noticed something peculiar about the way the girl was helped to take her seat among the watchers in the outer ring. He turned to the young chief. "What is it? Why . . . ?"

Miguelito's voice was sober as he said, "My sister is blind, Cor-dah-lee. That is why she sits in a darkened wickiup, alone and quiet. She has never been able to see a thing."

Stunned, Cordalee reached for the mescal jug. He took a huge swallow, gritted his teeth, and repeated the procedure.

"Damn," he said, returning the jug to Miguelito. "God damn."

He had said it in English, and for a moment the Indian only stared. Then, apparently liking the sound of the words, he raised the jug toward his lips and said, "Sí. God damn."

Hours later, the young chief's jug long since emptied, the two men staggered together across the village compound. The dancing and singing were still going on, the drums still beating, the mescal still flowing, but Miguelito's wife, one called Nondi, was ill in their wickiup and the Apache felt obliged to return to her for what was left of the night. Cordalee, on the other hand, had consumed all the mescal he could hold.

But the two of them had talked long together; they had become drunk together. No more was said about Mistan, for it was obvious that Miguelito had told all he was a mind to for now. But about most other things there had been much openness. Something had seemed to happen between the two men, and that it could be the earliest beginnings of a real friendship caused Cordalee to marvel greatly as he bade the chief good night and quietly made his way to his own wickiup.

But what he fell asleep with were visions of a beautiful, blind maiden, his imagined spelling of the word *nah-lin* dancing fleetingly before his eyes.

CHAPTER 6

That the fledgling friendship with Miguelito had its limits was not lost on Cordalee during the next few days around the ranchería. Not that he wasn't treated well enough; he figured few in his position would argue about that. He was provided with plenty of food and adequate shelter; he was allowed to roam about the village more or less at will; he was, as soon as the chief's wife was well, invited to Miguelito's wickiup to meet the dusky, dark-eyed Nondi, and several days later was even presented with a handsome pair of Apache moccasins, made by Nondi herself, and which, fitting as amazingly well as they did, could not have been a more appropriate gift, considering the sad state of Cordalee's own worn-out footgear. Indeed, everyone he met seemed friendly, grateful for what he had done for old E-kon-sen-de-he, and completely willing to accept his presence around their village. Some of the Apache men even taught him to play their favorite game, that of "hoop-and-pole," or *na-joose*. He wasn't much good at it, but it was fun and the Indians had an uproarious time with him as he tried to learn. On the surface, things were "plenty *bueno*," as Miguelito, mixing his almost nonexistent English and his Spanish in a way that seemed to suit him keenly, had learned to say.

But with the rosy haze of the mescal gone and the Apache's natural wariness returned, there were other things Cordalee could not ignore. First, even though he was allowed the freedom to go exploring outside the ranchería, he knew as he went that he was being watched by unseen eyes every step of the way. Too, he wanted desperately to meet the blind maiden, Mistan, and hinted at same more than once, only to be politely but firmly put off in each instance. He also tried hinting that it was about time his rifle and handgun, taken from him that first day, be returned, but this was met with almost no response at all and certainly not the rifle and handgun. More bothersome yet, he somehow suspected that even had he had someplace else to go, he would not have been allowed to leave Stronghold Mountain—a subtle undercurrent that began to pervade everything else he did. In fact, although he never saw anyone doing it, he was convinced that his wickiup was still being guarded at night, and he was sure it was being done for the express purpose of keeping him in rather than that of keeping anyone else out. He was, by most standards, being treated as a welcome guest; by several others, he was truly a prisoner among his hosts.

Too, he was frequently bored at having nothing of a worthwhile nature to do. He had even wondered if he might not be just as well off back at Fort Huachuca, enduring the endless drills, tiresome fatigue duties, and pointless war games of General Miles's peacetime Army. But no, he decided, Stronghold Mountain was better than that. It offered pure mountain air in the place of stifling desert heat; clear, trickling streams instead of the inevitable dry Arizona washes; the association with a people to whom the individual freedom to do as one chose was supreme, as opposed to bullying first sergeants to whom such notions never occurred. . . .

But still his uneasiness grew; he was not comfortable with his lot. He didn't like the idea—real or imagined—of being forced to stay among the Indians whether he chose to or not. And most of all, he guessed, he hated the boredom . . . the incessant boredom.

This was broken with explosive suddenness on the ninth day of his stay there when the "trading party" from Magdalena burst upon the ranchería, their mounts lathered, their pack animals' *aparejos* as empty as the day they had left, and one young brave sporting a painful gunshot wound in one arm.

The entire village was suddenly alive with curiosity and concern, and the people gathered quickly to see what had happened. Cordalee stood off to one side, watching, as the nine braves wearily dismounted. As the wounded man was taken off to be treated and half-grown boys rushed to take the horses and mules, Miguelito came over to listen to a small group of the returning braves, each of whom gestured excitedly as he talked.

After a few minutes Cordalee made his way across the ranchería to within a short distance of where this conversation was going on, but he was careful to remain to one side and not interfere. The talk between the Indians was purely in Apache and Cordalee understood almost none of it; but a deep scowl lined Miguelito's face, and his voice, as he barked an occasional question, was filled with anger and frustration.

Upon dismissing the small group of braves, he turned to spot Cordalee standing less than fifteen feet away. He came over to the white man, the scowl still on his face.

Cordalee said, "I take it the Mexicans at Magdalena didn't want to trade."

The Apache nodded.

"Well, why not? What went wrong?"

Miguelito only said, "A chief should ride with his men. I did not."

Cordalee gave him a skeptical look. "Do you really think that would have made any difference to the Mexicans? After decades of you Apaches constantly making war on them? Come now, my friend, did you really expect anything different?"

"There have been times when the Mexicans traded with the Apache," the young chief said. "And besides, my men were to dress as Mexicans. They even had some of those silly-looking big hats and some serapes. They were not supposed to look like Apaches."

"But?"

"The Mexicans were not fooled. My men approached Magdalena all at once, all nine of them. Somehow the Mexicans knew and were waiting. Only, some careless fool opened fire too early and my men were lucky enough to escape with only one wounded and none killed. They lost one mule and that was all."

"But they did no trading. They brought back no goods. That's what has you so upset, isn't it?"

The chief gave him an affirmative nod. "It's a long way to Magdalena. Much time, hard work, and one mule has been wasted. That's no plenty *bueno* with me, Cor-dah-lee."

"Well, why did you send them so far? There are towns much closer by. Why not Bavispe or Bacerac, the river towns? Or Oputo or Nacozari? Even Casas Grandes over in Chihuahua is no farther than Magdalena."

Miguelito shook his head. "We thought of Casas Grandes, but we would have had to cross the mountains, and the people of Chihuahua are even worse Apache haters than some of these in Sonora. And all of the other towns were too close; we did not want to show ourselves in places so near as that to Stronghold Mountain. We were afraid that if someone became suspicious we might be trailed here afterward."

"Well, someone became suspicious at Magdalena," Cordalee observed, "and now you are mad because your men came all the way back empty-handed."

Miguelito grunted disgustedly. "In the old days Apache men would have been ashamed to come back that way."

"Meaning they would have immediately set out on a raid, taken what they wanted by force, by killing and stealing. Is that right?"

The Apache did not say anything to this, and Cordalee thought he detected a certain not very likeable gleam in the chief's eyes. "What are you thinking, Miguelito? A raid, anyway? Are you thinking of making a raid on Magdalena?"

"I am thinking something like that, yes."

Cordalee frowned. He wasn't sure any of this should really matter to him. After all, why should he care what happened to this miserable little band of Indians? Still, he said, "But what about your plans to live peacefully here on Stronghold Mountain? What will happen to them?"

"We tried to deal peacefully with the Mexicans. They tried to kill us in return."

"Uh-huh. So you tear off like the Wild Ones of old, the *Netdahe*, as you call them. And what happens? One raid, Miguelito. One raid and you'll be at war all over again. Maybe even with the Americans. You know that, don't you? The Mexicans consider you Apaches wards of the United States, and have ever since the Treaty of Guadalupe Hidalgo. They will demand that the Americans come once more to get their naughty charges. And away you will go, the last free Apaches, on your way to far-off Florida, like Gerónimo. You will be hauled away on a train like cattle, never to see your homelands again. Have you ever seen a train, Miguelito? A cattle car?"

"I would not go," the Indian said stubbornly. "I would fight."

Cordalee scoffed at this. "And you would be defeated. Oh, not at first, I grant you. But eventually they would run you down. It would be as before—too few of you, too many of them. In the end, you would not have had a chance."

"I would still fight," Miguelito maintained, just as stubbornly as before.

"Then you would die, you and all of your people."

"All right. We would die."

"And then there would be no more free Apaches," Cordalee said, having saved his most convincing argument for last. "You would have failed all those who have kept your secret, who have relied on you to carry on and preserve their people's ways. They would hear of it, Miguelito. Every one of them would know, I can guarantee you that."

This hit home like a six-pound cannonball; Cordalee could see it on the chief's face. "All right," Miguelito said solemnly. "So what would you have me do? My people do not want to live like primitive savages. They want things like coffee, flour, sugar, salt, tobacco, mescal. They want vegetable seeds so they can raise many kinds of food to eat, and it is already past time to plant many things. They want to raise cattle, and to have good horses; they want calico cloth with which to make clothes, plenty of ammunition for their guns so they can hunt. What can I do if the Mexicans will not trade or sell these things to us? Tell me that, Cor-dah-lee?"

Cordalee had to stop and think on this a moment. He could see the Apache's predicament. What *could* he do? These Indians were like anybody else, it seemed. They had tasted some of the white man's comforts of life and they wanted them for themselves. They were willing to do whatever was necessary to get them, too. They might even get a new chief, if the old one couldn't handle the job as was expected of him. They might very well do that.

But what skin was that off Luther Cordalee's nose? He was virtually a prisoner here, a man who couldn't be given his own weapons back, a man who was willing to stay around only because he had no place else to go, no better friends. . . .

Suddenly he was considering this last thought very seriously. He really did have no better friends, no one whom he owed more. It was an astounding thought, but it was true. Even before he realized it, he found himself saying, "Listen. Maybe you just don't know how to go about this business of buying and trading—assuming you do have something to buy or trade *with*. Maybe we can figure something out; maybe you need to try again someplace else. . . ."

"How? Where?" the Apache asked, eyeing him.

Cordalee shrugged. "Well, I'm not sure. I haven't had time to think about it. Maybe if we went over to my wickiup and talked we could come up with something. Then you could call a council tonight and see what your people think. You can ask Nah-de-glesh, the shaman, Mistan. The wiser ones will know if your new plan is a good one. What say? Are you willing to try?"

Miguelito was silent for a few moments. At last he said, "I like it when you talk this way. I am willing to listen."

"Good. Maybe we could even drag up a jug of mescal to loosen our thoughts up a bit. How about that?"

"Yes," the Indian said, almost smiling. "I think there may be one or two left; that is a good idea. Come with me."

Presently, a jug in hand, they disappeared inside Cordalee's wickiup. Two hours later, they reappeared and the chief set about the routine of calling a council for that night after supper. A new plan would then be presented.

Cordalee was not invited to attend the council, but no one seemed to mind that he sat just outside his wickiup, watching, as those who were involved gathered in front of the wickiup of Old Man Din across the way. It was shortly after dark and only the faintest afterthought of daylight shown in the west, adding but dimly to the flickering glow cast by the cook fires of the ranchería. Overhead the sky was clear and stars were appearing faintly, one by one. From somewhere a coyote howled and another yelped in answer from not far away. The evening air cooled rapidly, and out away from the campfires the night blackness was like an impenetrable blanket, seemingly surrounding and isolating the village completely from the rest of the world.

Something about all of this caused Cordalee to shiver as he watched the proceedings taking place in front of the medicine man's wickiup. He had begun to pick up a few basic words of the Apache language, but at present was too far away to perceive any of these. The voices that carried to him were faint—all except Old Man Din's, which was of such a sing-songy high pitch that it carried clearly throughout the ranchería.

But it didn't matter; Cordalee knew well enough what was being presented by the young chief. He knew that Miguelito was outlining another proposed trip for the purpose of purchasing goods and, if possible, livestock. He even knew, finally, what means of purchase was to be employed by the Indians and certainly no longer doubted their abilities in this regard. He had seen with his own eyes a small sample of what they had to offer, and if a healthy poke of glittering gold nuggets—the Indian called it "yellow iron"—wasn't good enough to convince a man, then he didn't know what was. He had been rendered almost speechless when, upon his own strong insistence, Miguelito had gone off and come back with his sample of what he had to "trade." The Indian would not tell him where it had come from, only that he figured there was plenty to buy what his tribe needed, and maybe even more. Much more . . .

Anyway, a plan had then been discussed for making another trip, and the chief had listened carefully as the white man had outlined his suggestions.

"First," Cordalee had told him, "I think you should try a different town, one closer to the border and maybe even across into Arizona. I guess I would have to discourage the latter, though, as off-reservation Apaches would be considered highly unwelcome in Arizona these days. So I guess a border town would be best—say, Nogales, or even Sásabe, if you want to go that far."

Miguelito's expression was impassive as he asked, "Which one would you choose, Cor-dah-lee?"

"Well," Cordalee said, considering, "I think Nogales appeals to me most. It straddles the border, thus having a Mexican and American side. It is on the railroad between Benson and Hermosillo, a good supply route, and it has, I understand, a population of several thousand, counting both sides. It's not too close—I remember your earlier concern on that point—yet is not so far away as Sásabe. It's big enough that it would have almost anything you would want to buy, and it has enough people that you could probably come and go without creating too much notice—that's assuming you operate a little more subtly than your men did at Magdalena, of course."

"How would that be?" the Apache asked intently, all but forgetting the mescal jug they had been passing back and forth.

"Well, for one thing, I don't think you need to go in with your whole party of men; two or three should be plenty, just so long as they can handle the pack mules—which I'm sure they can. Too, you should make sure you're fully disguised. No one must figure out that you're Apaches. Wad your hair up beneath those big hats you said you have, tuck your breechclouts in . . . you know what I mean. And for God's sake, don't talk anything but Spanish. In fact, don't say anything you don't have to. Do your trading and get out. And don't show any more of that yellow iron around than you have to. It'll create enough curiosity as it is. No telling what will happen if you try to pay for fifty pesos' worth of goods with five hundred pesos' worth of gold!"

Miguelito gave him a quickly discerning look. "I had not thought of it before, but how are we to know what all the things we want cost? How are we to avoid showing a large amount of our yellow iron if someone asks it as the price of his goods?"

Cordalee frowned. "Well, you're right about that, of course. I guess I just hadn't thought quite that far yet. No question about it, you could get robbed any one of several ways if you're not careful. Worse, you could wind up with half of Nogales trailing you out of town, if they get the idea you've got a big strike located somewhere. Yes, that is a problem. Damned, if it isn't."

But the Apache was not quick to give up. He said, "You could help us, Cor-dah-lee. You could make it not so big a problem."

Cordalee looked at him. "Well, yes. I suppose I could. I could try to coach you about prices of things, give you an idea what to watch out for—"

But the Indian didn't let him finish. "No. That is not what I meant. I meant you could go with us. You could speak for us and help conduct our buying. You and I and maybe one other man could go in together."

Cordalee's eyes at first widened, then they narrowed. "You would have to place a great amount of trust in me. It would be very easy for me to misrepresent the price of something or another, then keep the difference in what you paid and what it actually cost. And I could just as easily betray you to the Mexicans or the Americans, either one. Especially the Americans. You wouldn't have a chance to escape if I did."

"Would you do those things to us?" Miguelito asked simply.

You're damn right, I would, Cordalee thought to himself. *Why in hell shouldn't I?* But then he thought, why *should* he? What did he have to gain? Repatriation to the United States? Hardly. He wouldn't likely be recognized in Nogales, unless some of his old troop happened to be ranging around on the American side, but he couldn't just go striding back across to take up residence, either. He was still a deserter from the U.S. Cavalry, and nothing about that was likely to have changed in just a little over a month's time. And what had he ever lost among the Mexicans? A friendship of ignoble proportions in Fronteras?

He met Miguelito's gaze; the Indian was waiting patiently for an answer. "No," he finally said. "I wouldn't do anything like that. If you want me to go, I will help you all I can. I won't betray you."

Miguelito rose then. "Then I would trust you to do as you say. I will call a council and see what the others think of our plan. Is that plenty *bueno* with you, Cor-dah-lee?"

"That's plenty *bueno* with me, chief," Cordalee said with a thin smile. "Only I think you should give me back my guns before we go. I may need them to protect myself with, you know."

The Indian made no promises, but he didn't say no. He simply stalked away to do whatever it was he had to do.

Now, the council an hour underway and showing signs of breaking up, Cordalee sat wondering idly what was to be its outcome. Suddenly he realized that the group in front of the shaman's wickiup was dispersing. Seconds later, the straight-shouldered form of the chief appeared stalking across the ranchería toward Cordalee's wickiup.

"Well," Cordalee said, rising as the Apache approached and came to stand before him. "What's the verdict?"

The young chief actually smiled, he was so pleased. "We will go to Nogales. Twelve men, including you and I. We will also take plenty of pack mules and yellow iron. We will leave *pasado mañana.*"

Day after tomorrow, Cordalee thought. Well, that's that. "Did you have any trouble convincing the others?" he asked.

Miguelito shrugged. "Some . . . There was one condition laid down."

"What was that?"

"If we fail once more," Miguelito said very slowly, "then we must make a raid. The council is split now and will not hear of anymore unsuccessful trading trips. We must do well this time, Cor-dah-lee. We must do very well."

"Well, that's about what I figured. We'll just have to be successful this time is all. And, look, do I get my guns back or not? I mean—"

Miguelito cut him off with a stern look. "*Pasado mañana,*" he said simply, and stalked off toward his own wickiup.

CHAPTER 7

They left out at sunup two days later, a dozen mounted men and eight pack mules, geared and supplied for at least eight days on the trail and a minimum of one day and night camped out of sight near Nogales. In addition to Miguelito and Cordalee, all were athletic young warriors within a few years of their chief's own age. They were, as Cordalee had worked hard to learn and remember, the Nedni, Juan Tomás, a couple of Ojo Calientes or Warm Springs called Gregorio and Hishee, an Aravaipa called Ben-ah-thli, and six full Chiricahuas called by the names of Tas-ah-kay, Antonio, Chivo, Dja-li-kine, Kentoni, and Cruz. All were armed, alert to the trail, and exhibited what Cordalee thought must be the same kind of tense excitement that would have once characterized the Wild Ones themselves when going out on a raid.

By early afternoon they were at the Río de Bavispe, where they stopped for a brief rest and to water their horses. They struck out from there following the Fronteras trail, and by dark were within a few miles of the deserted Batepito Springs rancho on the San Bernardino.

The next day, they left the main trail and swung slightly north through low desert hills and ridges. That night they camped at a small spring less than twenty miles from the Arizona border. Thus far, they had seen no other riders, and Cordalee had noted frequently how intent the Apaches were on not being seen themselves while at the same time averaging between thirty-five and forty miles a day—even counting the slow going of the first morning's ride down from Stronghold Mountain to the Bavispe. To the Indians this pace seemed nothing special, if not a bit leisurely; to their white companion it was a forced march of the highest order.

Two more days, during which they saw only one other group of riders several miles distant and going away from the Apaches' route of march, found them by nightfall within fifteen miles of Nogales. They camped again near water, on a cactus-covered hillside, with the desert mountains of southern Arizona rising darkly on the horizon to the north. Tomorrow, it was decided, they would move cautiously to within a mile or two of Nogales, find a good place for a camp where all but three of them would wait while the selected representatives went in to see what could be done.

Thus, breaking camp even earlier than usual the next morning, they were on their way before sunup, and by late morning had reached a point east and some south of the bustling border towns, at which another camp was soon established. It was a dry camp, located a good mile from the nearest water, but it afforded dense brush cover for shade and concealment, and even more importantly high ground from which the lookouts could scan the countryside for miles around without being seen. Their water jugs remained filled to the brim from the past night's camp and were adequate to last the camp watchers a full day before someone would have to be dispatched to refill them. Each man carried his own food supply, plenty for his needs, and the worst likelihood those remaining behind really faced was boredom during the heat of the day. This they expected to combat by enjoining in any of several games of chance, which was among their favorite pastimes anyway.

The three who were to go into town included, of course, Miguelito and Cordalee, plus Juan Tomás, who could also speak Spanish if the need arose. He was also, Cordalee had finally learned, considered something of a "subchief" to Miguelito, although in reality there was no such position traditionally held among the Apaches. He shared this unusual distinction with the Warm Springs brave, Hishee, and only for this reason had been left on Stronghold Mountain during the earlier trading trip; as a "subchief" he was to represent leadership and look after the tribe while the chief and his other "subchief" were away. Miguelito's early return had, of course, not been anticipated. Hishee had actually led the abortive excursion to Magdalena and was happy enough this time to remain in camp outside Nogales, but had refused to be left behind on Stronghold Mountain. Old Man Din had thus been left in command of the ranchería, with eight or nine young men and half-grown boys, plus half a dozen elder warriors, organized for its defense in the unlikely event something untoward should happen.

"A warrior should not be made to do anything he does not wish to do," had been Miguelito's explanation for his apparent pampering of Hishee, with the wry addition, "Besides, it makes the shaman feel important to be in charge. We must always consider that." Cordalee, who was constantly amazed at the occasional jabs of this sort taken at the otherwise seriously held medicine man, had laughed. The idea he had once entertained that the stoic redman lacked in any way a sense of humor was rapidly being eroded to nothingness.

It was with these and other thoughts in mind that he mounted his buckskin pony, took up the halter rope of the lead mule, and set out with Miguelito and Juan Tomás for Nogales, less than two miles away. All three men wore huge, floppy sombreros, brightly colored serapes, Mexican sandals—all found among the loot left on Stronghold Mountain by the Wild Ones before their surrender—while the two Indians had removed their headbands and effectively managed to conceal their long hair beneath their hats, and thus really did look like Mexicans.

Coming in from the south, the threesome stopped to survey the town. "Well, Cor-dah-lee, what do you think?"

Cordalee, who had not shaved for over two weeks now, scratched his beard. "I think we'll get away with it, if we're careful. At the worst, you two might be taken for a couple of stray Papagos. That'll be okay, just so it's no worse than that. Just keep your hat brims pulled low and let me do the talking, okay?"

They pulled their sombreros down almost to the point of blinding themselves and rode on into the Mexican side of town. This was smaller than the American side, but it was obviously growing and did contain the railroad station and its associated structures. Goats, burros, and dogs wandered aimlessly here and there, but across the tracks the inevitable plaza was cleaner and neater-looking by far than might have been expected of a Mexican border town. Leading off from the plaza, an equally clean-looking street led them to the first general merchandise store they had seen. Attentive to any unusually curious stares from bystanders and passers-by, Miguelito and Cordalee went inside, leaving Juan Tomás outside to guard the horses and mules.

Finding some but not nearly all of what they were looking for, they decided, after a brief look around, to shop for another, hopefully larger store. Going back through the plaza and up another street, heading north this time, they found one. The only trouble was, it was on the American side of the line.

"See that pile of rocks over there?" Cordalee asked of his two companions. "That's an international boundary marker. The store is definitely north of the market."

The two Indians looked at one another. Miguelito finally said, "I think there are just as many Mexicans on one side as the other. I don't see what difference it will make if two or three more go across to that store. Eh, Cor-dah-lee?"

Cordalee laughed. "No, I don't guess three more would hurt anything." Then more seriously, he added, "But keep your eyes and ears open. These Americans are just as suspicious as the Mexicans, especially if you let something slip or do anything out of the ordinary."

The young chief said something like "Humph!" and kicked his horse forward, heading for the store. They pulled up and dismounted, tying up their animals and leaving Juan Tomás once again outside to watch. Inside, they found this store's stock of goods much more to their liking. In less than half an hour they and the eager proprietor had assembled a pile of purchases that must have represented a good day's business in itself.

"Well, my friend," Cordalee said to the Indian in Spanish, "what do you think of that? Is it what you wanted?"

Miguelito cast a wary glance over at the storekeeper, who stood bent over a nearby counter, totaling up the bill. The chief's eyes settled back on the large stack of goods arranged haphazardly on one side of the room. He grunted his satisfaction, but dutifully did not say anything.

In addition to a large supply of coffee, five hundred pounds of flour, two hundred pounds of sugar and a hundred of salt, there were several bolts of calico cloth, a goodly supply of tobacco, ten or twelve large cast-iron skillets, twenty-five boxes of various American makes and calibers of ammunition, three hundred pounds of pinto beans, several bags of vegetable seeds, a large sack of potatoes, and even a supply of hard candy wrapped inside a cheesecloth and stuffed into a two-gallon can. In addition, Cordalee had been talked into purchasing himself a new pair of boots, a good felt hat, two pair of trousers, some shirts, underwear, and some badly needed articles for shaving.

Presently the storekeeper, who said his name was Johnson, came over and presented his bill. Cordalee took Miguelito's poke of gold and went over to watch Johnson, his eyes fairly bugging, weigh out that portion of it that was the necessary amount. Satisfied, he returned the remainder to the Indian, then said to Johnson in Spanish, "Will this stuff be safe here for a little while? We want to get ourselves some lunch and look around a bit before we load our mules and leave town."

Johnson, as did virtually all border-town American merchants of his day, spoke excellent Spanish. "Certainly," he said. "Your goods will be perfectly safe." But then his eyes narrowed slightly as his curiosity seemed to get the better of him. "You fellows never did say where you're from, though. I know you haven't been in here before . . . and, well, there aren't that many paying for their goods with gold nuggets such as that these days. Not that I mean to be overly inquisitive or anything. . . ."

Cordalee watched Miguelito stiffen, and quickly said, "It's best not to ask, señor. My friend gets nervous when he hears too many questions." He knew the storekeeper already suspected him of being an American—his gray eyes no doubt giving him away—but he saw no reason to admit even that.

Johnson nodded apologetically and watched them leave the store. Outside, Coralee asked, "Well, have we got all you came for, my friends?"

Miguelito said, "Mescal—we wanted to buy some mescal. And horses; we do not have enough horses at the ranchería."

Cordalee frowned. "Well, the mescal shouldn't be much of a problem. They sell it by the keg in the cantinas around here. But horses . . . well, we'll have to ask around about that. And, say, how about we get something to eat first? You ever eat a good enchilada?"

They went back across the line where they found a Mexican restaurant called Dos Republicas. The Indians relished the large bowlfuls of frijoles but were less enthusiastic about the hot red enchiladas that were served them. Still, it was good food and nothing was left on their plates when they were finished eating it.

Leaving the Dos Republicas and coming back out into the hot afternoon sun, they went into a nearby cantina where they purchased what mescal they figured there was room for left on the mules and a box of Mexican cigars for Cordalee. As the two Indians went outside to load the mescal kegs on one of the mules, Cordalee stayed inside to ask where they might purchase some good saddle horses. He was told that the pickings were pretty slim around Nogales, but there was a rancho down near Cananea where good horses were the stock in trade. It definitely appeared the best bet, though Miguelito, when told of it, mumbled something about it being a "plenty damn lota trouble, this *buying* horses," and not the way the old ones of his people would have done things at all.

They proceeded back to Johnson's store where they quickly began loading the remaining mules with the purchases they'd made earlier. They were just finishing this when three well-armed Mexicans came striding down the street and entered the store, casting suspicious looks at the small pack train forming out in the street. This fact alone might not have bothered Cordalee much, but something else about them did. There was a vague familiarity about one of them that he couldn't quite define. He stared after the threesome for a few moments, then turned to Miguelito.

"I think we should get on out of here, amigo. I'm not sure, but I think I've seen one of those fellows before—and I don't like the way any of them looked at us."

The two Indians agreed and all three soon were mounted and on their way out of town. In true Apache fashion, they rode directly south for about half a mile, then, dipping down out of sight in a sandy wash, turned east and gradually began to make their way toward camp. On arrival, they were still trying to make up their minds whether to remain for another day around Nogales, or to move immediately out in the direction of the horse ranch where they expected to complete their business the next day.

It was Cordalee who, though having wanted badly to spend some time around the Nogales cantinas at night, finally said, "I just didn't like the looks of those three Mexicans. I even saw one of them staring at us through the store window as we rode out. I wouldn't be surprised if Johnson told them all about your poke of gold and all the stuff we bought. And there were other people giving us the eye, too. As much as I hate to say it, I don't think hanging around here any longer would be a good idea at all. I think we should break camp right now and move on toward Cananea before nightfall."

The Indians once again agreed and immediately began changing back into their normal clothing. As soon as this was done, camp was broken and they were on their way again.

They had gone about two miles, the warriors Kentoni and Cruz ranging ahead as scouts, when suddenly someone detected a rising dust cloud behind and to the main party's right. Cordalee sensed but a moment's confusion among the Indians before Miguelito yelled something in Apache, and three men burst forward at a run with two of the pack mules. Then he yelled something else, pointing to a body of riders that numbered maybe fifteen, coming fast at them from about a mile away. They were being chased, no question about it!

Three more men with two more mules took off in one direction, and Miguelito, Juan Tomás, Gregorio, and Cordalee set off in another with the remaining mules. Before they had gone a hundred yards, even this group split, with Juan Tomás and Gregorio disappearing up a deep arroyo and Miguelito and Cordalee continuing straight ahead and entering thick brush. After a while, they were joined by the scouts, Kentoni and Cruz, who appeared out of the brush like a pair of ghosts.

A mile farther, and the body of riders who chased them had become but a dark patch against the dull gray slopes of a distant ridge. They seemed to be slowing down, and within moments came to a complete stop, milling indecisively. It wasn't hard to guess their problem. Their quarry had seemingly evaporated, leaving them uncertain as to which of several diverging sets of tracks to follow.

"Do you suppose they've figured out yet that they've set out to attack a band of Apache Indians instead of a sleepy little bunch of Mexicans with a packtrain of goods?" Cordalee asked, knowing that Miguelito had just pulled the most common Apache trick ever on them.

The Apache smiled slightly, but his eyes never for a moment left the group of riders huddling in the distance. "Who do you think those men are?" he asked.

"Well, if I had to guess, I think I would include those three Mexicans we saw in town," Cordalee answered thoughtfully. "I still say I've seen one of them before. . . ." Suddenly it came to him. Fronteras! The shooting, the man he had killed—a man named Jorge Ibarro . . . one of the men in Nogales had been this Ibarro's brother; he had almost surely led the charge after Cordalee following the shooting. Ibarro . . . Narciso Ibarro. Cordalee had seen him a number of times in Fronteras, and knew the man to be if anything a meaner character than his dead brother had ever been. Cordalee didn't think that Ibarro—actually the somewhat notorious leader of a Sonoran gang of bandidos—had recognized him in his Mexican garb. But the man had almost surely learned about the gold they had used to pay for the supplies at Johnson's store and had gathered up his men to come after them, naturally figuring to find them easy prey for his outlaw gang.

Quickly Cordalee related this information to Miguelito, who only nodded as if he had figured about as much. Presently the young chief turned to the other two Indians and said something in Apache, then he looked back at Cordalee.

"We should go now. I don't think they will follow us any further. See? They are going back. They know they cannot find us again."

"But what about that horse-buying business? We're heading due east, not south."

"We will have to forget that for now. We must rejoin the rest of our men, and that will take at least until tomorrow noon. By then we will be far away from here."

"But where?" Cordalee asked. "How does everyone know where to meet?"

"I told them before we broke camp," Miguelito answered with slight impatience. "If anything happened, we would scatter, then meet back at a place near where we camped two nights ago."

"Just like in the old days, huh?" Cordalee said. "Like the Wild Ones, all those times the U.S. Cavalry chased them but could never quite catch them. But how come you didn't tell *me* where the meeting place was? How come you told only your men?"

Miguelito asked bluntly, "Could you have found your way there alone, even if I had told you?"

Cordalee thought a moment. "No. I guess not."

The Apache grunted knowingly. "Come on, Cor-dah-lee, we must go. The trading trip is over."

The four of them filed through the brush, the late afternoon sun casting long shadows on the ground ahead of them. Only Cordalee looked back, and that was just long enough for him to see the small blot of riders disappearing over the horizon in the direction of Nogales.

CHAPTER 8

A long four days later they were back on Stronghold Mountain, bone-tired from the journey but thrilled by the deliriously happy reception given them as they arrived at the ranchería.

It was an occasion Cordalee would not soon forget. That night, sides of beef were once again cooked over pits of hot coals; tobacco was distributed; mescal was brought out; the drums beat and there was dancing. After several hours, things quieted down and Miguelito rose to deliver a speech. He spoke, of course, in Apache, so Cordalee understood little of what was said. But he could not help being impressed by the flair of the young chief's oration and the exuberance with which he was received. The Indian was unquestionably a good speaker.

The same seemed true of Juan Tomás, who followed with his own brief version; then came Hishee, Gregorio, Kentoni, and Cruz. . . . It went on until all had had their turn. Even Cordalee was asked to say a few words, with Miguelito as interpreter. Speaking in the most convincing manner he knew how, he mainly congratulated his companions and their chief for having so successfully eluded the Mexican bandidos who had tried to attack them. Apparently this was the right thing to do, for his speech was met with a smile of pleasure from the chief and a loud cheer from the people.

Next came the formal presentation of all the goods and a discussion of how they should best be divided. Cordalee, able only to follow the general line of thought and not the specifics of it, gathered that this was not a dissimilar act to that of distributing the booty from a real raid in times not long past. Some things, such as the supply of vegetable seeds, most of the ammunition, and much of the renewed mescal supply, were to be stored in a sort of extra-large, communal wickiup located near that of the medicine man, to be rationed out later as needed. Others, such as tobacco, some food stuffs, and a goodly portion of the cloth materials, were to be divided equally among the various families right then and there. This project went well enough until two women got into the inevitable hassle over a certain bolt of calico cloth, proceeded to engage in a bitter verbal contest, and finally went after one another in a pitched battle of the most infuriated sort. No one dared interfere, and the fight went its face-scratching, hair-pulling way until settled, the winner getting the cloth and the loser a face full of blood and dirt and a measure of leftover calico from another bolt, which on any other occasion probably would have suited her just as well anyway.

But this was the only disharmony exhibited, and the thing that eventually impressed Cordalee the most was his own rapidly growing acceptance by the tribe. Certainly there might yet be those not fully comfortable with his presence; he was by no means a true "white Apache," although he was aware that a certain tiny few actually had experienced such a distinction in the past. But the question nonetheless occurred to him: Was he in fact on his way to becoming one? Was that what the future held for him?

Several days passed. He became involved in helping the tribe plant corn, beans, potatoes, chili peppers, and a small patch of melons across the creek just beyond the horse corrals. Then he went on a hunt only generally supervised by Miguelito; he killed three deer, a bear, and three turkeys—only to be told afterward that the Apaches would not so much as touch the bear because bears were really people incarnate who had committed crimes in their earlier lives and were now being punished for them. It was okay to kill a bear, because that would put the poor souls out of their misery. But to eat them—never!

The same thing happened when he came in alone one evening with a string of fish—trout caught easily in a little pool of one of the nearby streams. The White Eye with the funny name could eat all the fish he wanted, but to an Apache this was as repugnant as eating the flesh of a dog. Ugh!

Thus Cordalee began in earnest to live with and learn about the Apaches of Stronghold Mountain. He began in a very serious way to learn their very difficult language, and a few of them, including Miguelito, began to take serious interest in him. And finally, he managed to meet the sister of the chief—the quiet, graceful *nah-lin* called Mistan.

It happened on the same late-June day that Miguelito, the shaman, Juan Tomás, and the elder Nah-go-ta-hay suddenly chose to ride out together on some mission or another that they would not tell Cordalee about. They were mounted on their best horses and were taking three extra-stout mules, *aparejos* empty, with them. Cordalee had asked where they were going, but they would tell him only that it was special business that must be tended to.

"When will you be back?"

"Six, maybe seven days," Miguelito answered. "You will be safe enough here, just don't wander too far away from the ranchería alone."

"Why?" Cordalee wanted to know. "I've roamed all over these parts by myself in the last couple of weeks. I won't get lost."

The Apache shrugged. "Still, I do not want you going beyond the trail guards. You must promise me that, Cor-dah-lee." He waited for the white man's slow nod, then turned to ride away, heading down the south trail, his three companions and the pack mules close behind.

Cordalee, puzzled slightly by Miguelito's words, watched them go. Was the chief concerned that he might yet try to escape? He thought about it a minute, then wagged his head—whoever knew what an Apache was thinking! He put it aside and turned to the planning of his day. Already he had some ideas. From the corral guard he procured his buckskin pony, and from the chief's wife Nondi he obtained a lunch of jerked venison and *zigosti* (bread). Then, mixing his much-less-than-fluent Apache with his reasonably fluent Spanish, he managed to ask for and received directions for finding a certain high ledge that Miguelito had told him about, which overlooked the "up-Bavispe" River but from which there was no safe way to leave the mountain.

By early afternoon he had located the ledge, lunched, then lounged around, lazily taking in the view of the river some several hundred feet below, not to mention the mesmerizing Sierra Madre looming awesomely in the distance. By three o'clock he was on his way back to the ranchería, following a narrow deer trail across pine-covered slopes, down and across steep little canyons, and finally coming upon a grassy glen with a tiny creek coursing down one side. It was, he knew, little more than a quarter mile from the ranchería. A well-used footpath cut through the glen, following generally the creek's course, and disappeared in the trees at the far end.

Cordalee had just paused to let his horse drink when he thought he heard a light peal of laughter coming from a thicket of willows growing a short distance away. He pulled the buckskin's head up, then listened intently for several moments more. He was about to decide it was nothing when he heard it again—laughter, followed by voices low and feminine.

For a moment he was almost afraid to move; he didn't know whether to go forward and make his presence known or, fearing that might cause some sort of embarrassment, to simply slip off undetected.

Before he could decide, two Apache girls suddenly emerged from the willow thicket. They stopped, startled to see him sitting there, and seemed about to turn and go back when two more girls came out of the brush, one leading the other. The first two Cordalee had seen before but did not know by name; the third he recognized as the Mexican girl, Paulita; the fourth was the blind maiden, Mistan.

After a moment's further hesitation, he kicked the buckskin forward and rode up to within a few feet of where the four girls had stopped. He didn't know if he was breaking some kind of taboo in approaching them this way, but he figured now that they had stumbled onto each other he might as well find out. He dismounted slowly.

"*Buenas tardes, señoritas,*" he said, somehow forgetting entirely the one or two Apache greetings he'd learned.

Mistan turned to Paulita, her hands reaching to touch the other girl as if for reassurance that she was still there. She said something in Apache, and Paulita's low answer included Cordalee's name, hyphenated the way virtually all of the Stronghold Mountain Apaches had come to pronounce it. It was Paulita who finally said to Cordalee, her Spanish, as always, clear and concise:

"We did not see you there, Cor-dah-lee. We would have avoided you had we known."

"Why? Am I diseased?"

She shook her head impatiently. "You are a man and we are unmarried girls of marriageable age. We have had our *goo-chitalth,* the Sunrise Ceremony of the Virgins. This is not entirely proper."

"I'm sorry for that," Cordalee said. "What are you doing here?"

"We were gathering herbs for the shaman, for when he returns. But we must go now. . . . We should not talk with you here."

Cordalee's eyes were singularly on Mistan, who stood calmly, her blind eyes seemingly cast off into the distance. "You are already talking with me here," he said. "And you have talked with me before. Have I ever said anything discourteous or improper?"

Paulita looked nervously at the other two girls. One of them, a rather fat, dour-faced girl, uttered something in Apache. Paulita turned back to Cordalee. "We must go," she insisted.

"I wish you would not be in such a hurry," he said, his gaze still firmly on the blind maiden.

Paulita started to answer, but was cut short by a low-voiced query from her companion. She looked in uncertainty from Mistan to Cordalee.

"What did she say?" he insisted somewhat anxiously.

"She asked what we were talking about? She wants to know what you have been saying?"

"Tell her I said I think she is beautiful. Tell her I wish I could talk with her. Tell her that ever since I first saw her I have wanted to know her."

Paulita obviously thought this was out of place; but, torn between further uncertainty and an impatient tug from Mistan, she finally turned and translated.

For a moment a hushed silence fell over the group as Mistan considered the white man's apparent rashness. Then the fat girl uttered a single, terse Apache word, at the same time flinging an angry glance Cordalee's way. Mistan immediately countered with a curt remark of her own, waving her hand impatiently and saying, *"Ugashe! Ugashe!"* The two younger girls seemed at first shocked, but then, hesitantly, they began to move off down the trail toward the ranchería.

When they were gone, Mistan said something and Paulita turned to Cordalee. "She wants to know what the man who saved the life of old E-kon-sen-de-he looks like." She waited a moment, and when he did not say anything, she turned back to answer Mistan. When she had finished speaking, Cordalee asked, "Well, what did you tell her? I notice it did not take long."

Paulita said, guardedly, "I told her you looked much better now that you have shaved off your beard and are wearing clean clothes."

Mistan said something else then, and once more Cordalee asked, "Well?"

Paulita actually blushed. "She says she is glad to hear that you are so handsome. She thanks Paulita for being honest. She wishes she could talk with you directly." She turned her eyes away, still blushing wildly.

He tried not to smile at the Mexican girl's discomfort, although he figured she had probably gotten what she deserved. He said, "Tell her I am trying to learn Apache. Her brother is teaching me, only it is going slowly because he is so busy. Tell her I wish I had someone like Mistan to teach me. I could teach her both English and Spanish in return."

Again Paulita translated, and after a moment Mistan replied, a slight frown crossing her face, her words coming in measured tones.

"She says she is not sure good would come of it," Paulita told him. "She is uneasy about the future . . . and she senses that you are very much a part of that."

"Why? What does she foresee?" Cordalee remembered well Miguelito's claim that his sister had a prescient mind.

"I don't think she knows for sure yet."

"Ask her anyway."

Paulita did, although it plainly was not to her liking. Mistan's reply came once again slowly and only after several moments of thought.

"As I said," Paulita told him, "she is not yet sure. Except that she thinks the Mexicans will have something to do with it. She is afraid that

someday many will come and that they will be led by a certain man, a
man who wishes only bad for our people—and maybe you, too."

This troubled Cordalee, but he had a natural optimism about him that
was already working hard not to take it too seriously. He looked at the
Mexican girl. "Ask Mistan if she is not sometimes wrong in her premoni-
tions. Ask if it might not turn out to mean little or nothing at all."

Mistan listened as Paulita translated, then nodded slowly. "Yes, sometimes Mistan is wrong," Paulita told Cordalee, but her expression did not
indicate that she placed much faith in the possibility.

"Well," Cordalee said finally, "tell her I hope this time she is wrong.
Tell her I am trying to learn to speak Apache well enough that I can talk
to her directly, and that I wish to see her again."

To this, the reply was, "Mistan says we must go now. She is glad you
enjoy talking with her. . . ."

Cordalee thought he knew when he was being put off. "That doesn't
say what I wanted to know, Paulita. Will she see me again? Ask her—"

But Paulita put up a hand, cutting him off. "I did not finish," she said.
"Mistan also says that she often comes to this place when there is someone
to bring her. Maybe someday you will see her here again. She does not
promise, but maybe that will happen." She hesitated a moment, then said,
"*Buenas tardes,* Cor-dah-lee."

He watched them pass from view on their way back down the trail, his
heart thudding with the excitement caused by the glimmer of hope
Paulita's last translation had given him. He tried to warn himself that it
might be no more than that, a glimmer; but despite this, his hopes soared
higher and higher, until by the time he himself had returned to the
ranchería he truly believed that Mistan had the same as agreed to meet
him again.

Yet, as he virtually haunted the pretty little glen for the next few days,
his high hopes were slowly ground to frustration, then actual despair.
Morning, afternoon, and evening he went, and not once did Mistan and
Paulita appear. Several times he saw them around the ranchería, sometimes separately, sometimes together. But he knew better than to approach
either of them directly, in public. He knew that was a breach of etiquette.
If Mistan wished to meet him, it had to be at a time and place of her
choosing, not his. And it could not be in public. Already he had discerned
that.

By the fifth day, he had almost given up. On the sixth, he didn't even
go to the glen. He rode off in the opposite direction and did not return
until almost sundown. He was once again dissatisfied, unhappy, and rest-
less.

On the seventh day, Miguelito and his small party returned. They came at night, and Cordalee did not see what they brought with them; the pack mules were in the mule corral the next morning, and there was no sign that he could see around the ranchería of anything new having been brought in.

Miguelito was, as could be expected, completely mum on the subject. Cordalee decided not to ask more than once, for he knew it would do little good. He was glad enough to let his curiosity rest for now, as his relationship with the chief seemed otherwise back to normal.

It rained a few days later—a real downpour—and the month of July and the wet season were fully upon them. For several days it came with little letup, except to settle finally into a slow drizzle that so seemed to permeate the body pores that after a while one was cold and miserable even when dry beneath a shelter.

Then it cleared off and the mornings were bright with sunshine again, though heavier than ever with dew. The hillsides were green and the air was clean and pure and charged with energy. People and animals alike felt good, and even Cordalee could not help concluding that Stronghold Mountain was indeed a paradise. It was such a beautiful, peaceful, happy place to be, that he gradually even began to get over the depression caused by his experience with Mistan. And even this promised renewed possibilities when one afternoon he suddenly saw her with Paulita, heading up the trail in the direction of the glen. Elated, he was about to follow along, but then was disappointed to see several other girls and a couple of older women taking the same path ahead of him. Dejectedly, he stayed behind. But his hopes were churning: Mistan had again begun going to the glen. Things were looking up all over. . . .

Then, just before sundown that same day, a strange Indian suddenly showed up at the ranchería, causing quite a stir among the people. He was an Apache about thirty years of age; a renegade—a bronco—from the United States.

His name was Makkai, and he wanted to know what a large party of Mexicans was doing camped on the banks of the Bavispe near the foot of the north trail.

CHAPTER 9

Makkai was a big, broad-faced Indian with a savagely untamed look in his eyes and extremely long black hair, worn without benefit of a headband, and thus making him look even wilder yet. He was armed with a good Winchester rifle, full cartridge belt, and knife. The horse he had ridden in on stood lathered and spraddle-legged a dozen yards away. Everything about the Indian spelled fugitive, wild Indian—*Netdahe*.

At present, a conference was going on near the center of the village between the newcomer, Miguelito, a couple of the elders, and "subchiefs" Hishee and Juan Tomás. A few feet to one side stood the medicine man, the chief's mother, and the warrior Kentoni. Other onlookers—including a purposefully inconspicuous Luther Cordalee—maintained a respectful, though curious distance. Notably absent from the gathering was the maiden Mistan, which seemed the case with most, if not all, of the unmarried girls of the tribe, even though Cordalee was positive that those who had gone to the glen could easily have returned to the ranchería by now.

Presently, despite the impending darkness of night, a group composed of Miguelito, Makkai, Hishee, and half a dozen others mounted and rode out in the direction of the north trail. After they were gone, Cordalee drifted over toward Juan Tomás, who apparently had been left in charge of the ranchería.

"Who is that Indian, Juan Tomás?" he asked.

The young warrior's face looked troubled as he answered. "Makkai is a wild Chihinne, Cor-dah-lee. I wish he had not come here."

"Why? What's he done?"

Juan Tomás shook his head. "I know only a little more than what he himself has just told us. He once roamed these very mountains, back before Nantan Lupan came the first time to take our people back to Arizona. After that he lived on the reservation near Fort Apache, until one day the soldiers gathered up all the peaceful Chiricahua and Warm Springs people there, drove them to a place where they could be put on a *besh-sinki-gaiya*"—railroad train—"and sent them off to a place far away. Makkai did not go. He stole away and left the reservation and has never gone back except to steal himself a woman now and then. He says the Warm Springs people never came back. He says they are gone from Arizona for good." The Indian paused, frowning deeply. "Is that possible, Cor-dah-lee? Do you know of such a thing?"

Cordalee was hesitant for a moment, before saying, "Yes, I know about that. They were sent to Florida, the same as was Gerónimo. I don't know if they will ever be allowed to come back."

Juan Tomás frowned anew at this, but he only said, "Well, anyway, Makkai is a bronco now and he says the White Eyes are looking for him everywhere. Not only that, many Indians are too—reservation scouts and police, he calls them."

Cordalee considered this, then asked, "Is Makkai alone, Juan Tomás?"

The young Indian grunted distastefully. "He is alone except for a young San Carlos woman stolen from her father's wickiup the last time Makkai entered the reservation. He left her tied and gagged to a tree near where the north trail reaches the top of the mountain. He even bragged about it. He said he didn't want her screaming and giving him away to the trail guards when he sneaked past them."

"Good grief," Cordalee said. "He actually sneaked past the trail guards?"

"I'm afraid so. They must have been asleep, for no one could get by their lookout without being seen, if they were alert. Needless to say, they will get a good piece of Chief Miguelito's mind when he sees them."

Cordalee wagged his head, suddenly realizing now why no young maiden had been allowed to be seen around the ranchería while the bronco was about. "Makkai must not think much of his woman, to leave her like that," he commented.

"Humph! She is lucky he did not kill her. The chief will probably have her brought back here, once he and the men have scouted the lower trail to see what the Mexicans are doing. She is lucky indeed for that."

"Yeah," Cordalee said. "Lucky."

It was after midnight when the scouting party returned, Makkai and his bedraggled woman included, and it was morning before Cordalee got a chance to ask Miguelito what had been learned. He spotted the chief outside his wickiup at sunup and sauntered over to have a visit.

"¿Cómo le va, Cor-dah-lee?" the Indian greeted. "You are out early this morning. I don't suppose it is curiosity that has caused that, eh, my friend?"

Cordalee smiled. "You know me better than that, chief."

"Ha! Well, even so," Miguelito said, smiling, "have a seat and some coffee. My wife might also have some breakfast left if you have not eaten, and maybe you will even be interested in what we learned last night."

Cordalee, declining breakfast, happily accepted the invitation of coffee and talk. He took a seat beside the small breakfast fire and the coffeepot and smiled politely as the dark-eyed Nondi appeared momentarily at the doorway of the wickiup.

"Well, I have already learned much from Juan Tomás about the bronco Makkai," he said to Miguelito, "but what of the Mexicans he said he saw? Did you see any sign of them?"

Miguelito poured the coffee, then took a seat opposite that of his guest. His demeanor was now more serious.

"They could not be seen from the head of the trail," he said, "but partway down we could see them camped near the first big bend in the river. It was a large camp, maybe twenty, twenty-five men altogether. We could see their campfires burning and could even hear them singing and laughing and playing their guitars. They must have had plenty of mescal, and from the sound of the voices, they had women, too."

"Do you have any idea what they are doing there?"

The chief shrugged. "It could be a packtrain taking supplies to the river towns. We did not get close enough to tell. But just in case, I had the trail guards doubled last night, and today I plan to take some men and try to get a closer look."

"Then you do think they might pose a threat to the ranchería?"

The Apache shrugged once again. "We have learned that one can never be too cautious when Mexicans or White Eyes come around."

"Yeah," Cordalee said thoughtfully.

Miguelito went on. "We will take the Bacerac fork of the south trail; Bacerac is a small town a few miles upriver from Bavispe—I know you have heard of it. Anyway, we must go that way as it is unlikely that we can approach that camp from the north trail without being seen and I do not want to wait a whole day—for nightfall—to check those Mexicans out better. From Bacerac we can work our way north, downriver, until we find them."

"But won't the people of Bacerac see you? I thought you wanted to keep your presence here a secret from the people on the river."

"No Mexican sees an Apache if the Apache does not want him to," Miguelito said contemptuously. "Besides, there is much cover on the river trail. We can pass by easily there without being seen."

Cordalee smiled. "And what if the Apache has a white man with him? Will you let me go with you?"

The chief studied him seriously. "Well, I suppose I could do that, if you will do as you're told. . . . Only I must tell you this. Makkai will be coming along, and few *Netdahe* ever had reason to hate the White Eyes more than he. So far, he does not know you are here, but if you come today, well . . ."

Cordalee's brow wrinkled as he considered this. After a moment, he said, "I can't hide from Makkai, Miguelito. And I want to go with you. If your *Netdahe* friend doesn't like that, then he'll just have to show what he can do about it."

A look of mild satisfaction came over the Indian's face. "Very well. Just remember, as long as you are my guest, you will be safe here at the ranchería. But when we go down to the river, you must be prepared to take care of yourself. Will you remember that, my brother?"

Cordalee, despite the little chill creeping along his spine just then, said, "I'll remember."

"Enju!"

Half an hour later a party of fifteen Apaches, stripped in their old fighting tradition to the skin, except for breechclouts and ammunition belts, stood assembled with their horses in the center of the ranchería. As Miguelito had indicated the case would be, Makkai was among them. The big Indian's eyes flashed immediately as he spotted Cordalee leading his pony toward the group. He hotly turned toward the young chief.

"Who is this *Indah*, Miguelito?" he demanded, *Indah* being a word Cordalee had learned was used to mean white man, as opposed to *Indeh*, which was used in reference to "the People," both words' literal translations being something else entirely.

Cordalee arrived just in time to hear and understand—generally—the question. Of Miguelito's reply he was able to understand less, although he did detect his own name and something about his being a friend of the Stronghold Mountain Apaches.

Makkai, hardly placated, barked back, "Did you ask this 'friend' to ride with us? This *Indah* is going to ride with the Apache?" Heavy scorn and anger marked his every word.

Miguelito's own terse reply was both cutting and final. "This man rides at my invitation. He has ridden with us before and has shown himself worthy. That is all I have to say. If you don't like it, you can stay here with the old men and the women."

Cordalee, once again understanding just enough to get the gist of it, thought Makkai might come apart at this; his eyes were like smoldering coals suddenly ignited to flame by a bellows, and his muscles grew taut, reflecting the tension in all those who stood around him. But it was clear that Miguelito was in change; he was not to be backed down.

Makkai, glowering darkly, turned to his horse, thus letting the moment and the decision pass to the young chief. But it was plain that he had suffered a slap in the face no Apache was likely to forget. But even an inveterate battler like Makkai could not ignore the fact that Miguelito had the overwhelming support of his men—thirteen solid warriors, not one of whom would hesitate a second to take the wild intruder apart at each of his joints. What he might do if and when the circumstances differed was another likelihood altogether. Cordalee couldn't help a little shiver at the thought of it.

But it was settled for now, at least, and presently Miguelito gave orders for the party to ride out. Splitting them into two groups, he sent Hishee and three men to join the trail guards at the head of the north trail—a precaution just in case the Mexicans did indeed try an invasion of the mountain stronghold from that direction. The second and larger group—Miguelito, Juan Tomás, Makkai, Cordalee, and eight others—set out immediately for the Bacerac fork of the south trail. Old Man Din, assisted by his crew of old men and half-grown boys, was once again left in change of the ranchería.

It took just over an hour of steady riding to reach the fork in the trail. Here they paused while Miguelito conferred briefly with the two trail guards who came down from their station atop a low hill overlooking both forks. Then, taking the easterly fork—the other branch continuing almost due south toward the towns of Huachinera and eventually Oputo—they began winding their way down to the Bavispe.

As they drew near the river, Cordalee pulled his horse up beside Miguelito's. "You were right about the cover," he said, "A full troop of cavalry could hide in some of this." The trail at this point, although briefly wide enough for two horsemen to ride abreast, was otherwise engulfed in thick brush. It did not look much used at all.

"There will be no problem until we each the river bottom itself," Miguelito replied. "Then we will have to be more watchful. There is no telling what or who we might run into there."

"What about the Mexicans you saw last night? Where will we be likely to find them? Mightn't they already be gone?"

Miguelito shrugged. "If they are coming up the river with a slow packtrain, they will do well to reach the town of Bavispe in a day's travel. If they are going the other way, toward Fronteras, they will be long gone and we have nothing to worry about. The only truly bad thing they might do is try to come up our north trail. If they do that, Hishee and his men will quickly make them wish they had not."

"Four men?" Cordalee asked doubtfully. "Four men and the trail guards against twenty-five?"

"One man and a few good boulders could hold off fifty on that trail, Cor-dah-lee," the Indian said with confidence. "Believe me, it has been done before. In the old days Apaches would laugh and roll rocks down upon anyone trying to come up a trail like that. Then they would laugh some more as men, horses, and mules all tumbled to the bottom. A hundred Mexicans and more could not take that trail today, my friend."

In less than an hour they had picked their way down the steepest section of the trail to a point about half a mile upriver from the sleepy little village of Bacerac. The town, a dismal conglomeration of adobe *jacales*, a few stores, and a church, sat perched atop a bluff overlooking the Bavispe. Very little activity could be seen from half a mile away, and Cordalee suspected that little more would be noted if one stood square in the center of the village's small plaza.

The Apaches did not tarry over this, however, mostly because the morning was already well along and there was little time to waste. Departing from the main trail, which was almost completely overgrown with vegetation at this point, they moved off through cottonwood, willow, and cane, avoiding all trails now, and moving at a goodly pace downstream in the direction of the town called Bavispe.

Shortly past noon they cautiously approached a ford in the river, crossed, and swung to the east for about a mile. The minute they reached high ground, Miguelito pointed toward the town less than two miles away. Beyond that, though not yet in sight, was San Miguel, an even smaller place yet. Like Bacerac, Bavispe was nothing to brag about. The Apaches had seen to that in years past.

Striking north once again, the party crossed what the Indians said was Ranchería Creek, then Azoria Creek, and finally the Dos Carretas trail, which wound its way through the mountains to the northeast toward Janos. San Miguel now appeared in the distance to the west ot them, and they could see that they had left Bavispe slightly behind. Quickly taking to the brush of the foothills, they circled around until they came upon the Fronteras trail about two miles north of San Miguel, heading once again down the twisting, cutting course of the cool-watered Bavispe.

It was decided that a brief rest for both animals and men was needed. Guards were sent both ways to watch the trail, and a temporary day camp was established out of sight of the trail. The horses, watered earlier on the Bavispe, were allowed to graze on the sparse grass to be found around the

camp, and the men lounged in the shade, lunching on jerked venison and
zigosti.

Less than an hour later, Miguelito motioned the men to catch their
horses and mount back up. The mid-afternoon sun beat feverishly down
and the humidity was high. The air was still, broken now and then by the
screech of a gaudy-colored bird and filled with the dull hum of incessantly
buzzing flies.

But even before the last man had mounted his horse, one of the camp
guards burst through the cane. Excitedly, he related something in Apache
that Cordalee understood even less of than usual. Maybe this was because,
as Miguelito had only belatedly thought to warn him, the Apaches traditionally used different words for things on the warpath than they used for
the same things at other times. It had not been made clear to him why this
was, but it was exactly what seemed to be going on at the moment. Still
he caught some of it—something about the trail . . . and Mexicans! The
Mexicans had been spotted on the trail, coming upriver, as they had been
expected to.

"Quick," Miguelito told them, "dismount. Leave your horses here so
they don't give us away when the Mexicans' horses come into sight. You,
Ben-ah-thli, and you, Chivo—stay with the ponies. The rest of you come;
we must get under cover so we can watch the trail." He motioned to the
somewhat confused Cordalee, and the next thing the white man knew he
was slipping through the cane behind the chief, excitement coursing
through his veins and making his heart thump hard and fast.

In a matter of minutes he found himself lying completely still amid
huge clumps of sacaton grass, within fifty yards of the trail. The Mexicans, spotted by the camp guard from a tall cottonwood when they were
still half a mile away, had not yet appeared. The Indians, except for
Miguelito and Makkai, who were only a few feet away, had seemingly
vanished into the ground around him. It caused him to wonder how many
times he himself had ridden past just such a party of ghostlike forms hidden alongside a trail in rocks, grass, or brush that should hardly have hidden a bird. The thought sent chills up and down his spine, as did that of
what was going to happen when the Mexicans came into sight. . . .

He didn't have long to dwell on it, for suddenly he both heard and saw
them, emerging from a willow thicket less than two hundred yards down
the trail. They were coming at a leisurely pace, laughing and calling to
one another, the thought of danger lurking along the trail apparently the
farthest thing from their minds.

As they drew nearer, Cordalee began to count them, but then became
distracted by the overall look of them. He recalled Miguelito's remark that

they might just be mule packers taking supplies to the river towns. The closer they came, however, the more he grew convinced that this was no regular packtrain. They were heavily armed, had but eight lightly packed mules, and the four or five females with them looked to be captive Indian women rather than Mexican señoritas brought along from Fronteras or wherever they had come from. The poor creatures were ragged and pitiful and showed every evidence of having been badly used by their captors.

The leaders of the loosely organized procession were dark-skinned, mustachioed, big-hatted, ammunition-belted, and were almost abreast of the Indians' hiding places when Miguelito reached over and touched Cordalee's arm.

He whispered quietly in Spanish, "How many do you count?"

"Thirty, *más o menos*," Cordalee whispered back. "Maybe more."

"Do you see anything else of interest?"

Cordalee looked. "The women—they are Indian, aren't they? Opatas, Papagos?"

"I think Opata," Miguelito said. "But is that all you see? Nothing more?"

"Well . . . I don't think this is a simple packtrain carrying goods. They look more like *bandidos* to me—" Suddenly one of the men riding toward the rear of the procession kicked his horse into a gallop, charging past the rear guard and finally pulling up beside the leaders. Cordalee recognized him immediately as he rode past. "Narciso Ibarro!" he breathed. "Our friend from Nogales, Miguelito! The man whose brother I killed and who chased me out of Fronteras! This must be his whole outlaw band!"

He half expected to hear Miguelito give the word for his warriors to open fire. Makkai, from his own place in the grass nearby, must have had the same thought, for his dark gaze was fastened on the young chief, plainly as if waiting for some word to act.

But strangely Miguelito said nothing. He only shook his head, and they watched as the outlaw band passed on up the river and out of sight.

CHAPTER 10

A furious Makkai rose up from the grass and glared at the young chief. His native tongue contained no profanity, but the look on his face was not so handicapped, no combination of American or Mexican oaths, even in the hands of an Irish soldier or an Arizona mule skinner, could equal what an Apache could do with one such look.

"Why did you not attack those Mexicans?" he demanded hotly.

"There were over thirty of them," the young chief said simply, defensive despite himself in the face of the gloweringly wild Apache confronting him, "and there are only twelve of us. We had nothing to gain by attacking them."

"Agggh!" Makkai spat derisively. "One volley from our *besh-e-gar*—guns, rifles—"would have cut their number in half. You should have ordered us to fire."

Miguelito shook his head. "No, Makkai. You are wrong. Sure, we could have won, but some of them would have gotten away. They would have reached Bavispe or San Miguel. They would have told their story and then everyone would know that once again there are Apaches in these mountains, and that they are up to their old tricks as well. That would only mean trouble for our people on Stronghold Mountain—armies hunting us, war again—"

"*Bah!*" Makkai said, his face a malevolent snarl. "That is not the way an Apache talks. That is the way a Mexican or a White Eye talks. Are there no Apaches left who will fight our old enemies? Only you—you who goes around running from fights and who gathers up no-good White Eyes for his friends?" His eyes settled harshly on Cordalee, who again was struggling to understand what was being said.

"We had nothing to gain," Miguelito repeated staunchly. "For the good of our people, we fight only in self-defense or in defense of our ranchería. We no longer make senseless war like the *Netdahe*. We are not such fools."

"You are not Apaches, either," Makkai snarled. "And *you* are no chief!"

"That is not for you to decide," Miguelito shot back, bristling.

Suddenly the big Indian made a quick move and something gleamed in his right hand—a knife! The other warriors, who had come up to watch from their hiding places of only moments before, all moved quickly back out of the way, as did Cordalee, who suddenly understood in the action everything he had missed in the conversation.

"I think I will decide," Makkai said angrily. "I think I will kill you, like I would a miserable dog." He assumed a fighting crouch, wielding the knife in a shoulder-high position, his elbows up and his arms stretched slightly forward.

The young chief, his own knife swiftly in hand, also squared around. "You will have to grow much smarter than you are now, Makkai," he said, and they began circling warily.

The big *Netdahe* struck first, a lightning backhand sweep that left a thin line of red across Miguelito's left shoulder. Just as quickly, the young chief's own blade flashed, missing but causing Makkai to jump back and take up a new stance.

Once more the two men circled. Makkai kicked out viciously with his right foot and followed with a catlike swipe of the knife. But Miguelito was ready for him this time; he ducked, then came up swinging with his own blade. The blade missed Makkai's jaw by a fraction of an inch, but the fisted handle caught the bigger Indian flush, stunning him and sending him stumbling back into a large clump of sacaton. He lost his footing and went down, his younger, lighter adversary, blood streaking down his left arm now, coming close behind.

But it was here that bad luck struck Miguelito—and saved Makkai. The young chief, his knife raised, was almost on his off-balanced opponent when his own foot struck something in the grass. Losing his balance, he went lurching forward and to one side of the now recovering Makkai, attempting too late to evade the other man's retaliatory swing.

The *Netdahe*'s flashing blade caught Miguelito under the right arm, ripping out the back and leaving a mean-looking gash just beneath the shoulder blade and armpit. A serious wound, both because of its depth and the quick blood flow, it immediately rendered the young chief's knife arm painfully useless; he went down, dropping his knife as he fell. Meanwhile, Makkai was quickly on his feet and set to pursue his advantage.

Miguelito managed to roll to his left, kicking out at his opponent as he did. But he missed and Makkai, slashing wildly, scored again as his blade struck the chief's right leg, laying open an ugly slit all the way to the bone for about six inches above the knee. Miguelito tried to roll away, but suddenly the big *Netdahe* whirled to stand crouching over him, straddling him, his knife within a foot of the younger man's throat. He obviously meant to drive it home and was only savoring the moment or two he aimed to give Miguelito to dwell on his fate.

But the young chief of the Stronghold Mountain Apaches had the blood of warriors flowing in his veins, no matter how much of it had already been spilled on the ground. He was no quitter; and the moment's respite given him by Makkai was a serious moment's mistake on the Wild One's part. The downed warrior twisted and brought his left knee up all in one motion, catching Makkai hard in the groin and avoiding the instinctive thrust of the blade at the same time.

Makkai wound up on hands and knees, trembling and sick with pain, while Miguelito rolled away, got to his knees, then wobbled to his feet.

As he did, he reached down and picked up his own knife with his left hand, and then just stood there, shaking, facing Makkai. Blood poured from his wounds; his right arm hung uselessly at his side. He probably couldn't have fought off a timid wood mouse just then. Yet there he stood, no less defiant than before, waiting to do further battle.

But Makkai was sick; the pain in his groin caused him to look almost as if he might vomit. Luther Cordalee looked around at the other braves, and his eyes locked with those of Juan Tomás. A quick understanding passed between them, and the young Indian nodded. He moved to step between his chief and the still kneeling Makkai.

"Enough," he said. "We will not do this way anymore. We gain nothing when Apache fights Apache. It is over." He looked toward his fellow warriors and Cordalee, the latter of whom and two more—the constantly paired Kentoni and Cruz—moved quickly to the side of the young chief, now clearly on the verge of passing out. As they half carried, half led him over to the shade of a nearby cottonwood, Juan Tomás continued to face Makkai, his rifle raised and its hammer cocked.

"You have caused enough trouble, Makkai," he said firmly. "We have given you shelter and allowed you to ride with us because you are *Indeh*. But we cannot abide your wild ways, your hatred, your attack on our chief. Your heart is bad, Makkai. You can only bring bad to the hearts of others if you stay. I ask you to go now and not to come back. I ask that you leave what is left of our people to search for peace in these mountains. I speak for all these men here when I tell you that you are no longer welcome among the Stronghold Mountain Apaches."

Cordalee, again picking up only the substance of the speech, so typically Apache in its manner, saw from beneath the nearby cottonwood the dark look Makkai gave Juan Tomás. He also heard him mutter something about the woman and horse he had left at the ranchería that morning, and he heard Juan Tomás bark back something in reference to the *Netdahe's* poor treatment of both, that he could take the horse he now rode in trade for the other one. In fact, the *Netdahe* was getting the best of the deal at that: a half-dead horse and a badly used woman for a good strong pony from the Stronghold Mountain herd—that sounded more than fair to Juan Tomás.

Makkai, bitter but helpless to do anything about it, rose and walked, slightly bent, toward the canebrake where the horses were being held. In a moment they heard him pounding off through the brush, headed downriver. Juan Tomás came over to where Cordalee and the others were trying to stanch the bleeding from Miguelito's wounds.

"How is he?" he asked Cordalee in Spanish.

Miguelito, still conscious and determined to answer for himself, said weakly, "I am alive. You are not going to get to be *Inday*"—chief—"that easily." Then he added, "I have to admit, though, you handled Makkai well. You are a good 'subchief,' my brother."

Juan Tomás smiled. "Haven't I always told you so?" Then he looked back to Cordalee. "How are his wounds? Can you stop the bleeding?"

Cordalee, who had already torn his own shirt into strips and was using them for bandages, frowned. "I don't know. The one on his left shoulder is not so bad. And his leg, maybe. But this one under his right arm is a problem. We might stop the bleeding, but it is a bad cut. It may never heal properly unless the wound is stitched up. If we had disinfectant and something to stitch with . . . something to kill the pain . . . a doctor . . ."

"I can stand pain," Miguelito put in testily. "I am no child."

Cordalee nodded. "Okay. But the main thing is, the wound needs the proper attention now, or my guess is you may never get much use of the arm again. You are very lucky an artery wasn't cut. An inch to the right and, well, Juan Tomás might be chief after all." Miguelito smiled wanly, but it was plain that he knew Cordalee was not joking.

Juan Tomás rose and drew the white man aside.

"Cor-dah-lee, can you treat Miguelito's wounds? Can you do this stitching? What do you need? I have an awl, some thread, a pair of tweezers my father gave me before he went back to the reservation with Nantan Lupan. . . ."

Cordalee shook his head. "Even if you had the right tools, I am not sure I could do it properly. He needs a doctor—a *real* doctor—Juan Tomás."

The young Apache's eyes were troubled as he asked, "It is that serious?"

"I think it is. Even if he does not bleed to death, he could become a cripple. It would be a sad state for a chief to be in—especially if it could have been prevented."

"But we have no doctor, Cor-dah-lee," the Indian protested. "How can we prevent it?"

"Surely there is one at one of the river towns. We are only a few miles from San Miguel. I could go there and find out."

Juan Tomás looked doubtful. "But how could we get Miguelito to him? Even if he would help an Apache, we cannot give our presence away to the Mexicans there. Everything we have done has been to prevent that. Miguelito himself would never hear of it."

Cordalee thought a moment, then offered, "Maybe I could bring the doctor here. I could lie to him, tell him a Mexican prospector has been shot. Then, when he is here, we can lie again, tell him you are Opatas or some such. Tell him you are on your way out of the area. Even if he suspects otherwise, what can he do about it? A couple of your men can hold him prisoner until the rest are gone, then turn him loose to go home. Surely we can pull it off somehow."

Juan Tomás' look was a studied one. "You think it is worth the risk, Cor-dah-lee?"

"I am certain of it."

"You must be sure to stay clear of your friends, those *bandidos* from Fronteras."

"I can do that."

Juan Tomás sighed. "Okay, but I will go with you and wait outside the village. We must get Miguelito to a safe place—back to the clearing where the horses are being held, maybe—and then we will go."

"Fair enough," Cordalee said and moved quickly toward the cottonwood tree where Miguelito lay.

It took less than half an hour for them to ride to San Miguel. They approached carefully, and upon nearing the outskirts of the tiny village, Cordalee left Juan Tomás behind within a grove of tall trees and entered the town. Shirtless but for the top of his long underwear, he rode straight up to the first cantina and dismounted. He saw no sign of the bandido band that had preceded them on the trail, and assumed they had gone on upriver.

It was dark and musty inside the saloon, and Cordalee figured he could easily pass for a Mexican himself. Only four men, playing cards, and the bartender were to be seen. Cordalee, addressing the latter in Spanish, asked if there was a *médico* in town. The bartender laughed. A *médico* in tiny San Miguel? Ha! That was a good one!

Well, Cordalee then wanted to know, what about Bavispe, or even Bacerac farther up?

Ah! Bavispe. Now that was a different story. Bavispe, it so happened, did have a *médico*—a *norteamericano*, no less. A man named Smith. All a man had to do was cross the river about a mile to the south and a little bit east . . .

Not waiting for the bartender to finish talking, Cordalee whirled toward the door. Minutes later, he and Juan Tomás were headed south at a gallop toward the Bavispe village *vado*. They didn't slow down until they reached the river, and then only to pull off the trail and find another place for Juan Tomás to hide while Cordalee crossed to the opposite bank and entered the town.

"Be sure and keep a watch out for the Ibarro fellow," the Apache warned. "It could go very bad for you if you are recognized."

Cordalee, taking ample heed of his friend's warning, took every advantage of the late afternoon shadows as he entered town at what looked to be its least busy section and stopped the first *peón* he could find to ask the way to the *médico's* residence. He also asked if a large party of men had come into town in the last hour or so. The *peón* said yes, but that he thought they were on the opposite end of the village plying themselves with tequila at a cantina there. The *médico* lived but a few houses away, just down the street to the left.

Cordalee rode cautiously in the direction shown him, and presently dismounted in front of a small adobe *jacal* that displayed a crudely lettered sign above its front door, which read: D. SMITH, MÉDICO. He knocked loudly. The door was opened by a barefoot urchin who turned and screamed, "*¡Papá!*" the moment he saw the tall white man standing there in his undershirt and blood-spattered trousers, then disappeared back inside the house. Seconds later, a slender, bearded man with deeply sunken eyes and sun-darkened skin appeared. As advertised, he was an Anglo, and he appeared to be less than forty years of age. He did not look particularly well, however, and Cordalee guessed that the man might have taken to drink.

He looked Cordalee up and down, then said softly in English, "Yes?" The man had not been fooled about Cordalee's nationality.

"You are the doctor of Bavispe?" Cordalee asked, using his native tongue in conversation for the first time in what seemed like years.

"I am. And you, sir? Who are you?"

"I am an American. I come from downriver, where a man has been hurt and needs your help. Can you come with me?"

The doctor stared at him. "What man—and how is he hurt? Why didn't you bring him here?"

"He's a prospector," Cordalee said, the planned lie coming more easily than he had expected it would. "It was an accident; we were afraid to move him. There's been a lot of bleeding and he has wounds that need suturing."

Now the doctor was outwardly suspicious. "What kind of accident? Did it have anything to do with those *bandidos* who just rode into town?"

"No. It had nothing to do with them," Cordalee said. "But we don't have time to be talking about it here. You must see for yourself. Have you a horse?"

Still the doctor was uncertain.

"You will be well paid," Cordalee said. "And your safety is guaranteed. I can promise you that."

At last the man shrugged and said, "Very well," then turned to call inside, "Benito! Ramon! *Mi caballo, mi silla de montar, mi silla de alforjas. ¡Andele! ¡Pronto!*" His horse, his saddle, his saddlebags—quickly! He told Cordalee, "You wait here. I will be only a moment," and disappeared inside.

True to his words, he was right back, hat on head and buckling on his gun belt. "You won't mind, I hope?" he asked with a sidelong glance.

"I guess not," Cordalee said reluctantly.

Shortly the urchin who had answered the door, and an older boy, appeared coming from around back of the house leading a jug-headed bay horse, saddled and ready to go. The doctor checked his bulging, oversized saddlebags, in which he said all of his instruments and most of his medicines were carried, then mounted. Cordalee followed suit, and they were quickly on their way out of town, passing only one or two rebozo-clad women and several half-naked, dirty children playing in the streets as they went.

The sun was disappearing behind the high ledges to the west by the time they crossed the Bavispe and Juan Tomás appeared from out of nowhere to join them. Dr. Smith immediately reined in, giving Cordalee a sharp look.

"Who is this Indian?" he demanded. "What is he doing here?"

"It's all right," Cordalee said. "He's an Opata. He's with me."

Smith still looked suspicious, but he agreed to go on. They struck an easy, ground-gaining gallop, Cordalee and the doctor traveling side by side and Juan Tomás lagging only slightly behind.

Twilight was upon them as they approached the Apache camp in the canebrakes on the east bank of the river. A camp guard challenged them, spoke a few quick words with Juan Tomás, then let them pass. "Another Opata?" Smith asked dryly as Cordalee motioned him onward.

They rode into camp and were met first by an anxious Kentoni and

Cruz. Moments later they were surrounded by the other braves. A still conscious but weakened Miguelito lay near a small fire in the center of the camp.

Juan Tomás dismounted and headed immediately for his chief's side, and Cordalee was about to turn to invite the *médico* to do the same when he heard an unmistakable click behind him. He whirled and found himself staring into the barrel of the doctor's revolver.

"You lied to me," Smith said angrily. "There are no prospectors here, and I know something about Indians, Opatas included." He brandished the six-gun threateningly. "Come on, man. I know an *Apache* when I see one. I want to know exactly what these fellows are doing here!"

CHAPTER 11

Cordalee took a moment to compose himself, then said, "I only lied because we were afraid you wouldn't come if you knew the truth. That man on the ground over there is a chief. He has been badly cut in a knife fight and needs your help badly. And, for God's sake, put that gun back in your holster." He indicated with a slight nod the several Indians standing tensely around them, rifles raised. "These men are agitated enough without you pulling down on me with that six-gun."

Smith looked around, then slowly lowered his weapon. "Then they *are* Apaches," he said. "You should have told me the truth, man!"

"Would you have come anyway?"

"I might have." He reholstered the revolver. "But of course you had no way of knowing that. You see, I spent three years as post surgeon at Fort Thomas near San Carlos and a year at Fort Apache. I was among the Apaches a good deal in that time. I would have been quite intrigued by the fact that there are still some of their kind left around here. Not surprised, mind you, but definitely intrigued."

"You resigned your commission with the Army?" Cordalee asked.

Smith smiled thinly. "Not exactly—at least not officially. I could have, but instead I just left one day, about a month after they rounded up all the peaceful Chiricahuas and Ojo Calientes and carted them off to Florida. I thought that wrong then and still do. I guess it sort of capped a long-building unrest in me. Anyway, I deserted. . . ." He paused, then added, "Not unlike yourself, possibly, I'd judge. I see you're still carrying an Army-issue revolver and carbine."

Cordalee nodded slowly. "I'm afraid you judge correct. Only I had a less humane reason than you. I simply hated the Army. I thought I hated Apaches, too, until I fell in with these fellows. How come you to wind up in a place like Bavispe?"

The doctor shrugged. "Some while back, I got to know some men of the Third Cavalry who came down here with Crook in '83. They told me of the sorry situation of the river towns along the Bavispe, the squalid living conditions, the miserable nature of the peasants. I thought I might do

some good here . . . and of course I thought I could hide here, with little
fear of being run down by the Army and court-martialed. My crime, you
see, was a matter of regret only after I had committed it." He looked
around then, adding, "Hadn't we better be seeing to your friend the chief
over there? I'm afraid his men are getting nervous again."

"You're right," Cordalee said, swinging down from his horse and handing the reins to one of the braves standing nearest him. "It's all right
now," he said in Spanish to Juan Tomás, who was looking up anxiously
from Miguelito's side a few feet away. "Come on, Doc. Let me introduce
you to Miguelito. I think you'll find him as interesting a patient as you've
had in a long time."

The physician, after a quick but thorough examination of Miguelito's
wounds, called for someone to fetch a shallow pan from among his gear.
He wanted it filled with water and set to boil atop the small campfire.
Then from his saddlebags he began to lay out his instruments and medicines. It was not a complicated assortment of either, but apparently was all
that was needed.

"First I must cleanse and disinfect these wounds," he told Miguelito in
near-perfect Spanish. "Then comes the suturing. That may hurt some, but
it is necessary. Do you want a painkiller?"

Miguelito eyed him, his feverish eyes filled with suspicions. "What do
you mean 'painkiller,' médico?"

"Laudanum, possibly—good whiskey, if you prefer."

The Apache thought about it. "I do not need a 'painkiller,' but I like
whiskey. I will have that, if you have some."

The doctor smiled and dug deeper into the saddlebags for the bottle he
knew was there. Miguelito took a long pull, then looked at Cordalee.

"My friend has found a smart médico, a man who knows good 'painkiller' when he sees it. I am pleased."

The Indians had been quick about fetching the pan of water, which
now sat over the fire. As soon as the water boiled, the doctor began his
cleansing of the wounds. Following this, he disinfected his suturing
needle with alcohol and began stitching the gash under the chief's right
arm and shoulder. Miguelito did not flinch, but he did take another long
pull on the whiskey bottle.

The doctor's fingers moved deftly at their task and he talked as he
worked.

"Who did this to your chief, my friend?" he asked Cordalee in English.

"A wild Indian not of Miguelito's band. He is gone now. He won't be
back, either—I hope."

A few moments later the doctor said, "I don't know your name yet, do I? What do I call you?"

"Cordalee. Luther Cordalee."

"What was your regiment before you deserted? Or do you mind telling me that?"

Cordalee shrugged. "I don't mind. Troop E, Fourth Cavalry. I was headquartered at Huachuca. Have you ever been there?"

"No. But I know of the Fourth. I was with the Sixth—did I say that already?"

"You said Fort Apache; I assumed maybe the Sixth."

The doctor grew absorbed in his task for a moment, after which he went on to say: "Yours must be quite a story, Cordalee. Yours and these Indians'. I knew of Gerónimo's surrender even before I came here. Everyone said he took the last of the renegades with him. I guess we all suspected there might be an exception or so to that. Fact is, word to that effect has been hot news around the river towns ever since spring."

"Oh?" Cordalee was immediately interested.

"Yeah. Sometime during May, I think it was. Some Indians were seen coming down out of the mountains downriver, inside the big bend. It was suspected that they were Apaches, although no one has had courage enough to go up into those mountains to find out."

"Who saw them?"

The doctor had straightened and was looking around, his mind now on something else. "I need more light. Someone bring a torch. This campfire isn't enough." Most of the Indians were sitting around at respectful distances from the doctor and his patient, and only Juan Tomás sat close by; it was he who fashioned and brought over the torch. "*Bien, bien,*" the doctor said. "That's fine. What was it you asked, Cordalee?"

"I asked who said they saw Indians inside the Bavispe Bend?"

"Seems to me it was some Mexicans from Fronteras. I never knew all the particulars. Someone told me they were chasing a white man, an American, for some reason or another. They saw the Indians, guessed them to be bronco Apaches—for those mountains have long been a notorious Apache hangout—and turned back home. They never got their American fugitive, either, as I recall. . . ." Suddenly he straightened and looked at Cordalee, realization coming sharply to him. "Well, if I'm not a thick-headed one!"

Cordalee saw no point in attempting to deny the obvious. He nodded. "I am the American they were chasing. And many of those same Mexicans just this afternoon rode into Bavispe and were sopping it up at a local cantina when you and I left town. They are led by the brother of a man I killed, in self-defense, in Fronteras, a man named Ibarro. Have you heard of him?"

The doctor had Miguelito sitting up now, and was wrapping a bandage across his upper torso. "There," he said, after a moment. "That should take care of that for now. I've wrapped it in such a way he can't raise his right arm more than an inch or two. It should be kept that way until the stitches are ready to come out." He looked at Cordalee. "You realize they'll have to come out, I hope." When Cordalee nodded affirmatively, Smith went on. "Okay, then, let's have a look at that leg. The cut on the left shoulder won't take more than a few stitches, but this one above the knee is at least as bad as the one under the arm, only not in so bad a place."

He got Miguelito to lie back down, and turned to the gash on the young chief's leg. "Hold that torch a little more this way, my friend," he told Juan Tomás in Spanish. Then he slipped back into English, and back to Cordalee.

"Well, well, so you have made an enemy of the infamous Señor Ibarro from Fronteras. I don't envy you that, let me tell you."

"Have you any idea what he is doing in Bavispe?"

Smith shook his head. "None—except the man has a reputation up and down the river as a hardcase of the worst sort. All across the Arizona-Sonora border, in fact, from what I've heard. I would steer clear of him if I were you."

"I intend to," Cordalee said, thinking of the close brushes he had already had with the man and his bandidos.

Shortly the suturing of the leg wound was completed, and then the bandaging. The doctor rose and began putting his things back inside his saddlebags. He looked down at his patient and said in Spanish, "You've stood a lot of pain, my friend. Even with the whiskey, not many men I know could have done that and never so much as whimpered."

Miguelito was groggy from the whiskey and looking sleepy. But he looked up at Cordalee and asked, "Has this man doctored me good, my brother? Do I owe him something?" His Spanish was slurred but understandable.

Cordalee said, "I think he has doctored you very good, Miguelito. But I don't know how much you owe him." He looked toward the doctor. "His fee has not been discussed."

Before Smith could say anything, the young chief was holding something out with his left hand. "Will this do?" It was a small poke of gold, which he normally carried inside his belt.

Smith took it and shook out a sample of its contents; he whistled his amazement. "This is ten times any fee I ever charged. Where on earth did he get it?"

"I don't know," Cordalee answered. "He has never told me."

The doctor said to Miguelito, "This is far too much, my friend."

Miguelito was taking another pull at his whiskey bottle, all but emptying it. "No matter," he said. "Take it. You are paid well for doing well. I may need you again sometime. . . ." His words trailed off and he seemed almost to fall asleep.

"He's right, you know," Smith said to Cordalee. "He will need me again when those stitches are ready to come out, but mostly to make sure infection hasn't set in. Is there a way I can be brought to him again? I know it is too risky to bring him into Bavispe."

Cordalee frowned. "I can't make any promises along those lines. I'm sure these Indians will not stay here beyond tonight. Do you think Miguelito can travel soon?"

"I don't know," Smith said thoughtfully. "He's lost a lot of blood; he's weak as hell. But I'm darned if I'll say there's anything a live Apache can't do. I wouldn't advise it, is all. He might reopen a wound, start bleeding again, and that could be fatal."

"Well, whatever happens, I will come after you if I can, and if the Apaches will let me. How many days should I wait?"

"I'd say make it a week or ten days, to be reasonably safe. The one wound will be slow healing, and neither of the two bad ones will be fast. Take these pills and give him two a day. And watch for infection; keep the wounds clean and change the bandages daily. If there is radical swelling and pus, come for me quick. You won't have a lot of time to waste."

Cordalee nodded that he understood, then stood up, wondering how this might all be worked out. The doctor asked, "Am I allowed to go now? I think I've done all I can for the time being. I have a Mexican wife and two stepchildren waiting for me to come home."

Juan Tomás had come to stand beside them and was obviously curious as to what they were saying. He listened as Cordalee explained to him in Spanish that the *médico* was finished, that he wished to be brought back in a week or so to remove the stitches from Miguelito's wounds, and that he now wanted to go home.

Juan Tomás gave him an inscrutable look. "Can we trust this man? You yourself said we should keep him prisoner until we are gone. Do you now feel that unnecessary?"

Cordalee spoke to the doctor in Spanish so there would be no misunderstanding with the Indians later on. "Juan Tomás is worried that you will tell someone of our presence here. We had thought you might not recognize these men as Apaches; that we might tell you they were Opatas passing through. They don't want the river-town residents to know they have been here. These Apaches are peaceful and mean never to go to war again. They want only to be left alone. Will you keep what you have seen here tonight a secret?"

Smith didn't hesitate to answer. "You can bet on it. I won't even mention it to my family. My wife's first husband—and the father of those two boys you saw back there—was killed in an Apache raid just two years ago. It would scare her to death if she even guessed these fellows were around." He looked at Juan Tomás. "Listen, my friend. As I have already told Cordalee, I once lived among your people in Arizona. I knew several of the Chiricahua head men when they lived at Turkey Creek near Fort Apache. I knew old Loco, Nana, Chihuahua, Mangus, Chato, Kaah-Tenny—even Gerónimo. I sympathized with them. I will not give your presence here away." Then he laughed and gave the small pouch in his hand a light flip. "Besides, where else can I earn fees like this? Half my patients can't afford to pay anything at all." Vaguely Cordalee wondered if the doctor hadn't seemed almost too anxious to appear convincing, but he decided perhaps not. After all, the man wanted to get home to his family. . . .

But Juan Tomás still seemed unsure. "What do you think, Cor-dah-lee? Should we believe this?" The Indian could hardly be blamed for his caution, considering past Apache experiences with promises made by white men.

Cordalee said, "I think we will have to trust him for now, Juan Tomás. As he says, we will need him again in a few days to take Miguelito's stitches out. And he seems to me to be an honest man."

The young Indian considered this for a few moments, then said, "All right. We will let you go, médico. I will send two men to take you as far as the Bavispe vado. You will go tonight." Then he turned and moved away toward the other braves.

Cordalee watched him approach Kentoni and Cruz and begin talking in low tones to them. Dr. Smith went over to his horse and began strapping his saddlebags back on.

In a moment he came leading the horse over to where Cordalee still stood.

"Well, my friend, as you predicted, your Apache chief has been among my most interesting patients. I hope to see him again in a week or so. I hope you will be coming to fetch me."

They shook hands, and in a few minutes Smith rode with his two escorts into the darkness and out of sight.

Cordalee walked over to Juan Tomás and said, "I'm surprised you let him go. He could be back here in a couple of hours with half of Bavispe and San Miguel."

Juan Tomás shrugged. "It will not matter. I have instructed Kentoni and Cruz to make sure he travels very slowly, and to go from where they leave him on back to Stronghold Mountain by way of the south trail. . . ."

"But," Cordalee said, "if we stay the night here—"

Juan Tomás shook his head. "I have already spoken with Miguelito about that. We will not stay the night here. We will be leaving for the north trail before the moon is up."

Cordalee could hardly believe that Miguelito meant to ride all the way to Stronghold Mountain that night. But the young chief was both stubborn and strong; no amount of arguing would dissuade him from making the trip. And thanks to the expert job of suturing and bandaging done by the good doctor from Bavispe, there was only the tiniest bit of bleeding from any of the wounds.

Nevertheless, it was a hard ride, covering more than twenty-five miles, several river crossings, and the steep north trail in less than ten hours. Even considering the frequent rest stops that were made, it was undoubtedly the longest day of Luther Cordalee's life—and he could imagine what it was like for the wounded Apache. Few but an Apache, he knew, could have endured what Miguelito had that day.

But the young chief, held in the saddle by Juan Tomás much of the way, made it to the top, and shortly after sunrise they were being hailed by Hishee and the trail guards. Not long after that they were entering the ranchería, and all of the people—including Kentoni and Cruz, already there—gathered around to meet them. Cordalee, along with Juan Tomás, helped Miguelito to his wickiup, and then stumbled across the compound to his own abode. Inside, he flopped down on the welcome bed of hides in almost total exhaustion. His only thought before falling asleep was that it seemed forever since he had last been there.

The sun was low in the west by the time he awakened, refreshed but aching all over from the long ride of the day and the night before. He headed immediately for Miguelito's wickiup, where he was met outside by Old Man Din and was told—in a somewhat difficult but eventually successful conversation in Apache—that the chief was doing well but was asleep just then. Maybe Cor-dah-lee could come back later when the chief was awake. Right now the White Eye friend of the Apaches might do well to pay a respectful visit to the wickiup of Nah-de-glesh. It was always a good idea to pay one's respects to the mother of the chief. Besides, there were questions that one had regarding the so-called *médico* from Bavispe who had ministered to her son.

Moments later, Cordalee was cutting across to do as the medicine man had suggested when he happened to pass the wickiup occupied by Paulita and her little brother, Nito. Someone rounded the far side of the wickiup just as he was passing and a collision took place before either of them could sidestep the other. It was Paulita, and the collision was so sudden and forceful that it almost knocked her off her feet.

"*¡Lo siento mucho, señorita!*" he said, reaching out to steady her. "I didn't see you coming. Are you all right?"

"*Sí,*" she said shyly, straightening her dress. "I am all right."

They stood awkwardly for a moment, then Cordalee said, "I was on my way to the wickiup of Nah-de-glesh. Are you sure you're okay?"

"*Sí, sí,*" she insisted, adding, her eyes downcast, "I am sorry also."

Cordalee stepped aside and started to move on past, but Paulita's low voice stopped him and he turned back. Her eyes met his as she said, "I—I am not supposed to tell you this. It is not supposed to be planned. . . ." Uncertainty seemed to claim her.

"What? What is not supposed to be planned?"

Her eyes dropped, but finally she said, simply, softly, "The maiden Mistan will be in the glen tomorrow." Then she whirled back toward the wickiup and disappeared inside.

For several moments Cordalee simply stood there. He had wanted to ask what time tomorrow Mistan would go to the glen. But then, as he at last turned to be on his way, he swore softly to himself that it didn't matter, that he would be there at sunup and would wait all day if need be.

CHAPTER 12

The forest was cool and whispery, a slight breeze rustling through the pine tops and a continually changing pattern of sunlight and shade covering the ground. Above, the sky was a depthless azure, and nearby, the crystal-clear waters of the tiny creek danced and shimmered and trickled. The air, cleared the night before by a light rain, smelled sweet and clean, and Cordalee told easily that his were the only human footprints made on the oft-used creek-bank trail since before the rain. He knew that he was thus far alone in the glen.

He walked slowly, taking his time as the trail wound its way among clumps of oak, willow, wild rose, and berry bushes, the fruit of the latter not yet ripened. He paused to watch trout swimming lazily in a small pool, envying them their apparent carefree existence. He studied the oak- and pine-clad fringes of the clearing, certain that deer hung there just out of sight, watching curiously. Then, spotting a huge hollow log lying alongside the creek bank, he went over to sit and wait.

It was, he judged, almost one o'clock; he truly had meant to come earlier in the day, but had been prevented from doing so because Miguelito had been in one of his talkative moods that morning.

He had gone over to the chief's wickiup shortly after breakfast to help Nondi change her husband's bandages, and had found Miguelito not only feeling much better than he had the night before, but anxious to discuss seemingly any and all things in great detail.

First, there had been the matter of his wounds, the stitches having to be removed. Was this really necessary? Did the chief's friend still think it safe to trust the White Eye doctor from Bavispe? And did he think it safe to bring the doctor to Stronghold Mountain?

But that wasn't all; more practical matters also the lot of an Apache chief plagued Miguelito. An example were the crops being raised across the creek. Two old men had been appointed as overseers of the farming activities and had been given their pick of the young boys to help. Crude hoes were being used to control weeds, while pickets were on guard constantly trying to shoo birds away and keep both deer and cattle out of the fields at night. Not that it would matter, the chief lamented, if the rains did not come in a more productive way. For almost two weeks they had had only light showers, barely adequate to keep the crops alive. If the weather did not improve, things would soon be bad indeed. Miguelito did not like the thought of a crop failure upon their first attempt at farming on Stronghold Mountain.

Cordalee had suggested why not build a fence of poles and brush like the ones around the horse and mule corrals, only higher, to keep the deer and cattle out of the garden plot; and since the creek was nearby, why not irrigate? It shouldn't be all that difficult to arrange. The crops were already planted in rows, and the field itself sloped away from the creek on a reasonably gentle grade anyway. He himself could show the overseers and their charges how to locate and build the ditches.

Miguelito, pleased immensely by these ideas, also wanted to know if his white friend knew anything about the raising of livestock. The tribe's small herd of Mexican cattle was scattered all over the mountain and was mixing with others that were completely wild. The men had gone out more than once to try to count them, with widely varying results; it was to the point now that no one knew how many there actually were. And worse, this year only about one cow in five seemed to have a calf at her side.

Cordalee was no cowman, either; but he did have a few ideas. One was to cease immediately the indiscriminate butchering of breeding stock, good and poor alike; learn to identify a good heifer and keep her for the purpose of raising calves while killing only barren cows, old bulls, and, if there were any, steers. Also, appoint a herdsman to learn the ropes of raising and caring for the livestock and begin gradually to herd the tamer stock so they could become accustomed to being handled by men on horseback; and take up the castration of bull calves so that interbreeding could be controlled, then go somewhere and purchase bulls of good blood so the herd could be built up. . . . There were at least a dozen things that could be done, and the sooner started the better.

Miguelito thoughtfully tucked all of this away somewhere in the decision-making recesses of his mind, and went on to other things. The tribe still wished to procure additional horses; would a trip to the horse ranch near Cananea still be worthwhile? Another trip for supplies would probably be necessary before fall; maybe this time horses could actually be purchased. Maybe, too, they could find a ranch with some good breeding bulls for sale. . . . The list went on and on, with Cordalee offering suggestions wherever and whenever he could.

Then, finally, the chief broached a cautious subject that heretofore he had been unwilling to discuss—that of the tribe's extraordinary financial status. He had decided that his friend Cor-dah-lee should be trusted with certain knowledge, of which only the principal council members themselves were thus far fully aware. It had to do with the Indians' yellow iron —gold to the White Eyes. It had to do with the Stronghold Mountain tribe's own supply of the strangely valuable metal, a legacy left them by the Wild Ones themselves when Nantan Lupan had first come to the Sierra Madre. Soon, Miguelito would take Cor-dah-lee to see its hiding place; possibly his friend could give an appraisal of its value and how long the supply might last.

But that was "plenty *bueno*" for now; the chief could see that his friend was getting strangely anxious to be on his way. Maybe tomorrow they could talk further about irrigating the garden plots and herding the livestock; and, as soon as Miguelito was well, they could go and see the yellow iron. *Enjul*

Cordalee idly watched the water in the creek trickle past, somehow disturbed now by his talk with Miguelito. He wasn't sure why. Certainly he didn't mind the prospect of helping the Indians with their many projects; he even looked forward to that. But it bothered him, the realization that for all their dependency on remaining isolated within their mountain fastness, the Apaches were rapidly moving toward a life-style that depended just as heavily on their developing some kind of rapport with their age-old enemies, the Mexicans and the Americans alike. How else could they expect to trade with them, raise crops and livestock the way they did, live within twenty crow-flight miles of their nearest town? And how long would it be before the Mexicans came to claim these mountains, just as the Americans had done in New Mexico and Arizona? Once, those areas too had been vast wildernesses, the Apache's right to which had been virtually uncontested. And the Indians had tried there, too, to make treaties and live in peace—first with the Spaniards, then the Mexicans, and finally the Americans. Always disharmony and war had resulted; inevitably the Indians had lost, having finally been so overwhelmed that now they were either living as prisoners on a tiny scrap of their former homelands or were banished from them altogether.

Cordalee shook himself, attempting to ward off the depression that he could feel coming on. At the same time he marveled at his own thoughts. Was it really him seeing things this way? Was it really Luther Cordalee— the fellow who'd once been so certain that the Apaches were incorrigible to the last man, woman, and child?

He started suddenly, thinking he had heard a noise from somewhere back down the trail. When he looked that way, however, he saw nothing. But then he heard the sound again, coming from the willows downstream: voices. He watched patiently until the two girls appeared, walking side by side, Paulita holding Mistan's hand, guiding her almost imperceptibly.

Somehow they did not detect him sitting there until they were almost upon him and he stood up. Paulita suffered a perfectly legitimate start, her free hand coming to her mouth and a little cry escaping before she realized who he was. Quickly she turned and said something to Mistan, whose own mildly alarmed expression then faded, to be replaced by a look of pleasant surprise.

"*Buenas tardes, señoritas,*" Cordalee said. "*¿Cómo están . . . ?*"

Paulita simply nodded, but Mistan rather surprisingly replied, "*Muy bien, gracias; ¿y usted?*"

"*Bien, bien,*" he responded, looking over at the proudly smiling Paulita and adding, "I see someone has been giving language lessons."

"Yes," Paulita said, "and don't you think she did very well with the greeting?"

"Tell her *muy perfecto*. And ask her if she is still willing to help me with my Apache. Tell her I have learned to understand much of her language, but that I am not yet confident with my speaking of it."

Paulita translated from Spanish to Apache, listened to the Indian girl's brief reply, then turned back to Cordalee.

"She says she will teach you what she can, but that she is ashamed to have only one language to share with you and I, who each have two."

"Tell her she should never be ashamed. She is the sister of a chief, and she knows just as many languages as most of the people of this world will ever know. Tell her how glad I am that she came today."

The afternoon flew by. There was nothing formal about the strange, three-way language study; it was more of a game really, a game of words spoken over and over in English, Spanish, and Apache. The words were at first both simple and basic: sky—*cielo*—*mie*; sun—*sol*—*holos* or *chigo-na-ay*; moon—*luna*—*klego-na-ay*, the full moon, or *tzontzose*, the crescent moon. Other oft-used words included: young boy—*niño* or *muchacho*—*ish-ke-ne*; young girl—*niña* or *muchacha*—*day-den*; maiden—*doncella*—*nah-lin*; earth—*tierra*—*terte*; water—*agua*—*quesa*; knife—*cuchillo*—*bešn*; tobacco—*tabaco*—*na-to*. . . .

Finally the afternoon waned; all too soon, it seemed, the two girls determined that they should return to the ranchería. Insisting that no *nah-lin* should be seen going or coming with a man, Paulita proposed that she and Mistan start back a few minutes ahead of Cordalee. To his question regarding future meetings, she was noncommittal, saying only that on most days she and Mistan would continue coming to the glen, sometimes with other girls but more often than not just the two of them; and if in the latter instance Cor-dah-lee should also happen along . . . well, it was an unusual situation this, and Mistan was not always predictable. Maybe Cordah-lee himself would have other things to do some days, also. They would just have to wait and see.

Which was precisely the way it turned out. Over the next six days, Cordalee and the two girls found themselves in the glen at the same time only twice. Beyond that, one day went by the wayside because Cordalee spotted the girls leaving the ranchería in the company of several other *nah-lins* and older women, thus canceling his own plans to follow along later; another day passed in which he showed up at the glen but Paulita and Mistan did not; two days were spent helping Miguelito's "farm" overseers to design and construct a crude irrigation system for the garden plots; and still another was exhausted while riding with Juan Tomás, the tribe's newly appointed herdsman, to count cattle, identify good breeding stock, and discuss in general Cordalee's suggestions for building up the herd.

But no matter what the occasion, Cordalee never ceased working on his Apache. It was a highly tonal language, but he was determined that he soon would master the tongue in a conversational way, and he could hardly wait until the day he and Mistan could visit without the need of an interpreter.

It was on the seventh day that they finally met again, and the distinct pleasure with which Mistan received Cordalee's almost flawless Apache greeting was lost neither on Cordalee nor Paulita. The blind girl's happy response in English caused even broader smiles yet.

But Cordalee knew that he wasn't ready yet to completely abandon his Spanish. He said to Paulita, "I guess we still have a way to go, but I think we're doing pretty good so far, don't you?"

"Yes," she said, her dark eyes suddenly becoming inscrutable. "Very good, I think."

After a moment the other girl asked something in Apache, and mostly out of habit, Paulita translated, "Mistan wishes to know where you were yesterday."

"It's good to know I was missed," Cordalee said, smiling. "Actually I would have been here, but Miguelito asked me to ride with Juan Tomás to look at the cattle. I've never told Miguelito about my coming here, you know. I don't think he knows about it."

"We have not told him, either," Paulita said, glancing at Mistan. "We have told no one, not even Nah-de-glesh or my little *hermano*, Nito."

Frowning, he asked, "Is it wrong—what we're doing here?"

The girl shrugged. "It is . . . unusual."

"Tell Mistan that I don't want to do anything that is wrong. Tell her I want to meet and talk with her, to learn her language with her; but I do not want to do wrong. If there is a more proper way we should meet, I'll gladly do that instead."

Paulita allowed her eyes to rest on him for an uncertain moment, then turned to Mistan. After a brief exchange, she turned back.

"Mistan says there is nothing wrong."

"But don't tell anybody about it just the same—right?"

Again she shrugged. "I would not. Mistan has not. You may do as you please. It cannot remain a secret forever."

He could see he wasn't going to get anywhere with this, and decided maybe it was just as well. Reticence, on any subject or question having to do with custom or religion, seemed standard with the Apache; Cordalee probably would do well to accept the fact.

Changing to something else, he said, "I'm going down to Bavispe tonight to fetch the *médico*. Did you know that?"

"Yes," Paulita said quickly. "Nondi told Nah-de-glesh only this morning that the chief's wounds were healing. Tell us, Cor-dah-lee, about the *médico*. We have been very curious about this—this sewing and unsewing of the chief's skin. Is this always the way the White Eye doctors heal wounds?"

Cordalee smiled. "No, not always. Only when the wound is bad and may not heal properly by itself. And when a scar might be prevented or lessened. Sometimes that alone is reason enough."

Paulita turned to relate this to Mistan, and following another brief discussion—which Cordalee understood most of anyway—asked, "Does that mean the chief will have no scars? We are not sure he would like that. To have been in such a fight and then have no scars to show for it! He may be very unhappy with your doctor, Cor-dah-lee."

Laughing, Cordalee assured them that Miguelito would have all the scars he needed; they simply wouldn't be as bad as they might have been, and the healing would be more satisfactory where the severed back and shoulder muscles were concerned. But no one need worry that the Wild One, Makkai, had failed to leave his mark on their chief. He had done that aplenty.

"I hate Makkai," Paulita said bitterly. "He is the worst Apache I have ever known. I hope he never comes back here. I hope he goes back to Arizona and the White Eye soldiers shoot a thousand holes through him."

"Do you think he will come back here? Or will he live alone in some other part of the Sierra Madre? Seems to me he'd be a fool to try going back to the U.S. now. Everybody and his mule is bound to be on the lookout for him."

Paulita only shrugged. She did not know.

"What does Mistan think? Does she see anything in the future about Makkai?"

At first the Indian girl shook her head slowly, but then she seemed thoughtful, and after a few moments related something to Paulita that made the other girl frown.

"Mistan does not think that Makkai will ever be caught or killed in the U.S. by the White Eyes," Paulita told Cordalee. "She does not know if he will ever again come to Stronghold Mountain, but he will come again to the river towns and will cause much trouble and unrest among the Mexicans. She worries that one day, maybe not so long from now, this will even cause trouble for our people here. She does not trust some among the Mexicans on the river and she is sometimes afraid because of this."

Cordalee, ever intrigued by a prescient mind, at the same time could not fathom one. "How can she mistrust people she has never met or known?" he asked sternly. "When has she ever known anyone on the river? Anyone at all?"

Mistan seemed to understand his question without a translation, and she responded directly. Paulita interpreted her reply. "Mistan says she knows only what her dreams tell her. They are not always completely clear, but she has seen what she has seen. There are two men she sees most often, and who she trusts the least. One is the Mexican who she has told you about before. He comes to these mountains with bad in his heart for the Apache, and he is on the river now. . . ."

Cordalee could guess well enough who this might be, and he knew that Mistan had heard all about Narciso Ibarro; but who was the other one? He was about to ask, but this time it was Paulita thinking ahead of him.

"It is your White Eye doctor, Cor-dah-lee. Mistan thinks he will be the cause of much trouble one day. She thinks that it is he among those who should be trusted the least."

Shocked, Cordalee demanded to know why, but the blind maiden could not—or would not—elaborate. She simply maintained that her dreams spoke only what was willed for her to know and no more. She had said all she could.

Their mood thus darkened, the meeting did not last long after that; within half an hour the girls had gone back to the ranchería, and very shortly thereafter a disturbed Cordalee followed along. He tried very hard but could not dismiss the implications of Mistan's words from his thoughts.

An hour later he rode out with Juan Tomás on the south trail, wondering darkly if there was such a thing as a fate that could not be controlled.

No answer came for this, however, and by the time they turned onto the fork in the trail that led to the river towns below, he was telling himself that Mistan's dreams were really no more than the overactive imaginings of a superstitious mind.

He was telling himself that. And he was trying desperately to believe it.

CHAPTER 13

A waning crescent moon was fading against the faint first light of day on the eastern horizon when Cordalee and Juan Tomás arrived back at the ranchería with Dr. Smith. Men and horses alike heaved weary sighs of relief as they pulled up at the corrals and the two lead riders began to dismount. The doctor, tightly blindfolded and hands tied since leaving the outskirts of Bavispe, sat waiting for someone to relieve him of his twofold handicap.

Cordalee went back and did so, then watched as the man dismounted. Smith rubbed his eyes and looked around. Stars still blinked above them; the dim shapes of the wickiups across the creek were just visible against the dark background of the forest fringe; and the high posts and poles of the newly completed fence around the garden plots rose starkly against the skyline. "This is scary as hell, I don't mind telling you," the doctor said. "Especially for a man riding into an Apache camp for the first time."

Cordalee's eyes narrowed. "I thought you'd spent a lot of time around the Apaches," he said as Juan Tomás led the horses away. "Surely you've seen their rancherías before."

"That was on the reservation," Smith said almost too quickly, "not in the middle of the wilds of Mexico, and certainly not at night after five hours of riding through God knows what blindfolded!"

"I'm sorry about that," Cordalee told him. "You can understand the reason for it, I hope."

"Oh yes, sure, I know. The Indians don't want anyone to know where they are. Well, I guess it doesn't matter now; the ride's over and I'm here. So what's next on the agenda? I feel like I haven't slept in a month."

"How about some breakfast?" Cordalee asked, feeling somewhat the same way. "The ranchería is asleep now, but folks will be up and around shortly, and Miguelito will probably want his stitches out first thing. After that you can sleep all day if you wish. The plan was that we take you back to Bavispe tonight."

"Oh, no!" Smith groaned. "Not again! Cordalee, I hope you realize that this damnable clandestine way of doing things is getting to be a real pain in the rear for me."

"You were paid well enough for it before," Cordalee reminded him coolly.

Smith raised his hands, palms outward. "Yeah, yeah, I know. Too well, probably. I won't say any more. Where do we go to eat breakfast?"

"Follow me," Cordalee said, waving for Juan Tomás—who had already finished unsaddling the horses—to come along, too. "My wickiup is over this way."

The sun was an hour in the sky when they finally presented themselves at the wickiup of Miguelito and Nondi. Apache men, women, and children gazed curiously at them from every corner of the ranchería, and not the least among these was the wizened, coyote-faced Old Man Din. This one presented himself straight away, smirking and muttering, at the wickiup alongside of them. He eyed Smith up and down contemptuously before announcing his presence and stepping in ahead of them.

Cordalee smiled. "You had better be at your best, médico. You're going to be under the observation of a real Apache medicine man this morning."

"Great," Smith muttered as he stooped to pass through the doorway of the wickiup.

Inside, the dark-eyed Nondi murmured a quiet greeting and moved to one side as Miguelito, sitting up on their bed of skins along the opposite wall, hailed the visitors heartily. Old Man Din hovered nearby, sprinkling hoddentin and mouthing incantations of the weirdest sort. Smith laid his saddlebags down beside the bed and looked around, as if testing the light coming in through the open doorway. Apparently satisfied, he said in Spanish, "Glad to see you again, chief. How's the shoulder?"

"Stiff," Miguelito replied. Then he smiled, "But it will be plenty bueno soon, I think."

Cordalee went over to sit cross-legged beside Nondi, and began rolling what was for him a rare cigarette as the médico told Miguelito, "Okay, my friend, I see someone has done a good job of changing your bandages. Let's have a look at that underarm."

It took less than half an hour for him to remove the stitches from Miguelito's arm and leg wounds, the chief jerking almost imperceptibly with each tiny yank but saying nothing. Presently, Smith drew back and settled his bloodshot eyes on his patient.

"Well, chief, I wouldn't try to use that arm much for another week or so—nor the leg, for that matter, at least for a few more days. But otherwise, I'd say you're going to come through this in fine shape." Glancing over at Cordalee, he added, "Give old George Crook a troop of physical specimens like this and he'd be unbeatable, my friend. Absolutely unbeatable."

"Yeah," Cordalee agreed unenthusiastically, wondering what Smith thought Crook's Apache scouts had been.

Smith turned back to Miguelito. "I guess that's about it, chief. Now if there's someplace around here a fellow could get some sleep . . ."

"Wait," Miguelito said, rummaging around in a pile of things next to the bed with his left hand. "Here." He tossed over a small pouch. Realizing instantly what it was, Cordalee almost groaned aloud, especially as he saw Smith's eyes light up with scarcely veiled excitement.

"You must have your own little mine of this stuff somewhere, eh, chief?" the doctor said. "Do you realize what this is worth?"

The young chief's face was unreadable as he replied, "I know how happy it makes you White Eyes to have it, what things some of you will do to get it. That is why I give you some of what I have. I am happy that you have fixed my wounds; you are happy to have some of my yellow iron."

Cordalee could sense Smith's inner battle—a hot desire to find out more as opposed to a cold awareness that to press too hard along those lines would be unwise, maybe even dangerous. At last the man said, "Well, it's good that we're both happy. *Muchas gracias, amigo.*" He was stuffing the last of his things, including the small pouch, inside his saddlebags.

But he was not quite through yet; the all but forgotten Old Man Din spoke up as if to remind Miguelito of something, and the chief told the doctor that, since he was already here, they would like to ask another favor of him. Two, actually. The chief's old aunt, E-kon-sen-de-he, was still having some trouble with her leg; the bullet wound Cor-dah-lee had treated appeared to have healed satisfactorily, but there was still some pain, and the old woman could not walk without limping. And there was the young woman brought to Stronghold Mountain by the Wild One, Makkai. She was sick and had much pain in her stomach. Could the *médico* not look at these two women while he was here? The medicine man had done all he could do and was now willing to accept the counsel of the White Eye doctor who sewed up people's skin and called whiskey "painkiller."

All but Old Man Din and Nondi laughed at this, and the doctor—not altogether gladly, Cordalee thought—agreed to have a look. Which fact meant at least another hour before either he or Cordalee got any rest, but it appeased the chief and the shaman, and that was something.

In fact, this was about all that was accomplished, because in neither case was there much the doctor could do. Both old E-kon-sen-de-he's limp and her leg pains were pronounced more or less permanent aftereffects of her wound; and Smith's only conclusion regarding the poor young creature Makkai had so brutally mistreated was that she was suffering from an internal injury of some kind that probably would soon prove fatal, no matter what he did. He gave her a bottle of laudanum to ease the pain and later told Cordalee and the medicine man that it could hardly be more than a matter of days before she was gone. A shame, he said, but discerning the cold facts was sometimes the only expertise a doctor had to offer. Cordalee agreed: a shame.

They then paid a brief courtesy visit to Nah-de-glesh, who had insisted she get to meet the White Eye *médico* when he came but was strangely withdrawn and quiet when the chance actually presented itself. Somewhat surprisingly, Mistan was there also, but she, too, was withdrawn and said nothing during the interview.

A few minutes later, as they crossed the ranchería on their way to Cordalee's wickiup, the doctor said, "That girl, the blind one, I do believe is the most beautiful Apache female I've ever seen. Too bad she's blind. Do you know what caused it, or was she born that way?"

"Born that way," Cordalee said, not really wanting to discuss it.

"And you say she's unmarried?" Smith went on, unmindful of Cordalee's terseness. "Lord, what a waste! What's the matter with the bucks of this band—too damned lazy to take on a wife who can't see to do their work for them?"

Cordalee's silence at this should have been enough to chasten a rock, but Smith hardly noticed. "Well," he said, "if it was me sitting up on top of this mountain with a woman like that around and a gold mine someplace near . . ." He didn't finish the thought, but a few steps later he asked, "They do have a gold mine someplace, don't they? They must have. And you claim you don't know where it is?"

"I don't even know *if* it is," Cordalee corrected pointedly.

Smith eyed him. "Okay, then, just where do you fit in to things around here? Seems to me you could really have it made—no work, no worries, squaws to pick from, a string of good ponies . . . and maybe a little share of those gold pokes Miguelito keeps coming up with. Hell, you could even pass for an Apache yourself, if it wasn't for those gray eyes and your hair not being any longer than it is. Come on, now, Cordalee, how is it with you, really? You're not just hanging around here for your health, surely."

"I'm sorry," Cordalee said stiffly, "but that's about it: my health. I like it here. I have no squaw, only one horse—and that borrowed—and no gold. But it's healthy and I like it."

They stopped in front of Cordalee's wickiup, and Cordalee told the doctor, then, "It's not much, I guess, but the bed's inside. Just make yourself at home. If you're not awake by the time you're to leave, I'll come and get you."

"Where are you going to be while I sleep?"

"I'll be around," Cordalee said. "I've got a thing or two to do, then I might even find a shade tree and take a little snooze myself. I haven't had any more sleep than you have, you know."

"Yeah," Smith said, eyeing the bed of skins through the doorway to the wickiup.

"See you later," Cordalee said, and started to leave.

"Wait," the doctor called. "There's something I think you'd like to know. I think I've about decided where this place is, at least generally."

Cordalee turned back, his eyes narrowing. "Oh?"

"Yeah. Like I told you before, the suspicion already exists that there are Apaches somewhere inside the Bavispe Bend. It's just that no one has had the guts to come see. Now, I've never heard of any Stronghold Mountain before—I guess that's just these Indians' name for it—but I can see the tops of the main Sierra Madre from here, to the south and east, and I'm pretty sure we're well west of the principal river towns. I figure we're somewhere near—or in—what the Mexicans call the Pinitos Mountains. How about it, Cordalee? Just for laughs, am I right?"

"I've never even heard of the Pinitos Mountains."

Smith grinned. "All right, then. Try this. There is a very old and overgrown trail leading up into the mountains from the river near Bacerac. And there are other trails farther south leading up from Huachinera and Oputo. Again, the Mexicans have so long been afraid to use them they are almost forgotten, but they're there. And I figure we rode upriver about as far as Bacerac before we started climbing last night. Come on, tell me if I'm right."

Cordalee stared at him for a long moment. "No. No, I'm afraid you're wrong," he said. "You're way the hell off." Then he turned sharply and walked away, the lie ringing in his ears no louder than the realization that it probably hadn't done the least bit of good anyway.

It was Miguelito who decided that Kentoni and Cruz, rather than Cordalee and Juan Tomás, should accompany the doctor back to Bavispe. He had, it turned out, more than one purpose in mind for making the change. Cordalee wasn't sure if it was because the chief had been listening to Mistan—which he probably had—or if the usual Apache caution had simply taken hold, but it was obvious that the Indian felt that the situation at the river towns warranted closer scrutiny than was now being given it. Too, Miguelito must have seen the gleam in Dr. Smith's eyes when the man had been paid for the second time in gold, for this seemed to enter strongly into the chief's decision. His instructions to Kentoni and Cruz had been explicit. Once the doctor was delivered home, they were to remain indefinitely on the river. They would stay hidden near Bavispe for the express purpose of keeping an eye on things—including the *médico* himself. Anything unusual or threatening to the Indians was to be reported immediately back to the ranchería.

Late that afternoon, after the trio had departed, Miguelito told Cordalee, "Kentoni and Cruz both speak some Spanish, and they are smart young men. We will soon see if the White Eye *médico* is a friend or not." Cordalee had already related to him the doctor's neat guesswork regarding the location of the ranchería, in addition to the constant but subtle digging for information about the gold. "What do you think, my brother? Do you doubt now that the *Indah médico* can be trusted?"

Cordalee, uncertain just how much his own thinking had been colored by what Mistan had told him the day before, gave it a thoughtful moment. "Well, I guess I do some, yes. You yourself have noticed how yellow iron makes us white men do strange and unreliable things. It's a definite risk to let him go back, even blindfolded."

"You think he can find his way back here?"

"I'm sure of it, if he really wants to. He says the Mexicans know the trails leading up from the river, but are too afraid to come looking for you here. They apparently know that these mountains are more easily defended than attacked. But that was before the American doctor came here, before he or anybody suspected that you had a gold mine hidden away somewhere."

Miguelito wagged his head sadly. "I did not know what to do. I hated to think of killing the *médico*. He has done me much good . . . See? I can already stretch my arm halfway up." He raised his arm—although not quite the full halfway. "But I cannot risk the ranchería on his account, either. Maybe I should not have paid him with yellow iron."

"I think that was a mistake, all right," Cordalee agreed. "The first time wasn't so bad, but this time . . . well, I suspect he's decided you're too free with what you have not to have one hell of a lot more stashed away someplace. And you know as well as anybody the hidden-treasure and lost-mine stories that have come out of the Sierra Madre over the years. Why, even I have heard of Tayopa, Scalp Hunter's Ledge, El Naranjal. Legendary products all of a big, mysterious land, lost centuries, the dark ages that have intervened since the time of the Jesuits, and wild Indians—Yaguis,

Apaches, raiding, terrorizing, making the great sierra even more fearsome and mysterious than ever, its few scattered Mexican inhabitants being rendered frightened and timid to the point of almost total withdrawal inside their miserable little towns and villages."

The Apache sneered. "Mexicans! You are right. They have long been afraid of us; they will never come here. Why should we worry about them?"

Cordalee knew this was old-time Apache pride talking and not the young chief's usual good judgment. He shook his head. "I'm sorry, my friend. We both know times have changed now. Gerónimo and the others like him are gone. The Mexicans know that, too. Braver, more desperate men will be coming to the Sierra Madre, to the river towns. *Bandidos*, killers, outlawed Americans. Men with the fever for gold and silver, hungering for riches they have heard about but have never seen. Stories of gold inside the Bavispe Bend could lend them a brand of bravery even you Apaches may not be able to scare out of them. You know that, my friend, I know you do."

They stood on the creek bank just across from the ranchería, gazing down the south trail in the direction Kentoni and Cruz had just ridden with Dr. Smith. The Indian's eyes seemed set on some faraway place only the mind itself could see. He knew. He knew all too well.

"Well," he said at last. "At least they do not know where the yellow iron is hidden. The *médico* did not find that out, did he, Cor-dah-lee?"

"Even I have not learned that, my friend."

The chief eyed him suddenly, the faraway look dying in his eyes. "You will," he said. "You will very soon!"

CHAPTER 14

A few days later the two men sat their horses at the base of a steep, point-topped mountain some six miles from the ranchería, near the north trail. It had rained the night before, and thick red mud stuck heavily to their horses' hoofs, causing them to leave outsized and irregularly shaped tracks on the trail behind.

Miguelito had stopped to point out where the narrow path ahead seemingly disappeared in a tangle of tall brush growing at the base of the mountain. The brush cover ranged all the way to the summit, which became at that point little more than a barren outcrop. The trail, Miguelito said, curled around to the north side of the mountain, then led to within a hundred yards of the top before fading completely. It was very rough and had been little used by humans in recent years.

But what Miguelito insisted was even more significant about the trail was a point about halfway up where suddenly the brush cleared away and a commanding view was offered of not only the ever-winding Río de Bavispe below, but of the broad plain stretching north of the Bavispe Bend as well. The view was so good that on even the most marginal of clear days, one could see all the way to Arizona. It was a perfect lookout and had been used as such many times in years past. On up the trail, beyond this open area and gouged into a rock slope, was a cave, so hidden by an overgrowth of brush and vines that one could ride past it a hundred times and never see it. At its mouth, the cave measured just four feet in width and was no greater than that in height. Inside, about eight feet in depth was added to these dimensions. According to Miguelito, the cave constituted a hiding place that only a handful of Indians had ever known about.

Cordalee studied the mountainside. "That looks like a pretty rough ride to me. You sure you're up to it?" The chief's shoulder was still lightly bandaged and quite stiff, as was his injured leg.

But the Indian had not learned to accept pampering gracefully. "I am no woman or child," he muttered, then urged his horse forward with an impatient slap of the reins. "Let's go, Cor-dah-lee."

The trail snaked its way up through the still wet brush toward the slight shelf where Miguelito had said they would find the lookout. Arriving there was like coming out of the darkness into bright daylight; all of a sudden their view went from a maximum of fifty feet to fifty miles, and the world became vast and distant and awesome again.

Cordalee whistled and said, "It's just as you said it would be. I do believe, if we had binoculars or a telescope, we could see everyone and everything between here and Fort Bowie."

Miguelito smiled, his gaze set somewhere in the distance. The Río de Bavispe curled like an endless worm below them, and the broad plain that spread eastward from the south-flowing San Bernardino River seemed much flatter than it actually was. The mountains farther east were hazy blue and much less impressive than the towering sierra to the southeast, which was hidden now by the brushy hillside at their back.

"I felt much as you do, the first time I saw it," Miguelito said reminiscently. "It was an old *Chihinne* warrior who once rode with Victorio who first brought some of us here. It was only a few months before he and others, surrendered for the last time, with Chihuahua and Gerónimo, at Cañón de los Embudos. We called him simply the Old One. He showed us the trail, this shelf, and the cave, which is on up the hill from here. He said someday we would find it useful to know the whereabouts of such a place. There are many caves in these mountains, but in the Old One's view this cave was especially well hidden. A week later he showed the shaman, three of the elders, and me the place of the yellow iron. It is far to the south of here, and he never said anything to connect one thing with the other, but we all knew why he had shown us both this place and then that one."

Already Cordalee had been told that there was no Apache gold mine on Stronghold Mountain, that the cave was merely a storage place for what had been gained some other way. He listened patiently as the chief went on.

"So we decided to bring the yellow iron here. Only we thought it best to bring it a little bit at a time, thinking that would be safer than if we tried to bring it all at once. We could never tell when we might run into a force of Mexican *soldados* or *bandidos*. Three or four Apaches with only one or two lightly loaded pack mules can almost always slip past the Mexicans without being seen or losing their mules. A larger group with many pack mules would still get away if seen, but might have to leave the mules, thus losing everything. It took about one trip every other full moon to bring it all here. You yourself will remember the last time the shaman, Juan Tomás, Nah-go-ta-hay, and I rode out."

"And didn't return for a week," Cordalee recalled thoughtfully. "Yes, I remember that quite well. It must be a long way from here, the old warrior's hiding place to the south."

"Yes, it is. One must ride all the way to the headwaters of the Río de Bavispe. An old *Netdahe* cache for food and supplies, it was. A place the Old One himself chose in which to hide the yellow iron."

Cordalee's curiosity on this subject, long subdued, could no longer be controlled. "But where on earth did it come from? Wherever did you Apaches find so much gold?"

Miguelito once again smiled, but only slightly. "I was not there when it happened, but I have been told the story many times. I will tell it to you as we ride up to the *cueva.*"

They reentered the thick brush going uphill. Miguelito talked as they went. "It was at a time when all of the Chiricahua and Warm Springs people were still in the Sierra Madre, still months before Nantan Lupan came to Mexico to get them. Some of our people decided to lead a raid toward the town of Ures. This was at the same time that a small group of others went north to raid in Arizona. I am told that what the White Eyes call 'Chato's raid' became a very famous raid indeed." His eyes snapped with satisfaction as he saw Cordalee nod in affirmation of this. "Well, we think our other raiders did all right, too. Even though at the time we were uncertain how much a very few pack mules loaded with yellow iron was worth, we did know how highly the White Eyes and Mexicans seemed to prize it."

"Your people stole it during the raid?"

"Yes, toward the end of what was otherwise only a mildly successful affair, I'm afraid. You see, our men had gone as much as a hundred miles south and west of Ures, attacking a ranch here, a small town there, but had been unable to locate the real prize they were after—a Mexican packtrain laden with goods and supplies. That, my friend, was as tender a morsel to us Apaches, in those days, as a fat cottontail has always been to a coyote. But luck had not been with the raiding party this time. For one reason or another, they simply had not been able to capture a packtrain. They were returning home, tired and only half satisfied with the loot they had thus far taken, when they passed below Oputo and swerved south. A few miles above the town of Nacori, they turned east again, heading in the direction of their base camp near the headwaters of the Bavispe. It was here that a small advance party of warriors stumbled onto a Mexican packtrain coming down from the mountains on a lightly used trail. A desperate fight ensued, with the main party of Indians coming up quickly to swing the tide totally against the Mexicans. There were, in fact, surprisingly few defenders of the packtrain, and instead of running away, they stayed to be killed to the last man. This was a real surprise to our men, who could not remember a time when any Mexicans fought so desperately to defend a simple packtrain. It was not until the fight was over that the Apaches realized why. Several of the Mexicans' mules were loaded with canvas or leather bags full of dust and nuggets of the yellow iron. To the Mexicans it must have represented a fortune."

He paused, his eyes on the trail ahead as they rode. After a moment he continued, "Our men were very disappointed. They had no use for the yellow iron; what they had wanted was guns and ammunition, dry goods, foodstuffs—things our people could use. But the wise old *chihinne* warrior counseled that maybe the yellow iron would someday be worth more than our war leaders realized. It was he who insisted it be brought back to the mountains, and that it be stashed away in case of later need."

The Apache suddenly pulled his horse to a halt in front of a vine-covered bluff that looked on first glance to be solid. Miguelito, nevertheless, turned. "The cave is here, my friend." He swung his good leg forward, over his horse's neck, and slid stiffly to the ground. He limped over to the bluff and began parting the vines and low-growing brush. Cordalee dismounted and went over to help out, and in a matter of a minute or two they had a man-sized opening cleared. The cave stood open-mouthed and dark before them.

Miguelito reached down and picked up a dry branch from inside, on one end of which a wad of tightly wrapped rags had been tied. Cordalee struck a match and the cloth flared. He could see several more such torches lying just inside the mouth of the cave as the flame illuminated the cavern.

Dark and dank, the crumbling recess was nevertheless more than adequate to contain the pile of dusty leather and canvas bags stacked against the back wall. Miguelito went over and lifted one of the bags, then returned to the opening.

"Here, look inside," he said, handing it to Cordalee. "Take it into the sunlight where you can see better."

The bag, which weighed about fifteen pounds, contained several smaller pouches, just the size Miguelito seemed always to carry with him. Some of these contained bright, flickering gold dust and flakes, others held variously sized nuggets, the largest of which appeared to be about the size of a child's thumb.

"Are they all like this?" Cordalee asked. "I mean, gold dust and nuggets in poke-sized pouches?"

Miguelito shook his head. "Only two or three of the big bags are like this. The others have no little bags; they seem to have been filled more hurriedly. Some are fuller than others, and in some the yellow iron does not look so pure."

Cordalee whistled in awe. "Somebody must have been working a red-hot vein and was in one hell of a hurry to get out of the mountains with it. I don't suppose they were afraid the Apaches would find them before they could get away, eh, my friend?"

Miguelito shrugged. "*¿Quién sabe?* Maybe those the Apaches killed were *bandidos* who had robbed the real miners of their yellow iron. Maybe that was the reason for their hurry. I know the Old One held a view something like this."

"But you know of no active mine works in the vicinity? You never knew where the packtrain was coming from?"

The Indian gave him a blank look. "I don't know. We never thought much about that."

"You never wondered if there might not be more where this came from?"

"No. Besides, our people did not believe in taking the Mother Earth's riches from her. We believed it was wrong to remove the yellow iron from the ground. We knew of many places where both yellow iron and white iron—you call that silver—could be found. We knew—and still know—of ancient lost mines where the remains of old *arrastres* and piles of what the Mexicans call slag are still in evidence. Mines for which the White Eyes and Mexicans will probably forever search and will never find. But never have we taken the riches from the ground; we have seen too many bad things happen to those who have."

"Like the Mexicans and their packtrain," Cordalee suggested. "It was okay to take the yellow iron from them, I take it, but not from Mother Earth."

Miguelito gave him a level stare. "I see nothing wrong with taking from our enemies. Didn't they take from us? Our land, our game, even our lives when they could?"

Cordalee had no answer to that. He went back to studying the gold. After a moment Miguelito asked, "How much is it worth, Cor-dah-lee?"

"Well, I'm no assayist, you understand. But from the looks of this and the number of bags in the cave, I'd say at least fifty or sixty thousand U.S. dollars, and that's a conservative guess."

"Will that last us a long time? Can we live and trade as we are now doing for many years with these riches to support us? Along with our cattle and crops, too, of course."

Thoughts of the future inevitably disturbed Cordalee of late. A gradual uneasiness had come over him that sometimes kept him from sleeping at night and frequently intruded on his daytime thoughts as well. Somehow, perhaps because of the things Mistan had said, perhaps because of his knowledge of history and its many tragic lessons, he was not optimistic about the future of the Stronghold Mountain Apaches. He hated to admit this, but he was having an increasingly hard time denying it even when everything about him wanted to cry out that there was hope.

But this was no answer to Miguelito's question. That had been simple enough: Would the yellow iron not meet their needs for years to come?

Cordalee finally said, "No one can predict the future, my friend; but, yes, I say your yellow iron will last a long, long time. You must become more judicious in how you use it, however. I have yet to see you pay for anything when you didn't want to give far too much. Maybe we should purchase you a scale and teach you to weigh out only what things actually cost. At least you'd have a basic knowledge to pull you through when you no longer have someone to advise you."

A clear look of surprise crossed the Apache's usually impassive face, and Cordalee himself felt a little shock at his own words. Why had he included that last statement? No conscious thought, that. But he'd said it as if he were definitely planning to leave Stronghold Mountain, as if this was clearly inevitable.

To Miguelito's questioning gaze he could only say, "I don't know what I meant by that, my friend. I have no plans to leave. I guess I have no plans at all, really."

The Apache's eyes held fast on Cordalee's. "I have been meaning to ask about that—your plans. It has occurred to me that you might wish to stay with our tribe permanently. I have even come to assume that. And yet I also know that you will one day wish to take a wife. Did you know that I am aware of your meetings with Mistan and Paulita?"

Cordalee shook his head. "No. I didn't know, but I'm not surprised. Anyone could have seen me going to the glen. Have I done wrong in that?"

A flicker of a smile crossed the young chief's face. "Where Mistan is concerned, only she determines what is right or wrong. It is the first time she has shown interest in any man. There are mixed opinions about her choice of an *Indah* who has not a drop of Apache blood, but some of us have hope that she has at least made a choice."

"But no one knows even that for sure. Right?"

"No. Mistan is unpredictable. What about you, my brother? You have not asked for her formally. Have you that intention or not?"

It was Cordalee's turn to smile. He couldn't tell whether this was more the Apache chieftain speaking or simply an Apache maiden's brother!

In any case, he almost surprised himself when he said, "I want to marry Mistan, my friend. I wish to know how one goes about that."

Miguelito's expression was completely sober as he replied, "Well, you must understand that she may say no. You also must understand that there will be those among our tribe who will be displeased if she does not. Many fear intermarriage with the White Eyes. They think it will eventually mean the dilution of our blood, until we are no more. My sister may even be among these; she is given to worrying about the future, as you may well have learned by now. She may, herself, refuse you for that very reason."

"What do *you* think, Miguelito? What is in your heart about this?"

"What is in my heart becomes confused with what is in my head," the Apache said. "My heart tells me that my friend, Cor-dah-lee, cannot be bad for my people, that his blood cannot hurt us. My head tells me, however, to heed the fears of the old ones. Bad may come of it, for both you and us."

"So?"

"So I have told myself I will neither work for or against you. I will let Mistan decide. If she says yes, then she is yours. If not, then there is nothing more to be said about it. Of course, my mother, Nah-de-glesh, will have a say, maybe more so than anybody else. It is she who must set a price for Mistan. If it is high but not unreasonable, you can assume her support. If it is beyond all reach, then her answer is no."

"It wouldn't have to be very high," Cordalee said, a sudden sense of despair coming over him. "I only have one horse, and he is borrowed."

"If it is not unreasonable," Miguelito said, "I will help you pay the price."

Cordalee decided to accept this without further question, but he remained disturbed by the general drift of what the chief had said earlier. "Do you think Mistan will feed and care for my horses if she finds them in front of her wickiup one morning?" He knew at least that much about the courtship process.

Miguelito gave him a look of total uncertainty. "No one knows what is in Mistan's mind, my brother. Nothing can be read in her blind eyes, and she will not tell until she is ready for others to know. You have only one way to find out; that is from her and yet you may not ask her directly. Assuming her mother's price for her is fair, you can only find out by tying your horses in front of my sister's wickiup and waiting to see what is done with them. Of course, that assumes the price even includes horses."

Cordalee sighed at the complexity of what he had thought might be a relatively simple procedure. Nothing, he told himself, is ever as simple as it seems.

"There is one whose eyes are read much more easily than Mistan's," Miguelito went on, paying scant attention to his friend's obvious inner torments. "Have you not noticed the look Paulita has for you, Cor-dah-lee?"

Cordalee's jaw dropped. "Have you gone loco?" he wanted to say, but then let the words die on the tip of his tongue as he realized that indeed he had seen the look in Paulita's eyes, the blush on her face, when she had been caught paying him the compliment. He had attempted to dismiss it as nothing significant, until now.

Miguelito apparently chose not to add any more fuel to his friend's troubled fires, for he said then, "Well, that does not matter so much. There are plenty of suitors around the ranchería for Paulita to pick from. Someday soon she will be taken and that will be that. Come, Cor-dah-lee, let's eat some lunch and start back down the mountain. It will be late when we get home otherwise."

Cordalee, his mind already six miles away and his stomach anything but hungry, only said, "Yes, okay . . . fine."

CHAPTER 15

The price for Mistan was four good horses, five head of cattle, and two jugs of mescal. Miguelito, serving as intermediary between Cordalee and Nah-de-glesh, related this information to the would-be suitor a week following their discussion near the gold cave. He also insisted that, although the price might be considered high by some standards, it was infinitely reasonable for a maiden of Mistan's stature. Even more important, it was seeming proof that Nah-de-glesh could not be counted among Cor-dah-lee's opponents in his quest for an Apache bride. That, the young chief stated firmly, was a plus of immense proportions in the white man's favor.

"I still don't have the horses or the cattle," Cordalee moaned in frustration, however. "Or even the mescal, for that matter."

"I told you I would help you if the price was reasonable," Miguelito reminded him. "I have more horses than that, the mescal is no problem, and there are plenty of wild *ganado* in these hills. All you have to do is bring in the required number and present them to my mother."

Cordalee looked at him skeptically. "That's *all?*"

"If Mistan is worth it to you, then it will not be too much for you to do."

"What will others around the ranchería say? I thought all the cattle in these mountains here already belonged to the tribe."

"The wild ones belong to whoever can catch them," the young chief said simply.

"Which is about like trying to lay claim to a herd of mule deer," Cordalee responded. "I know. I've seen some of those cattle—or caught glimpses of them going through the trees at a dead run at the first sign of a rider. There is no way I can just drive them in here, no way."

"I know," the Apache admitted somewhat ruefully. "But we do not own cattle individually here—all are turned over to the people as we catch them. This will even be the case with those you present as a gift for Mistan. Unlike the horses, I have no cattle of my own to offer you. You will have to catch your own somehow."

"What's to keep someone from accusing me of bringing in tame cattle that should already belong to the tribe?"

"No one here will mistake the wild ones for tame ones," Miguelito said confidently.

Cordalee allowed to himself that this was probably true. "What will happen to them if I do bring some in?"

"They will be corralled until they tame down, then they will be turned back out to join the rest of the cattle. Unless, of course, a good young one or two can be selected for butchering at your wedding feast. That would be up to Nah-de-glesh."

"My wedding feast!" Cordalee exclaimed. "We don't even know if Mistan will have me yet. No one but she will know that until I leave my horses in front of her wickiup."

Miguelito shrugged in reluctant agreement.

"Which means I could still be turned down."

"Yes, that could happen," the Apache said. "But that is the risk one must take. No real prize—especially one such as Mistan—should ever come easy. You must accept that fact if you really want her."

Cordalee sighed. He had said he wanted her, he had asked her mother's price. He could do no less than his dead-level best to pay it. "Okay," he said, "what do I do now?"

"First, you bring in five head of cattle—good young breeding animals preferably. Then I will loan you the horses and the mescal. After that, it will all be very simple. You'll see."

Next morning, early, he saddled his buckskin and with two long ropes of braided rawhide that he had borrowed from Miguelito slung across the big saddle horn, he set out riding south. He rode slowly, trying to recall what little he'd learned back in Arizona about the handling of cattle. Limited as his opportunities to be around and talk with genuine cowhands had been, one of the tales that had intrigued him the most, strangely enough, had to do with bringing in wild mountain cows that could not be gathered through regular means during the fall roundups.

A transplanted old Texan working on a ranch near Bisbee had described to him in detail a process for teaching even the wildest-eyed old "mossy horn" to lead like a pet pony. It had sounded like pretty harsh treatment of the "mossy horns" at the time, but Cordalee thought it might just prove useful in his present situation. It was the reason for the ropes.

Not that this alone solved his problem; he still had to find and catch five head—and not just any five, either. Miguelito had indicated plainly enough that "good young breeding animals" should be his goal. Old, tough, and weary critters—or those too young to otherwise count—would almost definitely be unsuitable for presentation to Nah-de-glesh.

Added to this problem was Cordalee's limited experience handling a rope. He knew there was no hope at all of his driving those wild creatures he'd seen scattered across the mountain. Not by himself. He would have to rope them one by one. And, although he could snake a pretty good loop over a horse's head in a corral, he'd never roped a cow before in his life, especially from the back of a horse. Moreover, it was anybody's guess how his Apache-broke-and-trained buckskin would react to such goings-on. Not happily, he figured.

Nonetheless, by the time he had gone a couple of miles from the ranchería, he had already shaken out a good four-foot loop and had begun to get his initially skittish mount settled down to the fact that it wasn't going to get whipped with the thing. He even took a couple of practice throws, without getting bucked off, and he was about to try latching onto a light log and give the buckskin a chance to pull against the rope, when he spotted half a dozen cows and a huge spotted bull grazing at the far end of a small clearing.

Head high, the cows cantered off into the trees at first sight of the horse and rider. The bull paused to give one nostril-flaring look back before he, too, whirled with a snort and disappeared.

As he watched them charge into the trees, wild and furious with alarm, Cordalee wished desperately that he had some help. But he knew it wasn't to be. Miguelito would gladly have come along, and so would Juan Tomás, but Cordalee had sensed that this was something he should do alone. He had already taken all the help he could respectfully afford to.

He spurred the horse forward, crossed the clearing, and entered the woods on the trail of the cattle. He found their tracks easily, numerous sets of cloven-hoofed prints pressed in soft dirt marked by the loose droppings and urine splotches characteristically left by disturbed bovines.

Figuring to give the cattle time to settle back down, Cordalee proceeded on at an easy pace. Ten minutes later, coming to the edge of another clearing, he found what he was looking for: six cows, one bull, and two calves, grazing peacefully along the opposite brush fringe near a small natural sink in the ground that was full of water. They did not see him, and he quickly eased back out of sight. After a few thoughtful moments, he dismounted and tightened his saddle cinch, then checked his ropes. One of these he coiled carefully and tied onto the saddle behind his rolled-up poncho. The other he left hanging from the horn. Then he remounted and, checking the breeze, began making his way through brush and trees to the other side of the clearing.

It took almost fifteen minutes for him to reach a point fifty yards from the nearest cow. Cordalee nervously picked out a young cow and moved farther along the brush edge. He got within twenty-five yards before being seen, and this, predictably, was by the bull. With a low bellow, the big brute whirled and once again with head held high, the small herd started to canter away. But Cordalee this time put the heel to the buckskin, which burst forth and was quickly among them. The young cow, for a moment confused, had broken away from the others and was just beginning to swerve back toward them when she saw the horse and rider bearing down on her, Cordalee's rope whirring in the air.

Again she swerved, but too late. A perfect loop settled over her horns and the slack was clumsily but effectively jerked out of the rope. Cordalee, half surprised at his success, quickly dallied the other end of the rope around his saddle horn and pulled the buckskin to a gut-jarring stop. Frightened, the horse backed away almost as if trained, hauling the young cow around. They stood facing one another, sides heaving, the cow bawling low and beginning to froth at the mouth.

For several moments it was a stalemate; then, without warning, the cow began her struggle. She pulled frantically, tried to run, tripped and almost fell. Twice Cordalee thought she would jerk the horse off his feet, but like an old pro at the business, the game buckskin whirled to face the cow and managed to stay upright.

Suddenly the cow gave up pulling and charged. Cordalee kicked the horse forward and off to one side and ran right past her. Desperately hanging on to the dallied rope end, he let the horse run, soon causing a violent yank at both ends of the rope and bringing horse, rider, and bovine all three to the ground. Cordalee came up still holding the rope but several feet from the struggling horse, and the cow just lay there, having been hauled around with such terrific force that he was at first afraid her neck had been broken.

Slowly, however, she began to get to her feet. The buckskin stood off to one side, spraddle-legged and dazed. Cordalee, spotting a thick-trunked pine ten feet to the left of the cow, sprang forward and quickly took a wrap around the tree with the rope. The cow tried to back away, then seeing she could not break his leverage, tried once again to charge. She came straight for the man and the tree, allowing him, darting to one side, to take up all but three or four feet of slack before she was jerked back. A quick second and third wrap around the tree, then a fast tie, and she was caught "hard-and-fast."

Luther Cordalee stood looking in disbelief at what he'd done. Somehow, amazingly, he had gotten his young cow just where he wanted her.

All he had to do was leave her there, pulling in ever-growing futility against a rope from which she could not escape, until she finally gave up fighting it entirely. He knew it might take all day, but eventually she would lead away from there as docilely as if she were a pet dog.

The old Texan from Bisbee had sworn it never failed.

His knees shaking and an overwhelming desire for a smoke growing within him, Cordalee stumbled over to his horse to think out what he would do while he waited. His elation was tempered only by the thought that he still had four more just like this one to go.

Predictably, beginner's luck didn't hold. He managed to get only one chance with his second rope that day, and this he missed by a mile. It was nearly dark by the time he returned to the ranchería riding a flagging horse and leading—to the astonishment of not a few Indians—an amazingly submissive cow, which he promptly penned.

Still, for the next two days he came home empty-handed and terribly discouraged. The third day was better; he caught a fat young heifer, swelling with calf. She was even easier taught to lead than the first one he'd caught.

The fourth day dawned clear with the news that Makkai's woman had died. An Apache wake carried into the night, unusual in its concern for one who had no family among the tribe, but maybe not surprising in that this was an unusual tribe. It was not like the old days anymore. . . .

Cordalee stayed around the ranchería until the fifth day, partly because of the wake and partly because the buckskin had about had it by now and needed the rest. After dragging in a third young cow that afternoon, it became plain that his mount needed more than one day off. It was completely done in. Cordalee had to borrow a horse from Miguelito and then spend half a day teaching it to stand for the rope. Even with this, the new horse, a perky gray mustang, would never be the roping horse the buckskin had already become. It inevitably spooked at the rope, and twice nearly threw Cordalee just as he was about to make a throw.

Two days passed before he was able to lay a loop across the horns of another wild Mexican cow and even then bad luck was on him; he missed his dally and lost not only the cow but one of Miguelito's rawhide ropes as well.

Finally he went out on the buckskin again, and brought in a yearling bull, still full of fight even after a full day tied to a tree. It would definitely be the last bull Cordalee would try to bring in. Not that the last of his five head wasn't just as bad—a waspy red cow with one horn broken

off at the end and a reckless proclivity for swiping constantly at both man
and horse with the other one.

Nonetheless, when he brought her in, it was plain to everyone that he
had done it: five good animals penned for everyone to see, that part of his
payment to Nah-de-glesh in full. And no matter how hard he himself still
found it to believe that he had accomplished the feat, the Apaches were
truly awed by it. Even Miguelito, it turned out, had doubted that Cordalee could capture five of the wild ones. The price for Mistan, on second
thought, was not a cheap one at all.

And Cordalee was ready to pay it; over a week had gone by since he
had begun. August had come, and although the days were still hot, there
was a biting chill in the morning air now; a man, it was said, if he was
going to take a wife, should do it before the cold nights of fall or winter
set in.

Cordalee pressed Miguelito for more detail on how next to proceed.

"It is simple really," the Indian said. "Tonight, you and I will pick out
your ponies and you will tie them in front of Nah-de-glesh's wickiup. If
Mistan accepts, by custom she must feed and curry the animals and then
take them to water. It will be she who takes the initiative after that. All
you must do is wait until she comes to you. You will see."

"When will I know if Mistan has accepted my courtship offering?"

"By morning," Miguelito said. "She will have to have help, of course,
since she cannot herself see to lead the horses to water and feed them, but
in the morning you will know."

"Are there those who still oppose me?" Cordalee asked then.

The Apache shrugged. "I suppose there are. But there are others who
will be equally happy to see you succeed. Especially one young man I
know who wishes a wife of his own. He is only waiting to see if Mistan
accepts you before tying his own horses in front of the wickiup of
Paulita."

Cordalee stared at him, and the young chief went on to explain, "I told
you before that Paulita has eyes for you, my friend. Everyone knows it;
everyone knows she will accept no one else as long as you have not made
your final choice. It is Gregorio who wants her. He will be watching almost as hard as you will to see what Mistan does with your horses."

Cordalee was half astounded at this. Paulita? He wagged his head.
Who could account for the way things happened?

Just before dark he tied four horses outside Nah-de-glesh's wickiup and
then retired to his own, self-conscious and jittery at having been seen by
the entire ranchería as he led the horses across and tied them. For a while
he had actually wondered how Mistan would know someone else had not

left the offering; but now he realized how little question there could be about who it was. Everyone would know, too, who had been turned down if she did not accept. They had watched for days as he went out after wild cows. This White Eye who was a friend of their chief's and could teach cows to lead as if they were horses. This presumptuous White Eye who wanted to marry the prize maiden of the tribe. This foolish White Eye . . .

He hardly slept all night. Like a kid anxiously awaiting his birthday, he tossed and turned and lay awake until the early hours of the morning when he finally did doze off—only to be awakened by a minor commotion outside, somewhere across the ranchería, a short while later. Groggily rising and looking out the doorway, he spotted a man just dismounting a lathered horse in the dim predawn light outside Miguelito's wickiup. The chief appeared, and the two men talked earnestly for a few moments before the first man remounted and rode back across the creek toward the horse corral. Cordalee could not tell who he was, nor could he see where he went after caring for his mount. Miguelito disappeared back inside his wickiup, and the ranchería was still. Cordalee went back to bed and presently fell to dozing restlessly once more.

Morning dawned mountain-fresh and cool, and the sun's initial rays pierced the wickiup's doorway, waking him with something of a start. His mind normally a bit slow on first rising, his first thought was somehow to wonder who had ridden into the ranchería during the early morning hours. An unusual event to be certain, it was made even more so by the fact that the rider had gone straight to the chief's wickiup. A message of some importance, undoubtedly. Its possible portent was completely forgotten, however, by the time Cordalee was dressed and had gone outside, his thoughts now fully on the horses he'd left tied in front of Nah-de-glesh's wickiup the past evening.

Somehow, though, he was afraid to look. He couldn't bring his eyes to cross the ranchería in that direction. People were up and about, and he realized that everyone else probably knew already the fate of his proposal. Two young boys, caught staring at him from across the creek, darted away, refusing to meet his gaze. One of them, he was certain, was Paulita's brother, Nito.

He was still standing there, cursing himself for his momentary attack of cowardice and thinking just the same of going down to the creek to wash his face and shave before checking at Nah-de-glesh's wickiup, when Miguelito appeared coming his way.

The young chief's expression seemed purposefully impassive.

"Well," he said, stopping in front of Cordalee, "have you seen yet, my brother? Have you looked?"

Cordalee sighed and let his eyes travel almost against their will across the way. They passed over a group of half-grown boys playing the hoop-and-pole game near the center of the ranchería; they moved past a wickiup with the familiar figure of a girl standing just outside and came briefly to rest there as Paulita saw him looking at her and ducked self-consciously inside; then they finally came to lock on their original target. He felt as if he had been struck a blow to the stomach, his hopes collapsing in a way he would hardly have believed possible. The horses he'd tied in front of Nah-de-glesh's wickiup were gone!

Desperately he whirled on Miguelito, a question he could not voice showing starkly in his eyes.

The young chief put a solemn hand on his friend's shoulder and stood that way a moment before a slow, mischievous smile crept across his face. "Don't look so sad, my brother. The horses are in the corral and now belong to my mother. Mistan sent for me before sunup and asked my help in leading them to the creek. She has already watered and curried them. . . ." He smiled more broadly yet at the disbelieving look on Cordalee's face. "Mistan has accepted you, my friend. She is yours."

Not coincidentally, that evening two horses were tied in front of the wickiup of Paulita—a present to the chief in the absence of the girl's parents—from the warrior Gregorio. These horses, too, were cared for by the time the sun rose the next morning, and the Apaches buzzed over the prospect of two marriages and not just one.

Cordalee, on the other hand, could not explain the way he felt—even to himself.

CHAPTER 16

Old Man Din squatted in typical Apache fashion before his wickiup, seemingly without taking notice of the two men sitting across from him.

It was mid-morning, and Miguelito had led Cordalee over to the medicine man's abode in order that the white man might receive certain instructions having to do with his upcoming marriage to an Apache girl. Undoubtedly, the shaman knew why they were there, but for the longest time now he had not said a word. Apparently he did not have great enthusiasm for his work this day. Still, Cordalee was keenly aware that much remained that he did not understand about these Indians, and so he waited patiently, as did the young chief.

When the shaman finally spoke, his words were in halting Apache, which Cordalee was generally expected to understand now without an interpreter. The shaman looked only at the ground, but he clearly addressed the white man.

"You are not yet an Apache, but you marry an Apache maiden and so you must become an Apache soon. To be an Apache is a thing of the heart. Your heart must be good for you to deserve this Apache maiden. In only this way can you become *Indeh*.

"You must also know things that you do not now know. There are taboos.

"After you are married, you must never again look upon the face of your mother-in-law. You must not speak her name. If you see her coming to your wickiup you must leave while she visits there, and you must not come back until she has gone. If you see her walking somewhere, you must go somewhere else so that you do not meet her. This is the way it must be, as bad things will happen if you do not do the way I have told you."

The old man's eyes now were cast somewhere across the ranchería; he looked neither at Miguelito nor at Cordalee, who felt a little shock run through him at the thought of never again being able to look upon or speak the name of Nah-de-glesh. Was the medicine man serious? Could this possibly be the way things must be?

"As a man married to an Apache woman, you should sire children and those children should be raised as Apaches. They must learn Apache ways . . . and they should be well spaced. One child every four years is all right. An Apache man who has children by only one wife more often than that is not a responsible man. . . ."

Cordalee's eyes flew up to meet Miguelito's. The Indian almost smiled, but quickly looked away.

"A man must practice the proper restraint"—a word or two here Cordalee was not sure about; he was forced to guess. "A man may marry more than one wife, but of course he must be able to afford them both. A poor man settles for only one.

"A man whose wife is pregnant should not go on the warpath. It will make him weak and his power will not be with him."

The shaman took a deep breath. He seemed a bit tired, his enthusiasm still lacking; he went on nevertheless. "A man looks to his wife's family as his own. If the wife's people go somewhere away, the man and his wife should go there also. If a man's wife has a sister and that sister becomes a widow, the man should offer to take the widow who is his sister-in-law as his wife also. If he cannot afford her, she may then be taken by another man. . . ."

Cordalee just stared; Miguelito smiled faintly once again. The instructions went on and on. The shaman told how it was that an Apache girl would come to the man that would be her husband. He told what a man must do in order to formally accept that girl as his wife. Cordalee thought the interview would never end. But finally it did, and the young chief beckoned for the white man to rise. They bade good day to the shaman and turned to walk back across the ranchería toward Cordalee's wickiup.

"Was he serious about all that, Miguelito?" Cordalee asked as they went. "Even the part about my never again looking upon or speaking to Mistan's mother?"

"He was serious. What he said are Apache ways."

They walked along slowly, Cordalee making no attempt to hide the fact that he was troubled. He said, "This is the second day since my gifts were accepted, and I still have neither seen nor been able to talk to Mistan."

Miguelito seemed sympathetic. "Have you been to the glen above the ranchería yet?"

"Yesterday, twice," Cordalee said unhappily. "No one was ever there."

"Well, don't give up; go again today. Let yourself be seen. Mistan will know, and she will be there in her own time. You must be patient with her; she is not an average maiden, my brother."

Cordalee sighed. "Tell me again how it will happen after that. I am not sure I understood all that the shaman said."

They came to a stop in front of Cordalee's wickiup, and Miguelito turned with an understanding smile to explain to this nervous suitor once again. "Mistan will come to you, my brother—to your wickiup one night, after dark. She will spend the night there with you, but before daylight she will steal away to her mother's wickiup and you will not see her all that following day. The next night she will come to you again. Only this time she will not steal away. When morning comes she will hang your bedding out to air and cook your breakfast. It is very important that you eat what she has cooked, for that is the way you show your approval of her as a wife. She will not eat with you, but she will stay until you are finished before returning to her mother once again. The next night she will be back at your wickiup, and the following morning she will repeat the airing of your bedding and the cooking of your breakfast. Only this time she will eat with you and she will not return to her mother's place. She will stay with you then as your wife, and she will never again wear her hair in the bow of the *nah-lin*."

"But, Miguelito, Mistan is blind," Cordalee worried. "How can she do all that stealing back and forth?"

The young chief simply smiled. "She will manage, Cor-dah-lee. There are those who will help her. This marriage of Mistan's is too important to us that you must worry about things like that. In fact, soon afterward, there will be a dance to celebrate the event. The ranchería will be so wild with happiness it will probably become the biggest celebration we have ever had at this place. For four days it will last. You will see."

Cordalee could only wag his head. He didn't want to appear indecisive; he most certainly didn't want to jeopardize either his stay here or his marriage to Mistan. But the adjustments he must yet make surely seemed immense in proportion to all that had gone before. He was beginning to doubt his ability to deal with it. Before, he had simply been a white man living among the Apaches; now, he was about to take a major step toward *becoming* an Apache. Could he do that? Could he really?

Miguelito seemed to sense his friend's concern. "Don't worry so much, my friend. Here, let's walk over to the horse corrals. Perhaps we should take a short ride and look at some of the cattle. That might take your mind off of the things that worry you. Maybe you can even show me how it is that you teach the wild *ganado* to lead like horses. I think that is a good power for a man to have, and I would very much like to have it myself. Later, in the afternoon, you can go to the glen and look for Mistan. There will be time enough for that, you'll see."

They rode among the trees south of the ranchería, their pace leisurely. They had talked of several things, among them the young chief's continuing concern that the band's horse herd still was not large enough to suit him. A few of his people did not even own horses, and although the chief himself had several, the tribe's total herd probably numbered fewer than did its people. And very soon they would need more supplies. Already they were running short of such basics as flour and salt. The same was the case with tobacco, coffee, and other staples, not to mention mescal. The people of the tribe had become spoiled by these everyday items of the White Eyes' existence, just as had the White Eyes themselves.

The conversation had suddenly grown sober, and Cordalee suspected that the chief's concern went deeper than just the number of horses his people owned or how much salt was left in the communal stores.

"What's troubling you, my friend?" Cordalee asked. "It's not something to do with that rider who came to your wickiup two nights ago, is it?"

Miguelito gave him a searching look. "You know about that?"

"Only that he came, talked to you, and then put his horse in the corral and disappeared. I saw that much. I have no idea what it was about. I'd almost forgotten about it."

"It was one of the trail guards with word from Kentoni and Cruz," Miguelito explained slowly. "I don't think his message was as urgent as he possibly thought it was, but it has caused me some concern anyway. Kentoni had come up the south trail to tell the guards that the Mexicans along the river were stirred up over some murders that have occurred there recently. Two men were killed near Bacerac one night about a week ago and another near Bavispe three days later. The night before you saw the messenger come to my wickiup, a young señorita was stolen from her father's jacal on the outskirts of Huachinera."

"How does that affect us?" Cordalee asked, puzzled.

"A long-haired Indian was seen carrying off the girl. Kentoni said that he slipped close enough to overhear some Mexicans talking. They think this Indian was also responsible for the killings downriver. They are in a dangerous mood over it, and Kentoni thought I should know. They seem to think the Indian is an Apache."

"Why, that's impossible! Who . . . ?" He broke off as Miguelito wagged his head.

"I think it was Makkai. I think he is getting his revenge both on the Mexicans and us at the same time."

"You think he might be trying to goad the Mexicans into attacking Stronghold Mountain?"

Miguelito shrugged. "It is possible."

"Do you think they might do that—attack us?"

The same prideful derision that he so frequently exhibited when talking about the Mexicans suddenly flared in the young chief's eyes. He didn't have to say anything.

"All right, all right," Cordalee said. "I know—no Mexican could ever be brave enough to try taking this mountain. Just the same, they're bound to know you're here now; Dr. Smith has probably seen to that. Which I know worries you. You can see the possibilities forming: Someday, just as it has always been in the past, you will be forced to either stay and fight or abandon a place you thought was yours and move on. You know how hopeless the fighting would be, so you're already thinking what it might take for you to flee. To move your people quickly, you'll need plenty of horses—more than you now have—and you don't want to be caught unprepared." He paused, then went on to ask perceptively, "Are you thinking of another trading trip, Miguelito? Is that it? Have you already decided that one will be made?"

The Apache nodded. "Yes, that is what I am thinking. I have just about decided . . ."

"There's more to it yet, though, isn't there?" Cordalee's eyes narrowed as he pulled his horse up and looked sharply at the young chief. "More to it than just Makkai's antics with the river-town Mexicans . . . am I right?"

Miguelito also pulled to a halt. Once again he nodded. "Kentoni also told the trail guards that he had seen our Dr. Smith on at least two occasions talking with Narciso Ibarro, the *bandido*. It bothers me a great deal what these two men may have found in common to talk about. Do you know what I mean?"

Cordalee did. "Apache gold, located less than twenty miles from Bavispe—not to mention the man who killed Ibarro's brother!" He groaned. "To think I had to go and tell Smith that, too!"

Miguelito didn't say anything; he simply stared straight ahead as if in deep thought.

"Well, anyway," Cordalee said. "Your mind is made up. You are going to make a trip after horses and supplies."

"Yes," the Apache said. "At least the horses."

"When?"

"I'm not sure yet. Soon, I think."

"Do you want me to go along?"

Miguelito seemed troubled at this. "Well, yes. I would want your advice and help, just as before. But your marriage to Mistan must not be postponed. It would have to be after you have had your wedding celebration. I would not ask it of you any sooner."

"How long would that be?" Cordalee asked. "Is it safe to wait?"

Miguelito shrugged thoughtfully. "Ten days, I think, *más o menos* . . . I am sure we can wait that long. Yes, assuming my sister is not too slow in coming to you, ten days should be enough. I have already mentioned the possibility of a short wait to the council, and they are so little afraid of the Mexicans that they are not much worried. Ten days or ten weeks, it will not matter to them. Do you think that would be enough time for you, Cor-dah-lee?"

Cordalee thought for a moment, then said, "Well, maybe I will see Mistan today. If I do, perhaps I can talk to her about it. If she does not object, then of course it will be all right with me."

The Indian smiled slightly. "Good. And I am sure you will see Mistan today. Just be sure and tell her what we are thinking. Maybe she will come to you that much sooner. That, too, will be good, don't you think?"

This time, although sheepishly, it was Cordalee's turn to smile.

After his talk with the chief, Cordalee was hardly surprised that Mistan did indeed show up at the glen that afternoon. He *was* surprised, however, at who came with her.

He had been sitting on the creek bank for nearly an hour, plunking tiny pebbles in the stream, when a rustle in the bushes just downtrail from where he sat startled him. Paulita and Mistan appeared coming hand in hand from only thirty or so yards away.

He would have expected almost anyone other than Paulita, now that she herself was pledged to Gregorio.

The girl herself explained, "I don't intend to stay, Cor-dah-lee. Mistan believes she can talk with you without an interpreter now. I only came to guide her here. She wishes to be alone with you and for you to take her back to the rancheria later."

Before he could even begin to form a response, she turned, whispered something to Mistan, and quickly was gone. Cordalee watched as she disappeared in the brush, then turned awkwardly back to Mistan.

"Please, I wish to sit down somewhere," the girl said in reasonably good Spanish, her sightless stare cast someplace beyond the creek. "Our time together may be short and I wish to talk much with you."

He helped her to find a seat on a nearby log, then sat beside her, although he was quite careful not to touch her. He could not help remaining somewhat in awe of her. And he did not know what she meant about their time together being short. As far as he could tell, they had most of the afternoon left to them. Or did her words contain some far-reaching import, relevant more to a lifetime than an afternoon?

He felt uneasy as he said, "Your Spanish is almost as good as mine. You amaze me how fast you've learned."

She shrugged it off. "I have been learning longer than you realize. My brother began teaching me even before Paulita came back to live with our people. And you, before you came too, of course. It was just that I had not learned enough yet and had not the chance to use what I had learned. Now, I no longer feel so uncomfortable with the language of our old enemies. And my brother tells me you are speaking good Apache now. Is that not true also?"

Cordalee looked at her in astonishment; her Spanish, in a longer speech, showed a good deal of imperfection, but was in no way that of the beginner he had thought her to be. "You've understood what was being said all along, haven't you? All those times Paulita was translating, you understood almost perfectly."

"I'm sorry," she said. "I did understand much of it, although never all. I did not mean to be devious. It was just that I had never spoken with a White Eye before. And I have learned much since you came here. Paulita was very good to teach me, especially since she, too, had eyes for you. Do you forgive me?"

"Yes," he said, "of course. I suppose I should even be pleased. I hadn't dreamed we would be alone together today. I almost don't know what to say.

"You know about your brother's plan to make another trading trip, don't you? You suspect perhaps that he wants me to go with him."

She nodded, then frowned. "My brother wants more horses so that our people can escape from the Mexicans if we have to. He also wishes to make plans known for a regathering place far from here in case we are attacked and the people become separated while trying to escape. Such plans have been discussed many times but a firm decision has never been made. My brother feels it must be made soon lest we find ourselves unprepared if the time ever comes."

"You disagree with that?" Cordalee asked. "He only wants to avoid another war, which he knows the Apaches cannot win."

She turned, and could she have seen, would have looked straight into his eyes. "I do not disagree. I only think we should leave this place now. I do not think we should wait. We will have to fight if we do, and like you, I do not think we can win."

"You sound awfully sure of that."

"Of what? That we will have to fight? That we cannot win? Yes, I am sure. We are in danger here. Our Stronghold Mountain is not the stronghold we would like it to be."

Disturbed, Cordalee asked, "Have you told Miguelito that?"

She shook her head. "No. It would do little good, I'm afraid. He does not want to leave unless we have to. The majority of the council feels the same way. They are split, but most have said stay. They do not wish to be moving around all the time, even though in days past that is about all we did. My brother knows this. The people here want to settle down and have a home. They want that home to be here."

"Who among the council wishes to leave," Cordalee asked. "You said they were split."

"The elder Say-la and two or three others," she said. "They are the same ones who are still against your marriage to an Apache maiden."

Cordalee didn't know whether to be surprised at this or not; his reception by the tribal elders had always been polite, even warm at times, but he supposed it had never been one of complete acceptance. It was the older men who found it hardest to break with tradition, who would always distrust the White Eyes the most. Their opposition must not have been overly strong, however—especially in the face of something Nah-de-glesh herself had sanctioned—for the marriage was going to proceed. Still it bothered him, and he wondered why it was they opposed him.

Mistan must have guessed his question, for she said, "It is Old Man Din who influences them, Cor-dah-lee. He worries that it is bad to dilute Apache blood with that of the White Eyes. He says there are so few of us here now that this is the way the White Eyes will finally destroy us completely. He says they will dilute our blood until there are no more pure Apaches left, until we are no more a people."

"And you? You hold no such view?"

"No. Obviously not," she said. "I would not have watered your horses if I did."

He stared at her. "Why did you water my horses, Mistan?"

She stared sightlessly back at him. "Why did you leave them there?"

There wasn't much he could say to this. They sat for several moments in silence before the girl finally spoke.

"Is the day growing long, Cor-dah-lee? Is the sun well down in the sky yet?"

He glanced to the west. "I would say maybe two hours yet before sundown. Why?"

"I should go back soon. I will be expected."

He was somewhat disappointed at this, and thoughts of his discussion with Miguelito that morning quickly came to mind. A sense of urgency claimed him. "Your brother wishes to hold a wedding celebration for us that will last four days. He wishes to conduct his trading trip as soon as that is done. He said for me to tell you that."

Her eyes were again turned toward his. "And you both wish that I would not be too long in coming to your wickiup . . . is that not true also?"

He gulped. "Yes . . . but not entirely for the same reason . . . I mean . . ."

She smiled. "I know, Cor-dah-lee. I know."

"When? When, then, will you come?" He wanted so badly to reach out and touch her, to hold her, that he almost trembled.

She put her hands out so that he could help her to rise. "You must take me back to my mother's wickiup, Cor-dah-lee. We can talk as we go."

"But when, Mistan?" he persisted. "When?"

"Soon," she said simply. "Very soon."

Nevertheless, it happened even sooner than he'd dared hope it might. The very next night, a good two hours past full dark, he heard a noise outside his wickiup. He had no idea who had guided her there, for she stood there alone, waiting, when he looked out. Quickly, he moved to help her inside, the happiness of the moment for him hopelessly beyond his ability to relate.

Next morning, she was gone when he awoke, but the following night she reappeared just as Old Man Din and Miguelito had said she would. The morning after that, he ate with relish the breakfast she cooked for him. Despite her blindness, and with only a modicum of help from him, she had managed the task very adroitly. When he was finished, he guided her back to her mother's wickiup, taking note of the fact that Nah-de-glesh did not present herself for him to see when they got there.

The nights and days that followed were if anything even happier ones than the first or second. They also passed more quickly than Cordalee could believe. In no time, it seemed, the first day of the tribe's celebration had arrived. As Miguelito had predicted, it was to be an almost unparalleled event in the tribe's brief history. In addition to the marriage of Cordalee and Mistan, that of Paulita and Gregorio was also to be celebrated. Preparations for the festive occasion were in full swing throughout the day.

All proceeded well and fully as planned—until along about mid-afternoon three riders appeared coming up the south trail and threw everything into at least a temporary state of confusion.

Miguelito and Cordalee just happened to be the first to see them coming and were consequently the first as well to determine who they were. They rode three abreast, and the two on the outside were easily recognized as two of Miguelito's trail guards. They were heavily armed and were clearly escorting the third man under guard.

He, too, was easily recognized. He was the *médico* from Bavispe, and behind him trailed a single, overburdened mule. On its back were four kegs of mescal that the good doctor claimed were gifts from the river-town Mexicans—gifts for their friends, the last free tribe of Apaches known to exist anywhere.

CHAPTER 17

"Why do you bring this man here this way?" Miguelito's stern Apache words must have blistered the ears of the two trail guards—the Aravaipa, Ben-ah-thli, and his young Chiricahua companion, Chivo. "At the very least you should have blindfolded him."

The two young men traded uneasy glances. Chivo finally replied, "He was halfway up the Bacerac fork of the south trail when we first saw him. He claimed he was coming as a friend and that he already knew the way. He said you yourself told him how to get here. Because of that, we saw no reason this time to blindfold him."

He paused, but Miguelito did not seem placated, so he went on, "We recognized him as the White Eye *médico* who doctored you when you were wounded. We thought surely he was telling the truth. Is he not your friend, *Inday?* Did you not tell him the way?"

Miguelito looked over at Cordalee, then at Dr. Smith. He spoke now in Spanish. "Tell the truth, *médico*. You were not told the way. Why did you lie to these men? Why do you come here?"

Smith seemed determined not to squirm under the Indian's stare. "I came for the reason I said I did. As a friendly gesture made by the river people. I told your guards I already knew the way because I wanted to see where I was going this time. I wanted to be trusted, not blindfolded and led around like some sort of spy."

Miguelito's expression remained stern. "You think I should trust you? Why? You come sneaking up here telling me the river people send the Apaches gifts of friendship, and you expect me to believe anything you say?"

"I hope you will, yes. I feel honestly that it is very important that you do."

"Why? Why is it so important?"

The doctor looked from one of his guards to the other, then back at the two men on the ground. They were near the center of the ranchería, and a small crowd of Indians had gathered curiously around them. He shifted uneasily in his saddle now, but still he seemed sincere. "Look, I'm not even armed. Don't you think I know that it's dangerous, my coming here like this? I would never try it if it were not important. Won't you just let me get down so we can talk? I can explain, believe me."

Miguelito looked at Cordalee, then at the two trail guards. He motioned for the doctor to dismount, then ordered the trail guards to take the man's horse and mule on down to the corrals before returning to their station—manned now by only two others—on the south trail.

"Come," he said in Spanish. "We will go to my wickiup and talk. You, too, Cor-dah-lee. You must help me decide if this *Indah* tells the truth or not."

They sat facing one another in front of Miguelito's wickiup, just the three of them. The doctor looked nervous, but he told his story in level tones.

"As I told you once before, the river-town Mexicans have suspected that your people were in these mountains for some time. You have not bothered them, and they have been afraid to bother you. I told them nothing of my contacts with you until recently, when some people began to be murdered down there. As you might imagine, your people were immediately suspected, and when an Indian was seen carrying off a young woman from her father's home, the Mexicans were certain that the Apaches had come to torment them all over again. Only then did I tell them what I knew of you, and then only because I wished to convince them that it probably was not your people who had done those things."

"Why? Why did you want to convince them of that?" Miguelito's eyes were dark with suspicion, his tone menacing. "How did you know it was not us?"

"Because you told me you wanted to be peaceful, and I believed you. Too, only one Indian was seen and at no time have there been signs of more than one where the murders were committed. I believe our villain is that wild Indian who knifed you, Miguelito. That is why I told them what I did. I think that man is trying to cause both you and the river people trouble. I have convinced them that I should come here with a peace offering, to see if you would help us track down and kill that man. Maybe you can even help us return the girl who was stolen to her family. It would go a long way toward establishing peaceful relations between the Mexicans and yourselves, believe me."

Miguelito and Cordalee traded glances. Because of what Kentoni and Cruz had related to them earlier, they could not deny the apparent credibility of the man's story. Still, Cordalee knew that the young chief could not be convinced so easily. The history of distrust between Mexican and

Apache was too firmly entrenched in his thinking; they had fought one another too long.

"Is that all?" Miguelito finally asked. "Have you nothing else to tell about the Mexicans?"

Smith sighed. "Only this. Narciso Ibarro and his gang are on the river again. They, too, are aware that there are Apaches in the area. They are less inclined to make peace with you than those who live on the river, however. I know; I have talked to Ibarro myself. Too, they are still looking for your friend Cordalee, here. They don't know he is living among you, but they may yet find that out. There are too few of them to attack you alone, but Ibarro would love nothing better than to stir the river-town people up until enough men there volunteer to help him. If he gets them, then of course he will come after you. I feel that if you help us now, that can be prevented. If you do not, well . . . who knows?"

Miguelito leaned back. Smith had definitely said the right things; he appeared to be hiding nothing—even his own conversations with Ibarro. Of course, he might simply be playing it smart in order to establish credibility. He could hardly be expected to be aware of Miguelito's prior knowledge of the situation on the river, but he could suspect it. It was not beyond reason that the Apache might secretly keep tabs on the river-town goings-on. If the Indians had spies out, Smith himself might even have been observed talking to the man Ibarro. Clearly candor—or what seemed candor—would be the best policy if a man wanted to fool somebody.

"What do you think, my brother?" Miguelito asked Cordalee in Apache. "Can we trust this man?"

Cordalee could only say, "I don't know, Miguelito. I really don't know."

The Apache looked around, then addressed the *médico* once more in Spanish. "As you can see, our people are preparing for a celebration. It will be a wedding feast and dance. Over there we are cooking a beef; nearby will be a big central fire for the dance. Your gift of mescal will fit well with the occasion, and you yourself will be allowed to spend the night here in one of our wickiups. Tomorrow we will talk more about what you have proposed. Maybe then we can decide." To Cordalee he then added in Apache, "Take him with you for now, my friend. Talk to him in your own tongue. Maybe you can learn more from him in that way. I will see you again in a little while, when you must begin preparing for the dance tonight."

As Cordalee and Smith walked toward Cordalee's wickiup, Smith said, "A wedding feast, eh? Well, well. My mescal sure did come at the right time, didn't it?" He seemed uncommonly pleased about that aspect of the situation.

"Yes, I suppose it did," Cordalee said guardedly as they stopped in front of the wickiup. There was no danger of disturbing anyone there, as Mistan would be staying at her mother's abode until time for the big feast to begin, but still he did not want to take this man inside. He motioned for Smith to sit down.

The doctor produced a pipe and filled it with tobacco. "I've seen parts of a couple of curing ceremonies held up near Fort Apache, but never anything having to do with a wedding. I wonder if they'll let you and me attend."

Cordalee smiled thinly. "*Me* they will. I don't know about you."

Smith gave him a thoughtful look, then said, "I keep forgetting . . . you're almost like one of them now. You talk their language, your hair is growing long like theirs, your skin is almost as dark as theirs . . . If it weren't for your clothes and those gray eyes . . . well, who'd know? Have you realized that, Cordalee?"

Cordalee felt his muscles grow tense. "I don't know. What if I have? What difference would it make?"

"Well, I'm not sure. I guess I just thought you might have reconsidered by now. Are you sure this is what you want? Do you never want to live around your own kind again?"

Cordalee shrugged. "I haven't missed them much so far."

"You could come back with me, you know," Smith persisted. "You don't have to stay here."

Cordalee stared at him. "And do what? Go live with the Mexicans, as if *they* were any more my own kind than these Indians?"

"They're Christian people, Cordalee. They're civilized."

Cordalee's jaw tightened. "Oh, really? Well, I think I'd prefer the worst of the Apaches I've known to Narciso Ibarro and his lot."

"Oh, come now!" Smith said, seemingly amazed. "That wild Indian on the river, too? That killer of innocent people and stealer of women? You'd prefer him, too?"

"Just about, yeah."

It was Smith's turn to stare. Finally he shook his head. "Well, you *are* one of them. I really had thought to urge you to come back with me, but I can see it's probably no use . . . no use at all."

Cordalee just shrugged. He didn't much like the man's attitude, but he thought it best not to prolong the discussion. He let it go at that.

Smith, perhaps sensing this, sought to change the subject. He looked around. "Well, well. So some young buck is getting married. Who is it, Cordalee? Any of those I've seen before? What are some of their names?— Juan Tomás, Hishee . . . ? I can't recall any others. . . ."

For a moment Cordalee did not answer; then he looked out across the compound and said, "It's me, Doctor. I am the one. I've taken as my wife the blind maiden Mistan. It's my wedding feast we are about to have here."

The other man's eyes at first grew round, but then he saw that Cordalee was not joking, and he could only wag his head. For a few moments he seemed not to know what to say. Then it must finally have dawned on him that for all practical purposes he truly was the only white man there. "Well, well," was all he could say. "Well, well."

A full moon rose as dark settled. The ranchería was alive with activity as the mescal flowed and good food was consumed with hearty abandon. Near the center of the compound a very large ceremonial fire had been built and its flames crackled and leaped against the darkened background. To the west of the fire sat the drummers and those men of the tribe who would later be willing to dance with the unmarried women and girls. Those who would be spectators sat well back from the fire, leaving an open dance area in between. Around the fire, but not too close, sat the unmarried women and girls, arranged in pairs. All about the scene there was an expectant air as the people waited for the dance to get underway. Cordalee and Mistan, she attired in a beautiful white beaded doeskin dress and he sporting a beaded buckskin shirt, clean trousers, and the moccasins long ago made for him by Nondi, sat with the spectators. On their left were the chief and Nondi; just beyond them sat Gregorio and Paulita. Nah-de-glesh was there somewhere but had carefully located herself so that no confrontation with her new son-in-law might take place.

Across the way, beyond the firelight, Dr. Smith was confined to his wickiup. Miguelito still had not decided what to do about the man and wanted him to know that his welcome among them remained provisional. A pair of young men had been left to guard him.

Just as everyone was becoming impatient, the medicine man appeared in festive attire on the west side of the fire. He came dancing out into the open, chanting and sprinkling *hoddentin* on nearly everything and everybody in sight. He was followed out of the darkness by five masked and body-painted male dancers whose identity escaped Cordalee entirely.

According to Miguelito, these were impersonators of certain Mountain Spirits sent by the Life Giver to minister to the spiritual needs of the People. They wore large, fanlike headdresses, and their costumes, Miguelito said, were kept in the most secret of hiding places when not in use. The body painting had been done for each dancer by the medicine man himself, and it went without question that they danced very much under his influence. The young chief did not try to explain all that they did because there were things he claimed he himself did not understand about their performance, but it was indeed an impressive ceremony. Cordalee did his best to describe the details of it to Mistan, who of course had heard the drums and the singing of such events many times but had never been able to observe one.

But all of this was just a prelude. The main dance was to be a social affair, not a ceremonial one. Almost as quickly as they had come the dancers ran from the scene and disappeared, and the medicine man retreated to the spectator section. The drums took on a different tone, the singing stopped. It was time for the women and girls to select their partners for the initial dance of the evening.

But first to move out must be Mistan and Paulita; they alone among the married women would dance tonight and then only the first dance. Cordalee was aware of this dance from instructions given him before the festivities had begun, but still he suffered some slight apprehension as Mistan rose and felt for his shoulder. A light touch there signaled her already predisposed selection for the dance. He rose, concerned only that in her blindness she might have difficulty with the dance. He need not have worried. She walked before him toward the center of the dance area as steadily as if she could see. And then she turned to face him. Paulita and Gregorio followed in like manner. The spectators cheered as the women and girls sitting around the fire also rose now and went in pairs to select their partners. In the morning, the men would be required by custom to give their partners presents for having chosen them, but tonight the pleasure was solely in the dancing for both males and females. The beat of the drums changed again as partners faced and the dance was formed. Mistan smiled and said, "Talk to me, my husband, so I will know for certain where you are."

Cordalee looked around. "What do I do, Mistan? I don't know how this dance is done." They stood three feet apart, still facing. Quite plainly, this was not going to be the Virginia reel.

Mistan was still smiling. "We are not to touch one another. When I dance forward, you dance backward. When you dance forward, then I will dance backward. Watch my feet so that you will go the proper number of steps each way. Can you do that, my husband?"

She was so beautiful there in the firelight that Cordalee almost said no, that he could do everything but keep his hands off her. But of course he could not tell her that. This was her night, and the happiness that radiated from her was almost more than he could believe. He would do nothing to spoil any part of it for her.

"I can do that, Mistan. For you, I can do anything."

It was a grand thing both to be a part of and to watch, the dancers moving in perfect rhythm with the drums and the singers, and all becoming almost hypnotic in their enjoyment of it. The Virginia reel paled to insignificance in comparison.

When it was over and they were back among the spectators, it seemed the dance had finished much too quickly. It would be their only dance of the night, for the rest would belong only to the unmarried ones. Still, Cordalee did not think he would ever grow tired of watching. It was such a sight as that.

Mistan clung to his arm as they sat back down and Miguelito treated him to a congratulatory pounding on the back. "You are going to be a plenty *bueno* Apache, Cor-dah-lee. Even the old ones and that cranky old medicine man of ours will have to admit that. You will see."

Cordalee smiled as a mescal jug was passed his way. He turned to Mistan and said, "I am very happy. Happier than I have ever been. Can you believe that?"

"I am happy, too, my husband. Happier than I have ever been."

It went on and on. They talked and drank and laughed. After a while, a still amazingly sober Miguelito turned to Cordalee and asked, "What about that *médico*, my brother? Did you learn any more from him? Did he ask you things that made you suspicious—such as about our yellow iron? What do you think of him now?"

Cordalee shook his head. "I'm afraid I learned very little, my friend. He didn't ask me much after he became convinced that I was one of you now. It even seemed strange talking to him in my own language. I think that if his intentions are bad, he'll likely not tell me any more than he will you."

Miguelito nodded his understanding of this. "What do you think about the river people? Should we try to make peace with them?"

"Do you think you *can* make peace with them?"

"I'm not sure," the young chief said thoughtfully. "My people have been very hard on them in the past. We have stolen from them and killed them as if they were vermin. I imagine they hate us very much and would make peace only because they are afraid and do not think they can defeat us in a fight. I am not sure if we ever *can* trust them and I don't know if they ever *will* trust us."

"But things have changed now," Cordalee suggested. "The Wild Ones are gone and you have done the Mexicans no harm for almost a year now. And they sent you mescal. Maybe they really do desire peace."

Miguelito took a deep pull on his jug. "They have sent out people with mescal before, my brother. At Janos and Casas Grandes and other places long before that. In each case, our people got drunk and when they were helpless they were slaughtered or taken as slaves. Many of my people here remember those times. I am not sure they will ever forget."

Cordalee, disturbed, looked at him for a long moment. "I don't know what to tell you, my friend. I really don't."

A soft tug at his arm caused him to turn. Mistan said, "Do not talk of such things tonight, you men. If you do, you will spoil it for me. And you, my husband, I want you to talk to me. Only to me." Her mouth was made into a tiny pout, but her blind eyes sparkled in the firelight.

Miguelito laughed heartily. "There you are, Cor-dah-lee. You have taken a wife and now you must talk only the way she wants you to. Ha! Ha!" His laughter was cut short by a sharp little elbow from his own wife, Nondi, but the good fun of it did not cease. "Look out there, woman!" he barked, feigning anger. "In the old days I would beat you. Maybe I still will!"

The festive atmosphere, if anything, increased in tempo as the night went on. The dancers continued to dance, the drums and the singing gained momentum, the mescal flowed, and the people rejoiced as the shaman reappeared, sprinkling *hoddentin* to the cardinal directions, to the fire, then on the dancers and finally the spectators.

Nearby, Gregorio was uproariously drunk. Miguelito and Cordalee were not far behind him. Most of the other men and many of the women were in much the same shape. At this rate, by tomorrow there would be no mescal left in the ranchería and many heads would pound. Only Mistan and Paulita, of those around them, seemed unaffected by the drink, and that was only because they had refused to take more than a small amount of it. For a while no one noticed that Paulita's eyes seemed constantly drawn toward Cordalee. Even Cordalee did not notice. Even Gregorio. For a while . . .

Cordalee was in the midst of passing a mescal jug back to Miguelito when a commotion suddenly erupted off to their left. Cordalee's eyes weren't focusing the way they should, and at first he could not figure out what was going on. Then Nondi screamed and the angry voice of Gregorio filtered through. There were more screams, and this time Cordalee knew them to be Paulita's. He came to his feet just in time to see what was happening. Gregorio was standing over Paulita, who was still sitting slumped on the ground. The young Indian was bent over just far enough that he could reach the girl, and he was attempting to pound her over the head with his fists. Not many blows were landing, but still some were. As others around them scrambled to get out of the way, Cordalee became intent on putting a stop to the incident. He was just preparing to lunge toward Gregorio when Miguelito stepped between them.

"This thing is between a man and his woman, Cor-dah-lee. You must not interfere."

But suddenly Gregorio landed a solid blow and the girl toppled over on her side, moaning in pain and covering her head with her hands. "There, you whore!" the enraged husband bellowed. "I will teach you to look upon another man in that way! I will teach you!"

Had Cordalee been sober, Miguelito's wisdom might have dissuaded him. But he was not sober and he could not bring himself to simply stand there and watch. Casting a surprised Miguelito aside, he dove forward, catching Gregorio off balance and taking him to the ground. They struggled for a few moments, then for some reason rolled apart. Gregorio, more enraged than ever, got to his feet and stood there glowering. Cordalee, breathing hard, rose more slowly and just stared at him.

"I will kill you, Cor-dah-lee!" the Indian hissed as he suddenly produced and fiercely brandished a knife. "I will cut your belly open, you worthless *Indah*."

Cordalee looked around. With eerie abruptness the drums had ceased their thumping and the singing had stopped. But for Gregorio's harsh breathing and the crackling of the fire, the entire camp was silent.

Once again, Cordalee looked around. All were backing away from him now and he stood there unarmed and feeling terribly alone. He looked for Mistan, but someone had pulled her back into the crowd and he could see her nowhere. Even Miguelito stood back. It seemed that the white man had committed an unpardonable act, and now he must pay for it. Dazedly he squared himself around to face the fierce young Apache.

But before anything else could happen between them, a voice cried out and a man came running across the dance area. Cordalee recognized him instantly as one of Dr. Smith's guards, but at the time did not connect the one with the other's actions. He simply stood there as the young man came bursting through the crowd to stop directly in front of Miguelito. Even Gregorio's stance suddenly became uncertain as he turned his attention to the newcomer.

For a moment the young guard seemed undecided as to just what he had interrupted. But then he said to the young chief, "It is the white *médico, Inday*. We turned away for just a moment and when we looked back he was gone from his wickiup. We cannot find him, *Inday!* The *médico* has stolen away!"

A quick frown crossed Miguelito's face and he was in the process of looking around when a shot pierced the night air. A yell of pain escaped from somewhere within the crowd and then there were more shots. From the moonlit darkness on the south, west, and east perimeters of the ranchería the muzzle flashes of no less than three dozen guns erupted. People screamed with pain. Men, women, and children either crumpled where they stood or turned to run as turmoil prevailed.

At first, Luther Cordalee could only stand there in a mescal-ridden daze. Then, ever so slowly, it seemed, the realization that the camp was under attack came to him. In frightened desperation he whirled to look once again for Mistan, but just as quickly he sensed how hopeless that was. She was nowhere to be seen. And there was no time to be looking. Starkly, he realized he had no choice but to run with the others who had not yet been shot.

CHAPTER 18

Only the darkness saved him, could possibly have saved any of them. Even so, the moment he felt safely beyond the village's firelit circle, he turned back, fearing still that Mistan might be left behind. All he saw was the great fire and bodies on the ground, many of them writhing in pain. There was wailing and screaming still, also. The gunfire had all but ceased.

And then he saw perhaps a dozen figures wearing great sloppy sombreros come darting in among the wounded and dead, watching with clenched fists as they coldly stopped here and there to fire into those still alive. He saw no Indians except those who had been shot and could not run. All others had apparently scattered in the instinctive Apache fashion and were now running for their lives. He sadly realized this was about the only thing they could do. All or almost all were as he was: unarmed and with no way to fight back; escape was their only avenue to survival . . . and to escape they could only run.

Still, Cordalee could not pull himself away. He crouched there in a clump of brush, his mescal-bleared eyes continuing to comb the bodies for a possible glimpse of Mistan's white doeskin. He did not spot anything that he thought could be her, and presently the sight became so awful to him that he could no longer look. He could only pray that some of the others had led Mistan away quickly enough; that somehow—somehow despite her blindness—she had found someone to help her flee.

Slowly he rose and backed away. He wondered if any others had lingered as he had. So far he saw no one. Except for the carnage being conducted back at the ranchería, he felt completely alone. He wondered how far he would have to go before he found someone. He wondered if he would find someone. These were Apaches he was following, and they would be making every effort not to be found by anyone other than their own kind.

He found a path and followed it. Almost straight overhead was the moon, its light very, very bright. He judged that it was midnight or just past and that he had perhaps five hours yet before he would see the first light of dawn—by which time or shortly thereafter the Mexicans would probably begin combing the hills for survivors.

He lurched along, still feeling the effects of the mescal but realizing that his experience of the past fifteen or so minutes had sobered him as nothing ever had before. Behind him, the ranchería soon was beyond view among the trees, although he could still hear an occasional shot and the gleeful yelling of the Mexicans. The forest was a maze of shadows and moonlit patches. He paused for just a moment to get his bearings.

He had left the ranchería going in what he considered a northerly direction. Because the village had seemed surrounded on all other sides, he was certain that most of the others had gone that way too. Once they had reached the protective cover of darkness, however, he had no idea what they had done.

He tried to figure out what trail he was on. Clearly it wasn't the main north trail; it was a much more lightly used path than that. Yet he felt disoriented. God, how he wished the effects of the mescal would wear off more fully . . .

He studied the stars. Northeast . . . he was going more northeast than north. He continued on, stopping every so often to listen for the sounds of others who might be nearby. Up ahead, once, he thought he heard someone call out, but it was only the one time and he could not be sure. Behind him now, the shooting had died but a dull roar could now be heard that caused him to look back. A red glow shone above and beyond the nearest trees, while a dense cloud of moonlit smoke lifted skyward. The ranchería . . . they were burning the ranchería!

Renewed anger welled up inside of him. He thought of Dr. Smith. Had the man been a party to this? Had he known what was going to happen when he came to the ranchería that afternoon? Well, of course he had. His appearance bearing four kegs of mescal at just the right time could be explained no other way. That he'd happened to choose the day of the wedding celebration was probably the only accident of the whole affair, and even that had been good luck for the attackers. The Apaches could hardly have been caught at a more vulnerable time. Probably Narciso Ibarro and his gang and no telling how many more from the river towns had done the actual damage, but it had been Smith who led them there, who told them about the Apaches and their ranchería, about Miguelito and his gold, about Cordalee. Smith was the key, no doubt about that. Smith and Ibarro . . . damn their rotten hides.

Cordalee thought then of the trail guards, and of Kentoni and Cruz on the river. Where had they been during all of this? Of course he had no idea about Kentoni and Cruz; almost anything might have happened to them. But the trail guards . . . why had there been no warning? Why not at least that? Well, they must have been overpowered before they could act. This was conceivable, for Smith had known of their presence; the raiders would have been well-advised on how to proceed . . . damn them again!

Cordalee turned back to the trail; once more he thought he heard someone calling out up ahead, only this time there were answering calls. Women, men—Apaches attempting to regather, a frightened people trying to find and help one another in a time of need. Now, too, Cordalee could hear the sounds of a creek trickling nearby, and suddenly he knew where he was, where the trail was taking him. The glen—the beautiful glen where he had met and talked with Mistan all those times! If fate was to be kind to him, if there was a place she might be, surely it would be the glen. He hurried on, excitement welling within him as more voices could now be heard.

He reached the glen, calling out himself now. A dark shape suddenly appeared before him. It was one of the old ones, Tan-ta-la, the ancient Chiricahua warrior. Cordalee recognized him the minute he spoke.

"Who are you? Quickly, say your name!"

"I am Cordalee. I am alone. I wish to come among you." He spoke in Apache and was somehow not surprised at how effortlessly the words came to him.

There were perhaps a dozen people gathered there, including children. Of the latter there were perhaps four or five, but they were no more than frightened little figures clinging to this or that adult and could not be counted easily. As best Cordalee could tell, only one fighting-age man was among them and that was a badly wounded Dja-li-kine, another Chiricahua. He had been shot in the back and must have made a Herculean effort to make it even this far. It did not look as if he would go any farther. Kneeling over him were a pair of old women, but as Cordalee looked at him stretched out there on the ground, it seemed unlikely that there was much anyone could do for him.

"Has anyone seen Mistan?" Cordalee asked desperately. "Did anyone see what happened to her? Anyone at all?"

No one said they had. All he got from them were hoarse little no's or saddened shakes of the head.

"Did anyone see Miguelito or any of the other fighting men? Has anyone even a gun?"

Again there were mostly headshakes; no one had seen anyone outside their own little group, and although there were a few belt knives among them, no one had a gun. Or so it seemed. . . .

A light tug at Cordalee's left sleeve caused him to turn around. A young boy stood at his side and slightly behind him. Nito! It was Paulita's brother, Nito!

"I have a gun, Cor-dah-lee," the boy said in a somewhat hopeful voice. "It's a very old gun and has not been shot in a long time, but it is a gun. If I give it to you, Cor-dah-lee, will you use it to shoot Mexicans? Will you?" There were tears in the boy's eyes, huge, glistening drops that shone brightly in the moonlight.

Cordalee dropped to one knee and put his hands on the boy's shoulders. Where he had come from, Cordalee had no idea, but there was no doubt that it was little Nito. And he did have a gun, which he immediately proffered for Cordalee's inspection.

It wasn't much—an ancient revolver that, had circumstances differed, might very well have been handed down from father to son. Cordalee could not quickly determine its make, but he did see that it was loaded with five cartridges that he could only hope were not as old as the gun.

"Will this gun shoot, Nito? Do you know when it was last fired?"

The boy shrugged. "I do not know, Cor-dah-lee. Miguelito gave it to me. He said it belonged to a very well-known *Netdahe* warrior who died here on Stronghold Mountain one day long ago. I do not know when it was last fired."

Cordalee grimaced. The weapon conceivably could prove useless or even dangerous to its user. But at least it was something better than what he already had. He said, "Thank you, Nito. I promise I will shoot the first Mexican I see with it. I promise you that."

A huge tear cut a dusty path down the boy's cheek and his eyes glistened even brighter, but he did not say anything more.

Cordalee once again gripped him by the shoulder. "Nito, have you seen Mistan? Did you see anything at all of her after the shooting started?"

The boy rubbed at the tears on his face as he slowly nodded. "She was with my sister, Cor-dah-lee. They left the ranchería together. My sister was the only one who stopped to help her. I tried to stay with them but my sister said not to do so; they were going too slowly. She told me to run ahead with these others, to the glen. She said that she and Mistan would catch up as soon as they could."

"You mean they're still back there? That I might have walked right past them?" Cordalee was dismayed. It seemed unbelievable that he could have done that, not because he might not have missed them, considering the condition he had been in, but because he did not think Paulita would have missed him. Surely they would have taken the trail—Paulita knew the way to the glen too well to have become lost. And even if she missed

the trail, there was still the creek; all she had to do was to find it and follow it upstream. They should easily have been at the glen by now. Unless
. . . unless maybe . . .

His eyes landed hard on the boy. "Nito, think. Were either of them injured? Could one of them possibly have been wounded?"

The boy dropped his head; a shudder ran through him as he said, "I
think . . . I think maybe . . ." He faltered, sobbed, but still did not look
up. "I think maybe Mistan . . . She walked bent over . . . but I do not
know for sure, Cor-dah-lee. My sister did not tell me that. I do not know
for sure."

Cordalee rose. "I'm going back, Nito. You stay here with these people
and do as they tell you." His voice was amazingly calm, but inside he was
shaking so hard he was almost sick. He turned to old Tan-ta-la. "You people must not stay here long. Come daylight you will be too easily found.
You must find a better place to hide."

The old one simply nodded. "I know, Cor-dah-lee. I know what you say
is true."

Cordalee hefted the revolver and stared at it, only briefly debating its
potentially limited worth before turning toward the trail.

Cold sober now, he made his way carefully along. He stopped frequently, listening, watching, hoping for some sign of the two young
women he so desperately wished to find. He even prayed, prayed as he had
never prayed before. He reached a point halfway back to the ranchería
where the heat generated by the burning wickiups could almost be felt
and the sky was red and the smoke beginning to pall the air around him.
Still he did not find the two girls.

He debated calling out, wondered if it would do any good. He even
thought of trying the call of a night bird. He considered that of the owl,
mainly because it was the only one he could think of. But he knew that
Apaches considered the owl—they called him *Bu*—bad luck. Would such a
call—could he approximate it—even be answered?

He went almost within sight of the ranchería, but he could hear the
Mexicans yelling at one another again now and caution took hold of him.
He must not be distracted nor take undue risks. He must concentrate fully
on the finding of Mistan and Paulita. He must.

He backtracked toward the glen. Finally, in desperation, he determined
that he must call out to them. They had been heading toward the
glen . . . they had told Nito they would meet him there. They must be
somewhere nearby.

He called at first in a low voice. Then he waited. He tried again in a somewhat louder voice. The low roar and crackle of the flames and the raucous yelling of the Mexicans in the background seemed to drown him out. He tried again, much louder this time. "Paulita! Mistan! Can you hear me?"

Nothing. There was no reply.

Perhaps they had somehow got by him and had arrived at the glen by now. Maybe he should go on back. He moved now at a faster pace than before. He ceased calling out, banking now that they would be where he expected them to be. He did not slow down again until he almost was there. He entered the glen cautiously, and again he called out, softly at first, then more loudly. At least he had expected to find the others still there.

But there was no one. He called the names of Mistan and Paulita, then Tan-ta-la, Nito, and finally the one or two others he recalled as having been in the group assembled there earlier. He was greeted with nothing more than the normal forest noises. He alone stood in the glen, listening to the trickle of the creek and the chirping of crickets and the echo of his own voice.

He didn't know what to do, where to look further. A feeling of hopelessness gripped him. He himself had told the small group not to stay there, but where had they gone? How had they disappeared so completely, so quickly? No sign remained of even the wounded man, Dja-li-kine. Nothing. They were gone, all of them, wraithlike, *Apachelike!*

Suddenly he was very tired, exhausted. He found a spot along the creek bank on which to plop down and try to rest. The grass there was cool and soft, inviting. He lay down, thinking of but a few minutes' rest but sensing even as he did that his body would likely not settle for just the few minutes. He was powerless to fight it. Slumber quickly began to claim him.

Strikingly, the last thing he saw before closing his eyes was the moon, cocked to the west now and gleaming both very brightly and very red, although at this hour perhaps more from the glow of the ranchería fires than anything else. It had been Mistan who had told him once about the Apache Moon; he knew what it meant. But this was different. There was blood on that moon up there, all right, but it had not been the Apaches who put it there.

His first thought upon waking was again of that moon. But the great orange orb that greeted him was not the moon. It was much too brilliant and it hurt his eyes, causing him to look away instantly, blinking and shaking his head. He was looking east, not west. What he saw was the sun, a good two hours in the sky since rising. It was morning. He had slept the rest of the night through!

But it wasn't the sun that had awakened him. Somehow he knew it had been something else. A noise? A subconscious feeling that something or someone was near?

He blinked again, intending to have a look around as soon as he could keep his eyes open long enough to do so. A voice saved him the trouble.

"Well, well! I've been wondering when you'd wake up. I thought maybe I'd have to bring you to myself."

Cordalee's head jerked around. The words had been spoken in English. It was the *médico*—Dr. Smith! He was sitting on the creek bank not twenty-five feet away, rifle held loosely in hand and his horse tied to a bush not a dozen yards farther back. Cordalee instinctively thought of the old revolver Nito had given him. What had he done with it? Had Smith already spotted it and maybe taken it away? No . . . no, he hadn't. Cordalee suddenly felt it against his right ribs; it was where he must have laid it last night, only now he had rolled partially atop it. As long as he stayed there, Smith could not see it. He made no move to rise.

"You're lucky I found you, Cordalee. Narciso Ibarro is also out looking for you. Fact is, I won't be surprised if he shows up here at any moment."

Cordalee stared at him between eyelids narrowed not just by the bright sunlight. "And if he doesn't, how am I so lucky it's you, Smith?"

Smith chuckled. "You know how, Cordalee. Ibarro wants to kill you, I don't . . . Oh, don't get me wrong—I didn't say I wouldn't. It's just that I don't have anything against you the way he does. I might even help you get away—assuming we can make a little bargain."

"Bargain?" Cordalee stared even harder. "Me bargain with *you*? After what *you've* done?"

Smith rocked back slightly. "Oh, come now, Cordalee. If you're talking about what happened back at that Indian camp—"

"It wasn't a camp, Smith. It was those Indians' home. It was a permanent village . . . at least it was meant to be that."

Smith sighed. "Well, whatever. The point is, they were just Indians. Savages, Cordalee, savages. You can't hold that against me, man."

"The hell I can't!" Cordalee said stiffly. "I can and I do, Smith. In every conceivable way, I do!"

Smith held up both hands. "Okay, okay. You hold it against me. I keep forgetting that *you've* forgotten you're a white man. And you've never been a Mexican. You don't know how generation after generation of those river people have suffered at the hands of the Apaches. You don't know how frightened they are of them, how they hate them, how impossible it is for them to rest knowing these Indians are up here. You don't know—"

"Don't give me that, Smith!" Cordalee seethed outwardly. "Ibarro and his thieves don't even live on the river; they only use it as a hangout, a place to go when things get too hot for them elsewhere. And you—you knew these Indians were peaceful. You knew that the one outlaw Apache who has caused trouble on the river in the past ten months or so was not one of this band. Admit it, Smith. You want Miguelito's gold. That's the only reason you helped stage this outrage."

Smith just wagged his head. "Well, I can see it's no use trying to reason with you. You feel the way you do because you chose the Indians to live with. I chose the Mexicans. And yes, I do want the gold. But this would not have happened if it hadn't been for the murders down below. The people there really are stirred up, and they really are frightened. I told my story about these Apaches up here only after it became apparent there was a need. I really didn't know if it was just the one Indian doing the killing or not. Believe me, I didn't. And when we discovered those two spies your chief sent down there to watch us, well . . ."

"You *what?*" Cordalee asked suddenly. "You discovered who?"

"Why, your two men, Kentoni and Cruz, of course. See?—I even know their names. We caught them both. How do you think we learned how many trail guards there were and how to neutralize them? Of course we caught your Kentoni and Cruz. They are under guard at Bacerac right now."

Cordalee couldn't believe it. "You lie! Kentoni and Cruz would never tell you any of those things."

"Oh, but they would," Smith insisted. "They did! Come now, Cordalee. You don't believe the Apaches are the only ones who know how to torture someone, do you? Why, Narciso Ibarro could make a loyal son deny his parents. He could—"

Cordalee started to rise, bunching his muscles as if to charge. "You bastard! Smith, you worthless bastard!"

The doctor quickly brandished his rifle. "Don't do it, Cordalee. You'll not make the first step, believe me."

Cordalee fell back. For just an instant his attention had been diverted by what he thought was movement in the bushes along the creek bank behind Smith, about two dozen yards from his horse. The horse had its head up, ears cocked. But Cordalee couldn't be sure what if anything it was, and he looked back at the doctor. He began to calculate his chances. They did not seem good, even with the old revolver he had almost forgotten about still on the ground beneath him.

"What do you want, Smith? You said a bargain. What do you want of me?"

The doctor almost looked surprised. "Why, the gold, of course. We couldn't find any live Indians to tell us where it is. Tell me how to find it and I'll help you get away. Your life for the gold."

"What if I don't know where it is? What if I can't tell you?"

"You know. I know you do."

"What if I say no?"

"Then I'll hold you for Ibarro. It's as simple as that. Your life for the gold, so you might as well tell me. If you don't, in the long run you'll probably give up both anyway. Ibarro will torture you until you tell. Believe me, if he can break those two Apaches we caught, he can break you. You lose both ways if that happens, for he'll kill you later on, anyway."

Cordalee wanted to ask why Ibarro hadn't got the location of the gold out of Kentoni or Cruz, but he knew why without asking. They didn't know; only a few among the tribe actually did. And Luther Cordalee was among those few. Damn!

He shifted his position so that his right hand was near the old revolver. He touched the barrel, felt for the handle. His finger found the trigger, his thumb the hammer. It was a gamble, he knew. Even if he could bring the old firearm to bear, it might not shoot. There was not much assurance of either thing.

"Well?" Smith wanted to know. "Make up your mind. Ibarro and I set out at sunup and I've been expecting to meet back up with him at any time."

Cordalee made a bid for time, to put the doctor off guard. "One thing . . . just one question first."

"What?" Smith was plainly impatient now as Cordalee thought he saw movement in that bush again, but still he could not tell what had caused it. "Say what and be quick about it, man," Smith went on.

"My wife. Have you seen anything of my wife—the blind maiden Mistan?"

Smith stared at him. "Jesus. No . . . no, I haven't seen her. My God, man, there are dead people everywhere in that camp back there! Everywhere. But no, I didn't see her there. She must have been among those who got away."

Cordalee's jaw was tense now as he went on. "Have you seen any of the others—the ones who escaped? Has anyone seen them?"

"No. They're Apaches, man. There's no telling where they are by now, and for sure there are too few of them to make a fight of it. Ibarro's men have no intention of even trying to run them down. He's after only you now, you and the gold."

"What about Miguelito? You've looked over the bodies for his, I'm sure. Was he among those killed?"

Smith shook his head uncertainly. "If he was, I didn't see him."

Cordalee was still trying to stall for time, hoping to distract the other man. "Well . . . ." he said, continuing to grip the old revolver as he carefully kept it out of sight.

Smith got impatiently to his feet, never once taking his eyes or his rifle off Cordalee. " 'Well' won't do, Cordalee. The gold—where is it? Do they have a mine around here someplace? Where do they get the gold?"

Cordalee never got a chance to answer. The movement in the bushes this time produced a sound loud enough for both men to hear. At the same time, Smith's horse shied, pulled hard on its reins, and broke free from the bush it was tied to. Smith whirled toward the horse, already cantering out across the glen. Cordalee never took his eyes off the bush, and because of that was the only one to see the buckskin-clad figure that suddenly emerged, racing toward Smith's back. Smith must have heard something then, for he just started to turn and was in the midst of saying, "What the—?" when the figure hit him from behind with such a jolt that his rifle flew one way, he the other. The figure stuck like a leech as both of them went to the ground.

"Get him, Cor-dah-lee! Help me get him!" The words were Apache; the voice was Paulita's . . . and Cordalee could not help remembering a similar occasion when the young woman had landed in the middle of his back.

But almost before Cordalee could move toward them, Smith had shaken the girl loose and was scrambling madly after his rifle.

"Don't do it, Smith," Cordalee called. "I have a gun here. Don't go for that rifle."

But the man never slowed down. He dove, rolled, and up he came with the weapon. Then he stopped, on one knee and half off balance, to stare for the first time at what his ears would not believe but his eyes could not deny: Cordalee's ancient revolver, pointed at full cock and square at his chest, from a distance of no more than twenty feet.

"Don't raise that rifle, Smith," Cordalee warned again. Paulita, who apparently lacked even a knife for a weapon, picked herself up and crouched, poised but a few yards away. A dark bruise showed on her right cheekbone where Gregorio must have struck her the night before, but she otherwise appeared unhurt. "I mean it, Smith! Don't do it!"

The rifle was a bolt action, possibly of foreign make, and Cordalee could only assume that a bullet had long since been placed in the firing chamber. Cordalee's grip on the revolver tightened, as did his stomach muscles. All too keenly he recalled his earlier doubts that the revolver would even fire. Somehow he knew Smith's rifle would suffer its user no such problem.

Which trigger was pulled first, no one would ever know. At first it seemed there was only one report, and because Cordalee saw Smith's muzzle flash before he realized that his own weapon had bucked then smoked in his hand, he thought fleetingly that only the other man's gun had fired. He fully expected to feel the impact of the bullet, to be hurled backward by its force, to know the hot burning pain of its penetration of his flesh. But none of this happened, and as he saw the other man crumple and fall, he knew that not only had the rifle missed but that the old revolver had both fired and hit. All he could do then was just stand there and stare blankly at what he had done.

It was Paulita who reacted most quickly as she darted to the fallen man's side, felt his wrist, observed his wound, then with dispatch unbuckled his ammunition belt and reached over to retrieve his rifle.

Then she rose and looked at the stunned Cordalee. "Come, Cor-dah-lee," she said in Spanish, perhaps more out of habit than anything else. "We must get out of here. The sound of those shots will carry far and the Mexicans will be here soon. Come and be quick about it!"

But still he just stood and stared. "Is he dead, Paulita? Is that man dead?"

Her eyes traveled only briefly to the body, then back to Cordalee. "Your bullet took him in the heart. He died as he fell. But that's no good to talk about now. If we don't hurry and get away, the others may catch us. Come, you must follow me."

He looked around dismally for Smith's horse, only to find that the animal had long since disappeared in the trees beyond the glen. Still he stood his ground as his eyes settled once again on the girl. "How can we get away on foot like this? And where are Mistan and all the others? Where do we go even if we do get away?"

Paulita wagged her head. "Now is not the time to worry about all of that. Later, when we are safe, then you can ask those things. Right now, you must come with me. Come with me and I will show you how to hide so that no Mexican can find you."

CHAPTER 19

They took off their moccasins and walked barefoot in the creek for nearly a hundred yards, following it upstream until they could leave it where the grass was matted and neither wet spots from their dripping feet and legs nor tracks would show. When they had dried their feet, they put their moccasins back on and moved off into the forest. When they encountered stretches of bare ground, they began to walk on their heels, so that only queer little indentations that in no way resembled human footprints were left for tracks. It was an old Apache trick that dated back to the days when the Apaches had no horses, Paulita said. Where they could, they avoided the bare stretches, choosing instead to step on rocks or clumps of grass or anything else unlikely to reveal even the little indentations.

But none of this was a fast way to go, and plainly Paulita was impatient to reach whatever place she was taking them to. More than once she motioned for Cordalee to come along faster. She pointed up ahead to a brushy, boulder-strewn hillside that rose abruptly beyond the trees—a mountain almost. It was where they were going and they must not dawdle in getting there. As if to accentuate this fact, a gunshot suddenly resounded from somewhere behind them, most likely from within the glen. This shot was soon followed by three more of startling clarity, fired in rapid succession.

Paulita said, "Someone has found the *médico*, Cor-dah-lee. He is signaling to his friends. Pretty soon they will be trying to find us." She paused. "We must hurry; we must reach that hillside."

They broke into the open a good hundred yards before achieving the foot of the slope, and they ran all the way as they crossed the opening. The hill was both rugged and steep, but the girl seemed to know exactly how she wanted to go. There was a trail, a deer path, heavily used. It angled its way up the slope around boulders and between brush clumps. The girl did not hesitate to take to the path and no longer seemed concerned about leaving tracks. In fact, she rushed Cordalee along so that he did not even notice that there were human footprints already on the trail, one set, moccasined, having both ascended and descended the slope within the past twenty-four hours.

Even with the trail, however, the climb was not easy. About a third of the way up the going became so difficult they were forced to stop and rest. Cordalee plopped down beneath a bush and said, "I hope you know where you're going, Paulita. We'll have no chance up here if they spot us. You know that, don't you?"

She only nodded and insisted that he should be patient. There was a place up there that would make it all worthwhile, he would see that it would.

Once again they began to climb. If anything the brush thinned out as they went higher, but the boulders only became more numerous and in some instances larger. One giant rock towered above Cordalee's head and seemed quite precariously perched. It even gave him a little chill to pass beneath it—which act the trail dictated he must do. Once past it, however, he paused to study it. Standing perhaps fifteen feet high and easily twice that in circumference, the boulder seemed more firmly positioned from the off side than it had from the direction in which he had first viewed it. He could see now that it wouldn't likely be budged by anything other than a force almost equal to its own in size and weight, and he had to smile at himself for his initial apprehension at having to pass beneath it. Why, the thing had probably stood that way for centuries—how silly to think it might topple and fall now!

But then he looked on up the hill and his smile was replaced by a new look of awe at what he now saw about a hundred feet vertically short of the summit. A second boulder, appearing even more precariously balanced than the first, loomed almost directly in line with where he stood. Now *that,* he told himself, should it roll, would create just the force necessary to roll the rock he stood beside, not to mention the numerous smaller ones strewn between these two and the base of the slope.

He looked at Paulita, who had also stopped and was following his gaze. "That is where we are going, Cor-dah-lee. There is a ledge on which that rock rests. But we must not just stare at it; we must go to it!"

"But why, Paulita?" he asked as she turned to resume the climb. "Why are we going up there? Besides that rock and the ledge, what is up there?"

"A place to hide, Cor-dah-lee," she said simply, neither stopping nor looking back as she scrambled up and over a particularly bad stretch of loose rock. "A place to hide."

But Cordalee was no longer willing to be put off. "Mistan is dead, isn't she? That's why you won't tell me anything, isn't it? She's back there someplace, dead. That's why you left her, why you were alone when you found me. Tell me—it's true, isn't it?"

Paulita reached a relatively level position and turned back to take the rifle—which Cordalee had been carrying ever since they had left the creek —so that his ascent of the bad stretch might be made easier. He handed the weapon up to her, but he did not resume his climb.

"Nito told me she might have been hurt," he went on. "Was she? Was she wounded, Paulita? Did she die before you left her, or was it just the old-time Apache way of leaving the hopelessly ill or wounded behind? Is that what happened? Did you leave her behind to die, Paulita?"

To say that the girl's look was not clearly readable would have been an understatement of immense proportions. But whatever was in her eyes just then was neither sympathy nor tender feelings. At first it might even have been hurt; but quickly after that it became something that made Cordalee almost regret that he had just finished handing her the rifle.

But she didn't shoot him, and just as he thought she was about to say something—whether in denial or admission of his accusation, he had no idea—she looked away. Something back the way they had come had caught her eye.

He tried to follow her gaze. At this point on the hillside they could see for miles. Nestled back there among the trees lay the glen, and beyond that a few wispy columns of smoke continued to rise from the burned-out ranchería—at this point nearly a mile away. Well to the south were the canyons of the Río de Bavispe and its tributaries, and to the southeast, stretching in a massive jumble southward, rose the mighty peaks of the main Sierra Madre. The view was a grand sight, awe-inspiring, almost frightful in its vastness but plainly was not what had caught Paulita's eye. That was something much closer by, something between them and the glen.

"There," she said, pointing toward a place in the forest where the creek could just be seen winding its way toward the glen. "Riders—I think there are three of them. And over that way, two more. They are Ibarro's men . . . They have spread out to look for us and they are coming this way."

Cordalee strained his eyes, finally picking up the first three men and then the second two, all less than half a mile away. "They're probably not the only ones, either," he said. "I'll bet there are at least that many more who we can't even see."

Paulita nodded ever so slightly. "Come. We must reach the ledge before they see us."

This time Cordalee scrambled after her without hesitation. He could see the lip of the ledge now and it appeared to extend a good twenty-five feet on either side of the big boulder. The trail, on the other hand, seemed not to lead all the way there, but rather to skirt on around the hillside, beginning at a point well short of the ledge and the rock. Still, there seemed no more immediate avenue for them to take. They clambered on up the trail, trying not to make noise but unable to avoid kicking a loose rock here and there, each of which typically went rolling loudly down the slope behind them.

They were almost there, within seventy-five feet of the ledge and about to leave the trail, when a shout sounded from behind and below them. Looking quickly back, they saw a rider just entering the open ground at the base of the hill.

"He's spotted us," Cordalee said. "He's calling to the others."

The girl quickly dropped to a crouch. "Follow me," was all she said.

Almost on hands and knees they began making their way toward the ledge. And because at this point there was almost no cover to hide behind, there was very little they could do but try to close the remaining distance as quickly as possible. Which they did, by scrambling madly upward, almost before the first shot rang out and a bullet went screaming past to ricochet off a nearby rock. They crawled out atop the ledge just as two more shots sounded, and they rolled back out of sight just as half a dozen more rifles opened up on the heels of the previous two.

For the first time Cordalee realized that not only were there the ledge—which was but a narrow, elongated shelf slightly tilted toward the hillside—and the boulder perched even more precariously than he had at first believed on the shelf's edge, but there was also a cave, low-mouthed and fully shielded from below. On first glance it seemed of inestimable depth, for its inside was darkened beyond the first few feet, and the roof of its mouth was just low enough that a grown man would have to stoop to enter.

More shots rang out and Cordalee quickly looked around for the girl and the rifle. A low moan greeted him. She had crawled farther onto the ledge and sat leaning against the rock face of the hillside several feet away from him. Her expression was unmistakably one of pain.

"Paulita!" Cordalee started to move toward her. "My God . . . are you shot?"

She shook her head. "No . . . it is only my knee. I hit my knee on that rock back there." As if to prove it, she reached down and grabbed the knee with one hand. Cordalee, hardly convinced, had started once again to move toward her when a bullet bounded sharply off a rock six feet overhead.

"The rifle," the girl said. "The rifle, Cor-dah-lee." It lay at her feet where she must have dropped it. "Quickly, before they start up the hill after us. . . ."

For a moment he hesitated, studying her. She continued to rub her knee, and the pain seemed to ease on her face. "Don't wait, Cor-dah-lee! The rifle . . . get the rifle!"

Quickly he grabbed up the weapon and bellied his way over to the edge of the shelf. He peeked over just in time to encounter a near miss by the next shot from below. It careened off into the distance. He edged over against the boulder, behind which he could stand and fire back. Shouldering the rifle, he eased to a point whence he could look down the hill. The look he got was a brief one. About all he saw was a puff of smoke, a pair of figures darting from bush to bush near the base of the slope, eight or ten loose horses milling nearby, and a quick blur of foreground as he dodged back behind the boulder. Just as he dodged, three more bullets whined past and ricocheted off the rock face of the hillside above his position.

He moved around to the other side of the boulder. There wasn't as much ledge left on that side, but there was more protection offered by the boulder. This time he got off a shot of his own, saw perhaps three more men moving up the trail about five yards apart and at least five more riders come charging across the clearing to dismount at the foot of the trail. Once again he drew fire, and once more he ducked behind the boulder.

He bolted another cartridge into the rifle's firing chamber, then looked over at Paulita. She hardly seemed to have moved from her earlier position.

"Paulita—are you all right?" She was in direct sunlight, and although it was still two hours before noon, the sun's rays were hot there on the ledge.

She only said, "The trail, Cor-dah-lee. Don't let them come up the trail!"

For a moment he considered removing Nito's old revolver from his belt and handing it to her so she could help out. But more shots suddenly rang out and he turned back to his post. Sinking to his knees, he found a position along the base of the boulder from which he could look over the edge without being easily seen. A lull in the firing allowed him a much better look this time.

He was not surprised by what he saw; he fully expected them to be scaling the hill and it came as no shock to him that they had spread out a bit now as they came. Actually, they were scattered all over, on either side of the trail. Their horses had been left to run loose in the clearing, and some had even trotted off as far as the nearest trees. If he had to guess there might even be as many as fifteen attackers down there, each anxious to get at their quarry on the ledge. He looked hard to see if he could locate Narciso Ibarro, for he never once doubted that his old nemesis was among them. But at this point he couldn't be sure; they were still too far away, their big hats shading their faces, boulders and bushes hiding this man then that man as they toiled along. Then someone must have spotted him, for in one swift instant a shot rang out, a small puff of smoke lifted upward, and a bullet whined just above him.

He returned the shot, then got off another as the attackers dove for cover before at least four return shots greeted his own. He moved quickly back. Well, at least he'd put them down for a moment. And the closer they came the harder it was going to get for them to come closer yet. At least such was the case as long as Cordalee didn't catch a bullet first, as long as he didn't run out of ammunition. Once more he thought of Paulita: it was she who had Smith's ammunition belt. Save what was left in the rifle and the four cartridges remaining in the old revolver, that belt contained all of the ammunition they had.

The girl had moved when this time he looked at her; she was now sitting upright just outside the mouth of the cave. She was bent forward, doubled up almost, and it seemed that just as he looked around she reached once more for her knee. Even before they had left the creek, she had donned the ammunition belt and had worn it, ever since, strapped diagonally across her breast and over one shoulder, just as the Mexicans always did. Apparently she had been thinking ahead of him, for already she had unbuckled the belt and removed it from her person. It lay at her side, and as his eyes settled on it she reached over and with some difficulty tossed it toward him.

The belt fell at his feet, and as he reached down to retrieve it he cast the girl another look of concern. "Are you sure you're all right, Paulita?"

He had his answer even before she had a chance to speak. The underside of the belt was slippery, sticky-wet to the touch. He looked at it, at his hands; what he saw and felt was blood. He looked in horror at Paulita, then moved quickly over to crouch at her side.

"No, Cor-dah-lee! Do not stop to tend to me!" She tried to turn away from him, but he grabbed her by the shoulders and would not let her do so. He could see now the blood on her dress; she had managed to conceal it from him before by contorting herself so that the wounded area was not in his view.

"My God," he breathed hoarsely. He tried to touch her, to get a better look at the wound.

"No!" she cried again. But then she relented somewhat. "Just help me

into the shade—inside the cave. Don't worry, there are no snakes in there
. . . I have already checked. Quickly, Cor-dah-lee . . . do as I say!"

He had no time to wonder when or how she had already checked the
cave for snakes. He had no time for anything but to do as she said. Trying
to be careful not to hurt her, he helped her inside the mouth of the cave.
She could not stifle a moan, and once more he tried to inspect her wound.
Again she would not let him. He was about to insist anyway when he
heard shouts from below, followed by half a dozen more shots, and he
knew that their attackers were bent upon their most serious rush of the
hill yet.

Extending for some distance on either side of the ledge and above it,
the face of the hill was a solid rock bluff. It did not look scalable anywhere Cordalee could see. The unfortunate aspect of this was that it appeared to leave the occupants of the ledge trapped with nowhere to go but
back down the hill, or at the very best, skirting the hill on the deer trail
that apparently followed the base of the rock bluff on around to no telling
where. The fortunate part was that the attackers seemed to have but one
workable approach to the ledge: straight up the hill, the latter part of the
ascent narrowing as they went until the deer trail was virtually their only
course to follow. This meant they could not make that final leg of the approach spread out as they now were. So, as long as he had ammunition
and hadn't caught a bullet, Cordalee could rather easily pin them down
and keep them from reaching the ledge. But then what? How long could
any of that go on?

Altogether he counted out twenty-four rifle rounds remaining, plus four
still in the old revolver. A quick look over the edge brought Cordalee sight
of half a dozen figures moving resolutely upward. He got off one shot,
which kicked up dirt and rocks in front of the closest man, then was
forced back behind the boulder as answering fire whistled and whined
around him.

Moments later he squeezed off another shot, then another, both hurriedly aimed and ricocheting off rock somewhere other than their targets.
But they were effective in that they sent men diving and scurrying for
cover. A couple even retreated twenty yards or so before finding something
suitable to hide behind. Others leveled a ferocious return fire on the ledge
and Cordalee was once more forced to duck behind his boulder.

Logically, he began to eye the boulder with more in mind than just the
protection it afforded. A good eight feet in height and easily that in diameter, the rock was, like the even larger one downhill from it, much less precariously anchored than he had at first thought. He had no idea whether

or not it could be rolled from its perch by a single man pushing on it. Certainly it occurred to him that the slide the rock's rolling might create would be devastating to anyone caught in its path. Not so good, however, was the fact that it might eliminate the trail—and his own and Paulita's escape—back down the hill. Present circumstances considered, he decided that this might yet be preferable to what would eventually happen when he ran out of ammunition and could no longer hold Ibarro and his men at bay.

But first he must get the rock to roll, and even that wasn't the only consideration. Just now, he knew, too many of the attackers were still near the base of the hill, from which they might very well see the slide coming and escape before it reached them. He never doubted that if he was going to get any of them, and then hope to escape the ledge himself—and with Paulita—he had better get them all. He would have to let them come closer, all of them.

But could he roll the rock? He was tempted to test his strength against it. But no, he had no choice but to wait. His timing would have to be right or all might be for naught.

He looked back at Paulita. She had moved farther inside the cave now, and even though they were but a matter of a few yards apart, he almost couldn't see her. "Paulita, I am going to try to roll this boulder down on them, but I'm not sure how hard it will be for us to get back off the ledge if I do. . . ." He paused. "Do you hear me, Paulita?"

For a moment he was afraid she wouldn't answer, but then she said, "Roll the rock, Cor-dah-lee! Roll it down on them if you can!"

He thought maybe she had not understood. "But we may be stranded here, Paulita. Without water, without food. Do you understand what I'm saying?"

"We won't be stranded, Cor-dah-lee. The Mexicans are our only danger. Kill them and we will be safe. The cave is . . ." She faltered, her body suddenly wracking with cough. Cordalee started toward her, but she said, "No! Stay there! I am all right. Roll the rock. . . . Just do that, will you?"

Still he hesitated. She *wasn't* all right. Damn it, he knew she wasn't. But what could he do, even if he went to her? He knew only that the urge to try to help her was strong in him. Very strong.

But again she stopped him. "Cor-dah-lee . . . the rock! Roll the rock . . . !"

A shout from back down the hill, followed instantly by more rifle fire, forced him to turn. Crouching low, he peeked over the edge from his vantage point alongside the boulder. Half a dozen figures could be seen moving quickly from place to place, first one man then another bobbing up and darting forward to the nearest cover. Their leaders were much closer now, too, perhaps within a hundred yards of the ledge, and several of the men nearest the base of the hill had finally moved up. Every man now seemed in on the charge—which suited Cordalee just fine. He didn't want anyone lagging behind. . . .

Too, they seemed to have concluded that the only feasible approach to the ledge was straight up the hill, for they were making no discernible attempt to flank him. Either that or they had simply realized he was trapped and could only have so much ammunition left with which to hold them off. All they had to do was keep the pressure on, draw his fire now and then, and wait him out. What could he do in the face of that?

He sneaked another look downhill. A shot greeted him but was apparently taken at random, for it fell far short of the ledge. A man jumped and scrambled up a short stretch of steep slope. He disappeared quickly behind a bush, but something about him captured Cordalee's attention for a longer time than it took for the man to simply make his short run. *Ibarro*, Cordalee told himself, *that man was Narciso Ibarro!* For the first time he was sure he had spotted his chief enemy among the attackers. Very carefully he catalogued the location of the bush in his mind.

A voice carried up to him. "Come and fight in the open, you gringo dog! Let me see you, and I will let you see me. Face me, you worm!"

Suddenly, at least three men were on the move below Ibarro's position; no longer were any of them visible near the bottom of the slope. Then came Ibarro himself. He left his bush and raced to a spot below and to the left of the big boulder Cordalee had marveled at when he himself had passed beneath it earlier. Quickly, the man went out of sight again.

"Come on, gringo! I know your name and I know what you look like, for the *médico* described you to me very well. I know you are the man who killed my brother. Come on and fight me like a man!"

"Go to hell, Ibarro," Cordalee finally shouted back. "You don't owe me any more than I owe you."

"What do you mean, gringo?" The man sounded perturbed, maybe even surprised. "What could you owe me?"

"I owe you for those people back there at the ranchería," Cordalee shot back. "For many friends and my wife, who are all now dead. I owe you an eternity in hell for that, Ibarro . . . and I'm fixing to start your payment right now!"

As he spoke he moved back from the edge, then rose and laid his rifle aside. He stood directly before the big rock, measuring it, reaching out to rest his hands against it, leaning only slightly, thinking to push but hesitating for fear he would find he could not make the thing move.

"I am coming, Cordalee! I hate your guts and I am coming to get you *now!*" The words rang loudly and gunfire erupted immediately on their heels.

Cordalee leaned against the rock and took a deep breath. Its surface was hot now from the sun's rays, but not enough so as to burn his hands. He leaned harder, set his feet firmly, began to push. He grunted, he strained. A few tiny pebbles and some dirt seemed to loosen beneath the rock. A slight creaking, a sort of scraping noise, came from the same place. But the rock hardly seemed to move. He strained harder. Nothing happened.

He relaxed and straightened. He was afraid he couldn't do it.

A low voice sounded from behind him. "You can do it . . . Cor-dah-lee." Paulita sounded weakened now; her words were little more than a loud whisper. "Push! Push harder, Cor-dah-lee!"

He looked toward her and saw only her feet and legs as she sat now almost in darkness. He felt the burning heat of the midday sun on his back and arms and face. He was sweating profusely. He turned back to the rock.

Once more he set himself. He heard Ibarro still yelling at him but no longer paid any attention to what was being said. Bullets continued to ricochet as a heavy covering fire was being laid down. Cordalee didn't care that they were probably on the move again. He had to roll the rock; it was that or nothing. Otherwise all would be lost.

He pushed with all his might. The rock moved, seemed almost to teeter, but would not quite go beyond whatever tentative midway point was required for it to roll. He strained and strained, and then was forced to step back once more. The rock settled where it had been all along.

"I can't do it, Paulita," he moaned without even looking toward the cave and the girl. "I can't do it!"

"Yes, you can, Cor-dah-lee," came the resolute answer. "You must. You must do it for . . . for . . ."

He turned as she seemed to catch her breath.

"For Mistan . . . Cor-dah-lee. You must do it . . . for her. . . ."

Yes, he thought. For Mistan. He must have that satisfaction. No matter who had pulled the trigger on her, it was Ibarro who had killed her. He was responsible for all of it. Cordalee must roll the rock.

Again he strained against it, groaning, cursing, sweat running down his forehead into his eyes. The rock groaned back; he pushed harder; the rock tilted. Harder, harder. Ibarro was screaming at him over the firing now, the bullets flying all around.

Cordalee strained harder than ever. One foot slipped but he did not re-
linquish his pressure. He reset the foot and kept on pushing, his body
straining until everything inside and out hurt. The sweat mixed with
tears. The rock would not go over. It balanced there but would not go.

"For me, Cor-dah-lee," the girl's voice intoned. "For me, too . . . *Make
it roll, Cor-dah-lee!*"

Finally the boulder creaked, tipped, ground away at its base. And then
it rolled. Just as Cordalee went to his knees in exhaustion, it left the ledge
with one mighty groan, its momentum at first ponderous and uncertain, as
if it might not even go all the way, as if it might stop after its first full
roll. But it didn't stop; it gained momentum; other rocks also toppled and
rolled; an ominous crashing sound brought surprised yells from below.

Cordalee crawled over to the edge. He saw Ibarro standing beside the
bigger boulder downhill, staring in wide-eyed terror upward. At the last
moment the man turned to run, but he must have known there was no
place to go. The boulder from the ledge struck the larger one just as he
passed beneath it and moved out of sight on his way back down. The
bigger rock shook but did not instantly topple over; for the briefest instant
Cordalee thought it might not roll at all, that the entire slide might stack
up against it and stop. But then the big boulder did roll, and it was as if
everything started anew except with ten times its original force. Cordalee
heard Ibarro's screams suddenly cut short in the resultant crash and roar.
He saw men farther down scrambling desperately only to disappear in
clouds of dust and bounding rocks. He saw horses running frantically
from the clearing at the base of the hill. He watched in fascination as the
entire scene grew in turbulence and devastation, until the slide, right
down to the last bounding rock, rolled and tumbled its way to the bottom,
covering as it went every living thing in its path with tons of debris.

Thick dust fogged upward from the base of the slope; small rocks gradually ceased trickling downward; the scene grew still. Cordalee stood and
watched until he was convinced that all discernible movement had ceased.
A deathly quiet settled around him. He did not move until a low groan
came from behind him and he remembered the girl in the cave. He went
instantly to her, crawling quickly inside to kneel beside her.

It took a moment for his eyes to adjust to the darkness, although as they
did he realized that the cave was neither as dark nor as shallow as he had
thought it would be. There was even a shaft of light somewhere back
there—daylight. The girl was curiously silent and he was just about to
reach out to touch her when he realized with a start that they were not
alone. There was someone sitting quietly at Paulita's side, across from

him, someone sitting so still that Cordalee had at first thought the person a white-colored rock resting against the cave wall.

But what he saw was no rock. The white was that of a certain doeskin wedding dress. The person was Mistan.

CHAPTER 20

"Is that you, my husband? I think Paulita is dead. . . . Can you tell?" Mistan spoke instinctively in Apache, while a stunned Cordalee, though he understood her well enough, would have been tongue-tied in any language.

His eyes, adjusting rapidly now to the dim light, settled on Paulita. She had sunk to a prone position and her head seemed oddly cocked to one side. He leaned over to listen first for a heartbeat, then for any sign at all of breathing. He reached shakily for her wrist. Her hand and arm were sticky with blood and the side of her dress was drenched with it.

He looked up at Mistan and finally said, "I think she's gone. . . . I can't find any sign."

"She spoke your name," Mistan murmured. "Her last words were of you."

Cordalee continued to hold the lifeless wrist in one hand as he stared down at the dead girl. All along she had been taking him to Mistan. Even when he had as much as accused her of leaving the other girl somewhere to die, she had been leading him to where she had left Mistan safe and well. It was why he couldn't find them during the previous night; they had come to the cave instead of the glen, and then Paulita, faithful Paulita, had come back for him. She had very probably saved him from death at the hands of Smith and Ibarro; she had brought him to Mistan— at the cost of her own life. . . .

"How did you find this place, Mistan?" he asked in a low voice.

"We were on our way to the glen," she said, also in low tones. "I had developed a pain in my side from running and we were hiding along the trail, waiting to make sure the Mexicans were not going to pursue us beyond the ranchería. Suddenly we heard the call of an owl"—Cordalee thought ironically of his own decision not to try that call himself—"coming to us—twice, then three times. Finally we answered it. It was Old Man Din. He was trying to find Miguelito and could not stay with us. He told us of this place and how to get here. It is one of the secret places the Mountain Spirit dancers use to store their costumes and is supposed to be

very sacred—not to be disturbed by anyone other than the dancers themselves or the shaman. But Old Man Din said it was no time to worry
about that now. It was a safe place for us to go, and so he told us about it
and how to get here."

She paused only momentarily, then went on. "It was very hard climbing up here, and very frightening for me, for of course I could not see.
When we got here, Paulita took me back inside this place somewhere—it
is a much deeper cave than I suppose you might think—and told me I
must stay there. I was very afraid—of being found by the Mexicans, of
snakes, of spiders, of just being so alone in so strange a place—but she told
me she was going back to find you, and so I did not argue. She told me to
stay exactly where she had left me and not to wander around as I might
wind up outside and fall from the ledge there or be seen by the wrong
people. She said not to leave the place where I was until she came back
and called for me. It was a very big risk for me, for if anything happened
to Paulita . . . well, you know how helpless I would be."

Cordalee actually shivered at the thought of it. What courage these two
young women had displayed—and for his benefit! He wanted desperately
to reach over and take Mistan in his arms. But somehow he couldn't just
reach across Paulita's body like that. He could only kneel where he was,
marveling at what he was being told.

"I had no idea you were here, Mistan," he said after a moment. "We
left the place where Paulita found me in a rush—I can tell you about that
later—and she never told me where we were going or why, except that it
was a place to hide. I . . . I thought you were dead."

Mistan wagged her head sadly. "Paulita told me not to call out until I
was sure it was her or you, or someone else among our people. When I
heard the shooting, I didn't know what to do. I heard you talking out
there, but of course I could not be sure what was going on. Only when
Paulita came inside the cave and I realized she was hurt and she called to
me did I make my way over here. Oh, my husband, what was all that ter-
rible noise out there? I was so frightened! It sounded like the whole hillside was falling!"

"That's about what it was," he said solemnly. "I rolled a big boulder
down on the Mexicans. I think I killed Ibarro and every man he had with
him. I'm sure I did, in fact. There's no way any of them could have survived such a rock slide."

Mistan accepted this with no great show of emotion; she only nodded.

"But not all of the Mexicans attacked us here," he went on. "There are
still others on Stronghold Mountain. We'll have to get away from here
somehow. The trouble is, the hill below us, and the trail, are destroyed. It

was the only way I know of to approach this place, perhaps the only way to leave it."

At this Mistan shook her head. "No, my husband, you are wrong. The old shaman told us so. He said it was one reason this was a good place for us to go. Only someone who knew the cave and this hill very well could ever trap us here. There is a way out the back."

Cordalee remembered the shaft of light he'd seen immediately upon entering the cave, and was already looking that way as the girl continued.

"He said that the hillside from the front is very deceptive, that there is a giant crack in its top that goes off the other side and breaks this cave open from the back. During the day you can see the shaft of daylight even from the entrance. . . . Can you see it, my husband? It is day, isn't it? Can you see that light?"

"Yes," he said hoarsely, almost excitedly. "Yes, I can."

"Then we can leave just like he said we could."

"Yes . . . yes, maybe we can." But then he thought: What then? Even if they got out, what would they do after that? "Mistan, what of Miguolito, the shaman, others who survived? Is there a way we can find them? Do you know where they might have gone?"

She shook her head. "I don't know all of those who did and did not get away, my husband. The old shaman said he could only hope that my brother was one of them, and besides the shaman, Paulita and I encountered only little Nito and three or four others after we left the ranchería. And there are you and I. That is all I know. The others will probably hide as we do, then steal away later in small groups, maybe even in twos and threes."

"But where will they go? Was a rendezvous ever decided upon? Will they be able to find one another again?"

"I don't know. As I told you once, my brother wanted to declare such a place. But many of our people didn't even want to think about having to leave this mountain. They wanted to live here always. They did not want even the possibility of such a thing as has happened discussed in the councils of our leaders. I don't know if a place was ever decided upon or not."

Cordalee grimaced. "A people on foot, mostly unarmed and not even sure where to go to find one another, and with some probably wounded . . . how can any of them hope to survive?"

"I don't know, my husband. Some always have, surely some will again." Then, as if enough had been said on that subject, she began to feel around, shifting her position uncomfortably. "Please, help me up from here. It is very uncomfortable, and we must do something with this dead friend's body."

He rose and helped her to step across the body, then for the first time since he'd found her again, held her tightly in his arms. "What will we do with her?" he asked sadly.

"We will bury her here, inside the cave where no one, not even a wild animal, will ever find her remains. In some dark corner where we can pile rocks on her. In a place from which her spirit can depart peacefully for the afterworld and never know the pain of this world again. That is all we can do for her, my husband, for we must also worry about ourselves. We must try, as Apaches always have, to find a way to survive."

Late that afternoon a body of riders, Mexicans, appeared at the base of the hill. Cordalee first heard them shouting to one another, then watched undetected from the lip of the ledge as they scouted around the rock slide. Plainly they had little idea what had happened, other than there had been a slide and that some of their fellows might be hopelessly buried beneath it. Apparently unable to see anything on the hillside worthy of further investigation, they soon gave up even their digging in the rubble for bodies and went away.

Cordalee watched them go and thought hopefully that they gave signs of having decided to leave Stronghold Mountain. They rode south through the glen and beyond, eventually going out of sight among the trees a short distance beyond the ranchería, seemingly following the south trail back toward the river.

And when they were gone, it was as if Cordalee and Mistan were the only ones left on the mountain. He saw no sign of anyone else, even though he stayed and watched until sundown.

Well after dark, when the moon was risen, they left the cave going by the back way the shaman had told Mistan and Paulita about. Even had Mistan been able to see, it still would not have been easy going. The way out led down through a gaping chasm that split the hill on its backside into what became then two hills. It was rocky and it was steep, and under any other circumstances Cordalee would much have preferred to have waited for daylight to negotiate it. But there were at least two good reasons why he could not do that. One, there might still be Mexicans about and for now darkness was the fugitives' only ally; two, neither he nor Mistan could go much longer without water, of which there was none in the cave or on the hillside.

It took them almost two hours to reach the bottom of the chasm, and this only after much stumbling and falling and scraping and scratching of hands, knees, and arms on the many rocks and scraggly bushes encountered along the way. When at last they reached level ground, they immediately began making their way westward, their sole intention being to relocate the creek that ran through the glen. When they finally found it, they at first drank sparingly of the cool, blessed waters; then, after a few minutes, they drank again, once more sparingly. They repeated the routine several times before their parched lips were thoroughly cooled and their thirsts quenched, then they quietly slipped off their clothes and bathed. However good the water tasted when they drank it, it felt even better when they soaked in it. But even this had its limits, for the night air had grown cool there on the mountain, and when they finally left the water they were chilled. They lay in each other's arms on the grassy, moonlit bank until they dried, serenely peaceful for the first time in a day's time. They felt clean, refreshed. They even slept for a while. But sometime past midnight, Cordalee awoke, and his brief sense of well-being had worn off. He awakened Mistan and told her, "We can't stay here. We must decide what we are going to do next, where we will hide when daylight comes. We cannot yet assume that the Mexicans have left the mountain for good."

Nevertheless, they had no concrete plan in mind as they dressed and began following the creek downstream. Almost like horses rushing to reenter a burning barn, they felt drawn toward the glen and perhaps even the ranchería farther on. Along the way, they found a few ripe-fruited berry bushes and paused to do what they could to pacify the gnawing ache of their hunger. All the while they listened carefully, and Cordalee watched, for signs of anyone else at all in the vicinity. There were none. The forest was eerily quiet, without a breeze. They were very much alone.

They approached the upper end of the glen cautiously. It was bathed in moonlight. It was hauntingly beautiful, at least to Cordalee, who could see it. They continued following the creek, until presently Cordalee saw something lying up ahead alongside the near bank, beside some bushes. He stopped suddenly. It was Dr. Smith's body, still sprawled where Cordalee and Paulita had left it that morning. The surviving Mexicans had not even carried it back to the river for burial. Cordalee led Mistan around and past where the body lay without saying a word about its being there. They went on, still without a plan, but as if drawn—drawn toward the ranchería.

The moon gleamed brightly as Cordalee caught sight of the first charred wickiup. Mistan, listening to what he described to her, was quite hesitant to go any farther. She said it was not good to look upon such a scene of death and destruction. She said it frightened her a great deal and that it could bring bad things for the future. But Cordalee insisted that he must see it, for there might be no other way for them to estimate just how many people—and which ones—had survived. Finally Mistan relented and allowed him to lead her toward it.

As they passed within the perimeter of the compound, even Cordalee began to suffer misgivings. Aside from any superstitions Mistan might harbor about evil portents, it would have been difficult for anyone previously familiar with it to look upon what was left of the ranchería, now so silent, so wasted; a place where little more than a day earlier children had laughed and run about, where grown men had played the hoop-and-pole game and gambled gleefully, where women had worked and gossiped and at times played games of their own; a place where a once primitive and warlike people had strived to become peaceful and adapt to a changing world, where warriors had voluntarily become gardeners and herdsmen; a place now so changed that even the most unimaginative man might view it and immediately be able to picture the cold, dead surface of the moon. For a moment, even Cordalee was no longer sure he wanted to go on.

But he knew he must, for whatever had drawn him there thus far drew him even more strongly now. He was just glad, for once, that Mistan could not see; he would never have wished the scene before them on her.

As best he could tell, not a single wickiup had gone unburned. Even the corrals across the creek had been pulled down and their posts and poles apparently put to the torch, for he could see little sign of them anywhere. Everything had been destroyed—even, he thought as they neared the heart of the compound, the bodies of the dead . . . even they seemed gone. My God, he told himself suddenly, the Mexicans must even have burned the dead, probably turning what had only last night been a great and happy ceremonial fire into a funeral pyre!

He pulled up so sharply that Mistan bumped hard into him from behind. Could it really be? The site of the ceremonial fire was no more than thirty yards away. He had been standing in almost this precise spot when the shooting had begun. People had fallen all around him. But now, everywhere he looked, they were gone. Simply gone.

He looked around, suddenly imagining the horrid smell of burning flesh. He even thought he could yet detect its odor hanging over the place. Except no . . . that wasn't so. There was no such odor; the air was clear. Even the smell of charred wickiups was no longer strong. He did not think any bodies had been burned here . . . but if not, what *had* happened to them?

He started as Mistan's voice suddenly came to him from where she stood at his side. "You are hurting my hand, my husband. What is it? What is wrong?"

Instantly he relaxed his grip and turned to her. "There is nothing here, Mistan. The entire ranchería has been burned to the ground. Worse, it now seems that not only have the living abandoned us, so have the dead!"

For the longest moment he would have sworn she was not only looking at him but was actually *seeing* him. And the most peculiar look had come over her face. He almost couldn't describe it, except that she seemed to be listening, but no longer to him; hearing, but not just his words; yes, even seeing, but not anything any man or woman with mere natural vision might see. "Mistan? What is it, Mistan?"

Her seeming gaze was now cast southward, distantly so. "There are no bodies here, my husband? They are all gone?"

"Yes. Yes, they are gone. I thought maybe Ibarro's men burned them, but . . ."

Even before he broke off, Mistan was shaking her head. "They were not burned. The Mexicans did not do that to them. They were still here just hours ago."

He gaped at her. "Mistan, what are you saying? How could you possibly know that—?"

She put out a hand, as if feeling for him, but in reality only to quiet him. "Trust me, my husband. I know what has happened here. I *know* where both the living ones and the dead have gone."

"But how?" he cried. "How could you . . . ?" But then he fell silent. Mistan was given to knowing things others did not; she had a vision-power that was something well apart from the limitations placed upon her by her own sightless eyes. Hadn't Miguelito and others told him so? Hadn't he himself many times sensed it in her, despite his own natural skepticism about such things?

She said, "The living ones came back here. At least some of them did. Even as we were climbing down from that cave back there, they were already here. They came to carry away and bury the dead—to a place where, like Paulita, no one will ever find them. They came with horses that some of them must have caught running loose in all of the confusion since yesterday. They have taken the dead and now are gone. They will not come back to this place again."

She stood there very calmly, and her tone was almost emotionless. She did not seem at all possessed, and yet it was as if she had witnessed everything she had said, as if she had actually been there when it happened and had only now remembered to tell about it.

"Who, Mistan?" Cordalee asked. "Who came? Was Miguelito among them? Was Old Man Din?"

"Yes, I think Miguelito, the old shaman, Paulita's brother Nito; there were others—some women, some children, a few men—I do not know for sure which ones. The dead number many more than the living: my own mother; my old aunt, whose life you saved when you first came here; my brother's wife; Paulita's husband . . . I cannot repeat their names, for it is bad luck to ever say an Apache's name again after he dies, at least for a very long time. . . ." She paused and no longer seemed unemotional. "There will be many such names among this tribe now, my husband. Many we will not say again."

"Where have the living ones gone, Mistan? Do you know that?"

Her unseeing gaze was turned as if drawn now to the south and east. "I think the way I am facing. Is that not toward the main Mother Mountains, the Sierra Madre? There are many old hiding places there. I think they will go to one of them."

"Do you think we can catch up to them? Can we ever find them there if we don't catch up to them soon?"

"I don't know, my husband. I have been there, but I cannot describe a thing to you I have never seen. We can only follow and hope to succeed. That is the only thing we can do."

"But if we don't catch them, how can we follow? Will they not try to cover their trail?"

Mistan shrugged. "There will be signs, my husband. There may be others such as you and I who they know have been left behind. Our people will not always leave tracks, but they will leave signs that only an Apache might know about. They have not forgotten us. I know they have not."

Cordalee looked back across the ranchería, to the west, and transferred the rifle he still carried from one hand to the other. He was about to say something when suddenly Mistan stiffened noticeably at his side.

"What is it now?" he asked, at first only mildly concerned.

"We are not alone here, my husband. There is someone else here! I feel it! You must look, look quickly, for he is not a friend! He is—"

A noise from across the way suddenly caused her to stop. It was the sound of someone or something moving rapidly through the timbered fringe of the compound. A figure leaped into full view less than fifty yards away. Cordalee never doubted that it was an Indian, but Mistan's warning that the man was not friendly caused him to lift his rifle to a ready position anyway.

"Who are you?" he called out in Apache. "Tell me your name."

The man appeared to be almost naked, wearing only a long breechclout and calf-length moccasins, and his hair was unusually long and unfettered, glistening black in the moonlight. Then something else glistened as the man made a sudden move—a rifle, of course!

"It is you who must answer that," he called back in clear Apache tones that Cordalee instantly found familiar. "It is you who must say who you are before you die!"

My God, Cordalee thought, *it is Makkai! Makkai, the Wild One! That crazy* Netdahe *come back to . . .*

Cordalee raised his rifle just as the other man fired. His finger was on the trigger and his eye tried to find the sights in the poor light as Mistan gasped beside him and seemed to fall back. He was firing even as the fear gripped him that she had been hit; firing in the direction of their attacker, pointing without aiming for he knew now he could never spot his target over the sights at night. The rifle bucked hard, belched flame, smoked again and again, until its firing pin had finally fallen on an empty chamber not just once but three times. Finally he lowered the rifle. The other man had fired only once; he had fallen and now lay still on the ground there in the moonlight—looking small and inconsequential. The last echo of Cordalee's shots died in the hills around him. All grew silent, just as it had been before any of it had happened. Cordalee scarcely heard anything other than his own breathing. Then he remembered Mistan, the gasp she had uttered upon Makkai's shot . . . He whirled, his eyes momentarily squeezed shut as he braced himself for what he so tragically sensed he was going to find. . . .

But then her voice came to him, low and shaky and desperately pleading. "My husband . . . Oh, please, my husband—speak to me! Are you all right? What has happened? *Oh, please . . . !*"

His eyes found her almost instantly. She was not at his feet as he had expected, but was standing half a dozen yards away, her hands still poised over her ears, which of course she had been trying to protect from the deafening noise of the shots as she backed away.

Then she was reaching out to him, feeling for him, but standing too far away to touch him. He struggled to make his own voice and leg muscles come back to life. "This way, Mistan . . . over here. I'm all right . . . except I thought . . . I thought—" But then her arms found him and suddenly he was holding her, unable to choke anything else out as she trembled violently against him.

He, too, felt shaky, and for quite a long while he didn't say anything. He just stood there, holding this young woman who was his wife and giving silent thanks that they were both still alive—thanks not only to the One God he had known all of his life, but to the One whose hand he now felt must surely rest as much as any other on his shoulder: to the Apache god, *Ussen.*

CHAPTER 21

With the moon at their right now, they crossed the creek and left the ranchería behind them. They walked past the demolished horse and mule corrals, and the garden plots—their fences knocked flat and the plots themselves having been trampled under by what must have been the dozens of horses' hoofs of Ibarro's men. It was a monument of sorts, it seemed, to Ibarro's determination to destroy everything, and Cordalee did not bother to describe any of it in any detail to Mistan. He told her only that there were no horses there, that the corrals had been torn down. The rest of it meant nothing now.

Behind them they had left Makkai lying where he had fallen, dead of two bullet wounds to the body. They didn't know where he had come from or how he had got there or why he had come. Likely it had been for no other reason than to visit the scene of the vengeance his hatred had helped wreak on the Stronghold Mountain Apaches, and perhaps to kill any survivors he found there himself. Apparently he had been too late to encounter those who had come earlier for the bodies of the dead, and unfortunately for him he had discovered Cordalee's rifle more accurate than his own—for which he'd had only the one bullet left anyway. Because of this, they took only his knife and left his rifle where it had fallen beside him. It did not bother them that his death would go unmourned.

In an hour or so the sky in the west would lighten, the day would begin to break; they would need every minute of that time to put distance between themselves and the ranchería, to find a place to hide during the daylight hours. For certain, Cordalee did not want to be around in case any of the Mexicans had still been within earshot of the gunfire exchanged between him and Makkai.

He didn't know if they could make contact with any of the surviving Apaches; he didn't even know if they could successfully follow them. They could only hope that Mistan foresaw correctly the direction they would take and the places they might go, that the signs she said they would leave would be signs Cordalee's non-Apache-trained eye might detect.

They avoided well-worn paths, especially the obvious south trail, but made no other attempt to cover their tracks. Neither did Cordalee make any serious effort to locate what tracks might have been left by the survivors. He knew there would be little chance of his picking up their trail at night, even less of being able to follow it. His main concern was to be somewhere they could hide come daylight. Later they could begin seriously the search for signs of the other party's passing.

Just before sunup they found their hideaway: a brushy foot slope that was about three miles south of the ranchería and overlooked the south trail from about a quarter of a mile away. Nearby was a tiny spring, its water, although not the best, at least drinkable. Scattered all about the spring were more berry bushes loaded with ripe fruit.

For the first couple of hours past sunup, they both slept. Later, Cordalee woke and kept watch while Mistan continued to sleep. He watched most carefully the south trail for any sign of movement going either way on it. By noon, there had been only a few head of cattle going or coming from water back to the north.

The afternoon passed much as did the morning, and by shortly before sundown Cordalee and Mistan had decided to resume their travel. They drank their fill of water at the spring, took Cordalee's shirt and fashioned something of a bag from it by tying off the sleeves and the bottom, and filled it with berries via the neck. Then they cautiously reentered the forest, Cordalee now hoping he could find at least some sign of Apaches before dark.

They had no luck, and were beginning to despair when along about an hour past full dark they decided it safe to angle on over to the south trail. They reached the path just as the waning full moon rose in all its orange-red splendor and began casting both soft moonlight and long shadows across the trail. They came to the Bacerac fork of the trail—where the trail guards should have been but were gone now without a trace. At first Cordalee had no idea which way to go, until finally he happened to look down and saw the first clear sign of friends having passed by.

At first he wasn't sure, for it had been pure luck that he even saw it at all: a single line of lightly colored pebbles uniformly placed about four inches apart and extending for a full two yards in length, aligned in the middle of the trail so as to point clearly down the fork that led on to the south. He still had his doubts about its makers, until he described it to Mistan, who immediately recognized it for what it was: a definite sign that could only have been made by Apaches for other Apaches to read. Quickly Cordalee's spirits soared. He immediately led Mistan on down the right-hand fork.

A short distance farther, and he found another line of pebbles, carefully aligned in similar fashion to the first. Twice more it happened—the correct course verified beyond a doubt now. Briefly, Cordalee had considered destroying the first line of pebbles they found and would have considered doing the same with the others had Mistan not in each case said otherwise.

"They are there for *any* of our people who are lost to find, my husband. Not just the first ones who come along. We must leave them as they are."

And so they did. Except the very next thing left for them to find after the fourth line of pebbles clearly was *not* intended for them to leave as it was found. About a mile from where the trail had forked, they came upon a place where someone had killed and partially butchered a horse. The carcass was but a few yards off the trail, and both haunches had been cut away. A small fire pit was located a few feet away, and next to the pit a sharpened stick lay pointing toward a nearby juniper tree. Cordalee carefully described the scene to Mistan, who immediately responded with her own appraisal of it.

"Only Apaches would have done this way, my husband. Only Apaches can build a fire and cook over it in such a way that no one but them ever sees the smoke. Look in the tree, my husband. I am sure that stick you found points to something left there for us."

It did. Hanging from one branch, out of reach of most wild animals, was a chunk of meat, bound and held by a long rawhide strip. Cordalee immediately retrieved the meat and found it already cooked, probably having been baked in the coals of the fire pit sometime the night before. There had been a time—long ago, it now seemed—when he had said he would never eat horse meat. But that had been then. He had no such inhibitions now. He sat with Mistan and ate, slicing the meat into edible-sized chunks with Makkai's knife. Had he at that moment been asked to make the comparison, he would have in all good conscience said it was the best meat he had ever eaten.

They rested for a while, then moved on. The mountains sloped rapidly downward now and were becoming, though still quite brushy, much less forested. They were moving toward an upstream fork in two minor tributaries of the Río de Bavispe and would emerge, as best Cordalee could remember from things Miguelito had told him about the south trail, at a point very near the small river town of Huachinera. And therein might lie their greatest challenge yet: not only in the fording of one and perhaps two of the streams, but slipping past a Mexican village as well. Cordalee

only wished—and he voiced the thought to Mistan—that whoever among their friends were ahead of them would wait for them to catch up.

"They do not even know for sure that we are alive, my husband," was Mistan's answer to this. "Anyway, it is better this way, when we are so few and our enemies are so many. If we go in ones, twos, or threes, and if some are attacked, then only one, two, or three may be lost. If a larger group goes together and then runs into trouble, then many might be lost at once. A few can hide better than many, also. It is the way Apaches have always done before, and it is the best way now. Think about it, my husband, and you will know I am right."

They kept on until about an hour past sunup, still finding signs here and there that they were on the right trail. With the daylight, they had even begun to find a few horse tracks and moccasin prints, easily less than a day old, and it was hard for Cordalee not to want to press on. But with daytime upon them and Mistan having become both tired and footsore, he knew they must find a place to hole up for the day.

And so they stayed the main part of the day alongside a tiny rippling creek with plenty of brush located about a hundred yards off the main trail, resting, sleeping, eating what was left of their meat and berries, and watching—Cordalee watching—always for the slightest sign of anyone approaching on the trail.

At sundown they were on the move again. At about ten o'clock that night, with the moon still struggling to lift itself above the horizon, they came to a spot overlooking one of the upper Bavispe River's westernmost tributaries. Huachinera, located on a rocky bluff overlooking the confluence of this and a second tributary, was but a few flickering lights at that time of night. Because there were several trails leading toward the nearest of the two streams, Cordalee was not at all sure which way to go to best avoid the village; neither was he sure that they could ford the creek and be well past the town by morning. But then he found another pointed stick lying in one of the trails, and finally he decided to give it a try.

By midnight they were at the stream, where they were forced not only to remove their moccasins but their other clothing as well in order to make the crossing without soaking their buckskins and ruining them. They tied their things in bundles and held them high over their heads as they went and were lucky that the stream where they forded it was no deeper than four feet. Two hours later, they were a good mile beyond the village. A short while after this, they came to a well-defined trail leading generally to the southwest. Mistan, upon hearing how it looked, said that this was probably the main trail that came all the way from Janos and would eventually wind up in Oputo, thirty miles away. Many times the Apaches had

used this trail in days gone by, even riding fearlessly straight through the river-town plazas as they went. A short way south from where they stood should be a now-deserted rancho called Tesorababi, and beyond that a fork in the trail, the main branch going west toward Oputo, the other, much less defined, striking northeast into the main *cordillera*—the vast Sierra Madre itself.

"We are getting close now, my husband," she said. "I can feel it. Our people will be waiting for us at last. You will see."

But it wasn't to be so easy as that. Massive darkened ridges, broken by deep and treacherous *barrancas*, faced them, towered above them. They had not yet entered the main mountain range, were yet at its skirts. Mistan, of course, could not see this; she could only recall the difficulties of travel there whether afoot or horseback from times back in her memory; Cordalee *could* see it. Even at night—perhaps especially so—it was frightening in its immensity.

They made the ruined Tesorababi before daybreak, skirted it, left it behind and found a resting place by sunup. They slept till nearly noon, when the hot sun awoke them. They decided to move on, as no longer were they quite so fearful of discovery by the Mexicans. They passed the fork in the Oputo trail, found the expected line of pebbles aiming up the lesser-used fork. They wound their way up and over a ridge, came to a stream and a place where a large buck mule deer had been butchered. A haunch of cooked meat hung in a nearby tree. Cordalee retrieved the meat; they ate and rested for over an hour; they then went on, carrying the balance of their meat with them, until dark claimed the land and they decided for the first time in three nights to rest and travel from then on only in the day.

The next day found them toiling mostly upward, moving into a forest of oak and then pine. Good water flowed in almost every canyon. Horse and moccasin tracks showed clearly now on the trail, as no longer was any attempt being made to hide them. An abandoned camp was found with as many as five now cold campfires; it was a place where appearances indicated that several groups of travelers had come together. Enough refuse was scattered about to indicate that some of them had been there for at least a full day, waiting most likely for others to catch up.

Mistan and Cordalee spent another night beside another stream, finished off their meat, picked a few more berries. Mistan was continually tired now and their moccasins were worn nearly through, their feet so bruised and sore that their pace had to be slowed even more than the increasingly rugged terrain dictated.

Another day and another night passed. Still they toiled on without finding their people. Cordalee became discouraged and even Mistan began to wonder. Their pace slowed to a crawl. If anything the signs on the trail indicated they were falling farther and farther behind, not catching up at all.

The days were hot and the nights were cold, and Cordalee was finally forced to discard his buckskin shirt altogether, for it had finally been ruined completely for that or any other purpose by its use as a berry bag. During the day, he was burned deep copper by the sun; at night he shivered in Mistan's arms. But like any other Apache he was learning how to endure.

The trail became not only toilsome but treacherous, the ridges steeper and rockier, the *barrancas* deeper. They spent all one day just crossing one tremendous canyon. The next day they could not even go on.

Finally Cordalee killed a deer; they built their fire and cooked the meat and cut out pieces of hide to put inside the soles of their badly worn moccasins. They rested a day and went on. But Mistan was becoming ever more weary; she had grown gaunt and was requiring more and more frequent rests, after which she inevitably remained tired. More than once they were afraid they had lost the trail, and once they went over half a day without finding a track. That same night it rained; what tracks there had been were washed out; creeks rose and were difficult to cross. The travelers became dispirited, and their wills to go on flagged to almost nothing.

They decided to camp alongside a large rushing stream (they did not know they had come upon the main upstream stem of the Bavispe) in the bottom of a great canyon and to stay there for a few days until they were more rested. Possibly, they kept thinking, other stragglers would come up from behind and at least they would have company. Surely some would. But none did. They spent two days and two nights at that place; Cordalee killed another deer; they ate well and rested much. Still they were alone. They finally decided to ford the stream and continue on.

The rain had eliminated all hope of finding any tracks not freshly made. And there were deer paths everywhere. But one trail seemed more prominent than the others as it wound upward and out of the canyon. They took this trail for that reason alone. About midday they achieved the top of a ridge that broadened quickly and somewhat surprisingly into a great shelf of indeterminate length and breadth. It was covered with stands of pine and oak that were interrupted here and there by grassy clearings, and trails went everywhere. The only fresh tracks were those of deer and other wild animals; there were no distinguishable signs of Apaches anywhere.

Despondently, Cordalee and Mistan stopped and ate some of the cooked venison they had carried with them; then they rested for about an hour. When they were ready to move on, they once again took the most prominent trail. It led more or less up the shelf, and at least the walking was less difficult than any they had known in days.

Not that this lasted long. The shelf eventually began to narrow perceptibly and the immediate terrain grew more mountainous as the shelf swept its way upward, toward the mighty backbone of the Sierra Madre.

They came upon a small stream of perfectly clear water, coursing its way through thick forests. They began to follow it upstream. After about half a mile, they came upon a small clearing, very serene, very grassy. It reminded Cordalee of the glen back on Stronghold Mountain, and it made him sad to think about it as he looked down at Mistan at his side, at her now terribly begrimed and tattered doeskin wedding dress that never again would be beautiful or even much useful. For a few moments he was even more depressed than earlier.

But then he saw something at the head of the clearing that he would swear was the low, rounded top of a wickiup . . . then maybe even that of a second. Excitement rose within him, and he began to hurry Mistan along, telling her as they went what he saw. And he was not mistaken; what he saw *was* a wickiup, except it was not just one or even two; there were five. But they had been hastily constructed, probably never intended for long-term use. Cordalee's heart sank as he looked at the signs.

Having been occupied for perhaps no more than two or three days, the camp had not been in use since the rain. The people had moved on, and there was no telling where. They had been waiting for stragglers again and perhaps had at last given up on any more arriving.

All Cordalee found were a few discarded odds and ends of their belongings: a worn-out blanket, a dirty headband someone had no longer wanted, a young man's broken back scratcher, a child's crude doll, probably mislaid and left for lost . . . Little else, besides the wickiups, remained as evidence that they had ever been there.

"They're gone, Mistan," he said forlornly. "Gone with no indication that they'll ever be back."

What had been a look of happy anticipation faded completely from the girl's face. "There are no tracks, my husband, to show which way they went? No little line of pebbles? No sharpened sticks lying in a trail?"

Cordalee looked at her, so drawn of face, so disappointed. She had been so sure, when he'd first told her of the place, that their people would be here, that at last someone would call out to them in welcome. So sure. He hated terribly to tell her no to all of her questions, but that was the only answer there was.

But then suddenly, even before he could speak, she asked, "How long have we been wandering alone like this, my husband? How many days?" Cordalee stared at her. He almost had no idea. It seemed months . . . but more likely it was a matter of about two weeks since that night when they left the ranchería on Stronghold Mountain. He told her that: about fourteen days.

She explained, "When someone has been too long alone, too long away from others, they sometimes go inside themselves. When they try to come back among their people, they are then strange and not quickly ready to get along with others the way they once did. Perhaps that is what was wrong with Makkai, who knows . . . ?" She paused, that all-seeing look creeping into her expression again. She seemed deeply thoughtful.

But Cordalee was only perplexed. "What are you saying, Mistan? That we have become strange and that your people no longer *want* us to come among them? That they are avoiding us?"

She shook her head. "No . . . not that. But they may not want us to hurry among them without first having seen us and watched us. They may be now . . . right now . . ." And then her face lighted up; excitement plainly stirred once again within her. "Look around, my husband! Look all around! Tell me what you see!"

Obediently, he looked. He saw the empty camp, the clearing, the trickling stream, trees, high hills rising on either side of where they stood, the haughty high peaks of the *cordillera* overshadowing all else. He started to look back at Mistan, but then something caught his eye well up on the side of the nearest hill. Something moved. A lone figure rose and crawled out atop a rock. A man called down to them. His words were spoken in clear, ringing Apache tones.

"Who are you, down there? Tell me your names!"

Cordalee's heart, or something, at least, was in his throat. He almost couldn't speak as he heard Mistan gasp, then felt her hands gripping his arm as tightly as he knew she could grip. They both had recognized the voice. It was Miguelito's.

The question was repeated, only louder this time. "WHO ARE YOU PEOPLE? TELL ME YOUR NAMES!"

Finally then, with all his strength, Cordalee reared back his head and answered: "IT IS WE . . . YOUR BROTHER AND YOUR SISTER! OUR NAMES ARE MISTAN AND"—and then he said it, said it the way they always did, and he said it with pride—"COR-DAH-LEE!"

Up on the hillside half a dozen other figures began to rise and show themselves, and the answer came: "Wait there, my brother and sister! Your people are coming down to you!"

And they did. It took nearly an hour, for they had been camped atop the hill for three days, waiting and watching, and not all were with Miguelito on the hillside. They came in twos and threes, men, women, and children—until in all twenty-one of them had appeared, some still bearing unhealed wounds from that awful night on Stronghold Mountain. They embraced the two wanderers with tears in their eyes and smiles on their faces. They were conspicuous not so much for their own presence, but for all of those who were missing. They brought food, what spare clothing they had, eight or ten horses, a small number of blankets, and what precious few weapons had been salvaged during the massacre. But mostly they brought themselves and talked of what they had been through and of a new ranchería to be built right around where the present five wickiups stood. They were so few; they were almost as thin and used-up as Cordalee and Mistan; their young had been taken right along with their old, and they were deeply saddened. But they were still Apaches, and there was a spirit within them that would not die.

That night their fires burned within the new ranchería. They ate fresh venison; their newly made drums beat and the old medicine man sang; they tried to think and talk not of the past and those no longer with them, but of things to come.

Not many nights hence, a full moon rose to frame the highest peaks of the sierra in bold moonlight. It was not a red moon; there was no blood on it. But it was nevertheless an Apache Moon, for nowhere did it shine more brightly than right there on what was already being called "New Stronghold Mountain"—by the last free tribe of Apaches on earth.

AUTHOR'S POSTSCRIPT

This book is fiction. The incidental uses of various historical personages, certain factual events and circumstances, real places and place names, have been made strictly for the purpose of authenticity. None of it is meant to establish, relate, or compete with historical facts of any kind.

This is not to say, however, that such a "last free tribe" of Apaches did not exist. It did. Its members not only must have disdained surrender to the U.S. Army, they persisted in Mexico well into the twentieth century. Quite possibly some of their descendants are still there.

As for Luther Cordalee, his character, too, is rooted in fact. Supposedly, an American Army deserter from Fort Huachuca actually did wander into Niño Cochise's band of Apaches in northern Sonora in the late 1880's, but was not long afterward killed while fighting alongside of them. More importantly, non-Indians could—and did—make good Apaches. And although the stories of Apache ruthlessness in dealing with their adult male captives are many and cannot in general be denied, it should also be noted that youthful captives who were allowed to live freely among the Apaches have been described as quick to favor life with their captors over a return to "civilized" society. Some had literally to be forced to return "home" upon later being "rescued" by their "own kind." Luther Cordalee, although the exception rather than the rule as an adult, would very definitely have been one of these.

J.P.

James Powell is a native of New Mexico, and currently lives in Las Cruces where he works as a range conservationist. He is the author of many Western novels, of which the most recent are *The Hunt, The Malpais Rider,* and *Deathwind.*